With Love from the Morisaki Bookshop

Satoshi Yagisawa was born in Chiba, Japan, in 1977. He is the international bestselling author of *Days at the Morisaki Bookshop*, his debut novel, which was originally published in 2009 and won the Chiyoda Literature Prize. *More Days at the Morisaki Bookshop* is the sequel, and both books are brought together in this beautiful collector's edition.

With Love from the Morisaki Bookshop

SATOSHI YAGISAWA

Translated from the Japanese
by Eric Ozawa

**MANILLA
PRESS**

First published in the UK in 2024 by
MANILLA PRESS
An imprint of Bonnier Books UK
4th Floor, Victoria House, Bloomsbury Square, London, WC1B 4DA
Owned by Bonnier Books
Sveavägen 56, Stockholm, Sweden

Published by arrangement with Harper Perennial,
an imprint of HarperCollins Publishers LLC. All Rights Reserved.

Days at the Morisaki Bookshop

Originally published as 森崎書店の日々 in Japan in 2010 by Shogakukan Inc.

Copyright © by Satoshi Yagisawa 2010
English Translation Copyright © by Satoshi Yagisawa 2023
Translated from Japanese by Eric Ozawa
Santōka Taneda poem translation by Bruno Navasky, used with permission.

Designed by Leah Carlson-Stanisic
Artwork by Ksusha Dusmikeeva and GoodStudio at Shutterstock, Inc.

More Days at the Morisaki Bookshop

Originally published as 続・森崎書店の日々 in Japan in 2011 by Shogakukan Inc.

Copyright © Satoshi Yagisawa, 2011
English Translation Copyright © by Satoshi Yagisawa, 2024
Translated from the Japanese by Eric Ozawa

Published in one volume as *With Love from the Morisaki Bookshop* in 2024

A CIP catalogue record for this book is available from the British Library.

ISBN: 978-1-78658-496-0

Also available as an ebook and an audiobook

1 3 5 7 9 10 8 6 4 2

Typeset by Envy Design Ltd
Printed and bound in Great Britain by Clays Ltd, Elcograf S.p.A.

MIX
Paper | Supporting
responsible forestry
FSC
www.fsc.org   FSC® C018072

Manilla Press is an imprint of Bonnier Books UK
www.bonnierbooks.co.uk

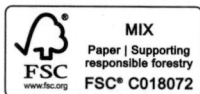

Days at the Morisaki Bookshop

SATOSHI YAGISAWA

Translated from the Japanese
by Eric Ozawa

Part One

1

From late summer to early spring the next year, I lived at the Morisaki Bookshop. I spent that period of my life in the spare room on the second floor of the store, trying to bury myself in books. The cramped room barely got any light, and everything felt damp. It smelled constantly of musty old books.

But I will always remember the days I spent there. Because that's where my real life began. And I know, without a doubt, that if not for those days, the rest of my life would have been bland, monotonous, and lonely.

The Morisaki Bookshop is precious to me. It's a place I know I'll never forget.

When I close my eyes, the memories still come back to me so vividly.

It all began like a bolt of lightning out of the clear blue sky. No, what happened was more shocking than that, more shocking even than seeing frogs raining from the sky in a downpour.

One day, Hideaki, the boyfriend I'd been going out with for a year, suddenly blurted out, "I'm getting married."

When I first heard him, my mind was filled with questions. Now, if he'd said, "Let's get married," I would've understood. Or if he'd said, "I want to get married," I still would've understood. But "I'm getting married" was just weird. Marriage, after all, is a covenant based on mutual agreement, so grammatically the sentence was completely wrong. And what about the casual way he said it? It was so brusque. The tone of his voice was exactly the same one he would've used to say, "Hey, I found one hundred yen on the side of the road."

It was a Friday night in the middle of June. We were having a nice dinner together after work at an Italian restaurant in Shinjuku. The restaurant was on the top floor of a hotel, so we had a beautiful view of the city at night, all the gleaming neon lights. It was our favorite spot.

Hideaki, who was three years ahead of me at work, was someone I'd had a secret crush on from the day I started. Just being together made my heart bounce inside my chest like a trampoline. That night was the first time we'd been alone together in a while, so as I drank my wine, I was in an especially good mood.

But then . . .

Without thinking, I replied, "Huh?" I thought maybe I had misheard him. But he repeated what he'd said, matter-of-factly. "So, it looks like I'm getting married next year."

"Married? Who's getting married to whom?"

"I am. To her."

"Huh?" I was still puzzled. "Who's she?"

And then, he says the name of a girl in a different department of the company—without the slightest hint of guilt in his voice. She had been hired at the same time as me, and she looked so pretty that even I wanted to wrap my arms around her.

Compared to her, I was taller and more ordinary-looking. I couldn't understand why he'd even consider getting involved with me when he was going out with someone as pretty as she was.

When I asked him, he said they'd been together for two and a half years. In other words, they'd been together even longer than we had. Of course, I had no idea that he was with anyone else. I never suspected it. I never considered the possibility. We'd kept our relationship a secret at the office, but I had just assumed that was to avoid making things awkward for others at work. Yet, from the very beginning, I was never his first choice, I was just someone to fool around with. How did I not realize that? Either I was slow—or there was something off about him.

Anyway, the two of them had already met each other's parents. The engagement gifts would be done next month. I felt dizzy. It was as if a monk had rung a temple bell inside my head. I could almost hear the gong.

"So, having the wedding in June would be great, right, but she didn't ask, and now, of course, it's too late for this year, which is why ..."

I sat there in a daze listening to the words coming out of his mouth. Then, I muttered, "Oh, that's good." Even I was surprised by what I'd said.

"Oh, thanks, but you know we can still see each other sometimes," he said with a big smile. It was his usual smile—how sporting of him. He didn't have a care in the world.

In a melodrama this would've been my moment to get up and throw my wine in his face. But I'd never been good at expressing my feelings like that. It's only once I'm alone, mulling things over, that I can figure out what on earth I'm really feeling. And besides, the temple bell ringing inside my head was getting too loud to think.

Still in a daze, I said goodbye to him and went back to my apartment alone. And when I finally regained my presence of mind, I felt a sudden wave of grief come over me. Far more than anger, I felt grief. A grief that was so violent, so intensely palpable, that I felt like I could reach out and touch it.

Tears poured from my eyes. It felt like they would never stop. But no matter how much I cried, I couldn't seem to get a hold of myself. I hadn't even turned on the lights. I just collapsed in the middle of the room, sobbing. The dumb thought popped into my head that if only all these tears were oil, I'd be rich, but it was so dumb that it made me cry more.

Someone help me, I thought to myself. I was serious. But I couldn't raise my voice. I couldn't do anything but cry.

After that, it was just one awful thing after another.

Because we worked in the same office, I had to keep seeing him no matter how much I hated it. And he kept contacting me as much as ever, which was excruciating. And to make things worse, I was always running into his fiancée in the breakroom and the cafeteria. Whenever it happened, she would greet me with this radiant smile, and I couldn't tell whether or not she knew about us.

Before long, my stomach refused to take in any food. I couldn't sleep at night. My weight dropped precipitously. And, despite my attempts to hide it with makeup, my complexion became so pale that I looked like a corpse.

In the middle of work, tears would come streaming down my face. I cried so many times, hiding inside a stall in the bathroom, muffling the sound of my sobbing.

After two weeks of this, I'd reached my limit, physically and psychologically. I finally went to my supervisor and handed in my resignation.

On my last day of work, Hideaki came over and said in a cheery voice, "Just 'cause you quit, doesn't mean we can't get dinner, right?"

I had lost my boyfriend and my job all at once. I felt almost like I'd been cast off suddenly into outer space.

I'm from Kyushu and came to Tokyo for work after graduating

from a local college in the south. Because of that, the only people I knew in the city were basically the people from the office. And because I'm shy and have never been good at making friends, in all of Tokyo, there was no one I was close to.

When I look back, the word that sums up the life I'd lived up till this point, all twenty-five years of it, is "adequate." I was born to an adequately wealthy family, graduated from an adequately good school, got a job at an adequately good company.

Meeting Hideaki meant so much to me at the time. For someone as passive as I was then, finding a boyfriend like him was nothing short of a miracle. I liked him so much that I could barely stand it. The downside was I never saw this shock coming, and I had no idea how to cope with it.

The coping mechanism I ultimately went with was to devote my life to sleep. Even I was surprised by how sleepy I was. I know it was probably my body's way of helping me avoid reality, but once I buried myself in my covers, I would fall asleep right away. I spent days in a deep sleep in my little room, drifting all alone through outer space.

I probably spent a month like that. I was ignoring my phone and then one night when I woke up, I noticed I had a voicemail. I didn't recognize the number on the screen, but I gave it a listen. All of a sudden, I heard a cheerful voice saying, "Hey, hey!"

"Takako? How're you doing? It's me. It's Satoru! I'm calling from the bookshop. Give me a call. Later's fine. Oh damn, I got a customer. Gotta go. Talk soon."

I sat there for a moment, puzzled. *Satoru? Who?* I had absolutely no idea. He said my name, so it couldn't be a wrong number. What was the bookshop? Bookshop . . . I turned the word over again and again in my mind—and then it finally hit me.

Satoru was my uncle Satoru! Come to think of it, I had heard from my mother a while back that he'd taken over the bookshop in Jimbocho that my great-grandfather started. The last time I'd seen him I was in my first year of high school, so we hadn't seen each other in almost a decade, but I was sure that was his voice.

And then I had the sneaking suspicion that my mother was behind this. Yes, it had to be her. She was the only person I'd told that I'd quit my job and broken up with my boyfriend. She must have asked him for a favor because she was so worried about me. But even so, that wasn't a good enough reason.

To be honest, I wasn't really that fond of Uncle Satoru. He was so unconventional that he was hard to figure out. He was completely uninhibited, no matter who was around. He was always making little jokes and chuckling to himself. It was odd, and it made him come off as a bit of a weirdo, which bothered me.

But when I was little, I loved his personality. We used to play together in his room when my mother took me back with her to Tokyo to visit her family. But as I approached puberty, his eccentricity became extremely off-putting, and I started secretly avoiding him. And then, on top of that, he suddenly got married—even though he didn't have a steady job yet. From then on, one way or another, he seemed to cause trouble in the family.

That's why when I came to Tokyo I never once thought of going to see him. I was trying not to have anything to do with him.

The afternoon after I got his voicemail, I reluctantly called him back. I could just imagine my mother flying into a blind rage if I didn't return his call. Given that my uncle was in his midtwenties when I was in grade school, he must be already past forty.

On the very first ring, someone answered.

"Hello, this is the Morisaki Bookshop."

"Hi, it's me, Takako.

"Oh, hey!" I could hear my uncle shouting on the other end

of the line. That's the intensity I remember from the old days. I rushed to hold the phone away from my ear.

"It's been so long! You been okay?"

"Ah, yeah, well . . ."

"I knew you were in Tokyo, but you never came to visit me."

"Sorry about that. I've been busy with work," I apologized automatically.

"But you quit, didn't you?"

He cut to the quick. I mumbled a response. This was not a man you could expect delicacy from. My uncle just kept on talking, telling me how this was just like the old days, talking on and on—until he suddenly came out and said, "Listen, I've been thinking, if you don't feel like working right now, how about you come and stay here?"

"Sorry?" His sudden offer caught me off guard.

But my uncle kept pressing me for an answer. "The money you're spending on rent and utilities is nothing to sneeze at. If you come here, it's all free. Well, I mean you could maybe help me out a little at the bookshop."

When I asked him about it, he explained that he was running the shop all by himself. He needed someone to open up in the mornings for him while he went to his appointments at the hospital to be treated for his back pain. My uncle lived in a house in Kunitachi, so I'd have the place to myself when the shop was closed. He assured me I'd have total privacy. The place had been a residence until some years ago, so it was fully equipped with a proper bathroom.

I thought it over for a moment. I knew my current arrangement couldn't last forever. If I kept on living this way, I was going to run out of money soon. On the other hand, I didn't like the idea of anyone interfering in my life.

"But I'm sure I'd be imposing," I said, attempting to decline the offer.

My uncle did not take the hint at all.

"Imposing? That's nonsense. It would be my pleasure to have you."

Did Aunt Momoko agree too? I started to ask the question, but I quickly caught myself. That's right. His wife, Momoko, had gone and left him years ago. It was a pretty big deal in our family. When she ran off, he seemed so depressed that my mother was really worried his health might suffer too. I remember feeling sorry for my uncle when I heard the news, but it left me with a strange feeling. It didn't make sense. At their wedding, the two of them had seemed so deeply in love. Aunt Momoko was so kind and good-natured. She was hardly the kind of person who seemed likely to run off.

I was remembering all this and mumbling my way through the conversation. My uncle, meanwhile, was trying to rush ahead with the plan. "Great. It's decided then."

I tried again to hold him off. "But what about all my things?" I said, but he told me he had space in his house in Kunitachi for all that. I could send everything there and just take some smaller bags with me to the shop.

It looked like I'd been outmaneuvered on all fronts.

"Trust me, Takako. This'll be better for you too."

But how was I supposed to trust someone I hadn't seen in a decade?

"Well, I'll start getting things ready over here," my uncle said, and then, without waiting for a response, he told me a customer had just come in and we'd have to talk later. Then he hung up.

I sat there for a while in a daze, listening to the dial tone.

2

Two weeks later, I was standing in Jimbocho Station. How had it come to this? In an instant, my life had changed so quickly that I was still reeling from it.

After the conversation with my uncle, I had a phone call with my mother. "What'll it be?" she asked. "Come back to Kyushu or go to Satoru's place?" I reluctantly chose my uncle's. I knew that if I went back home, I'd probably be pushed into an arranged marriage, and I'd never come back here again. After all the trouble I'd gone through to move to Tokyo, I couldn't stand the idea of going back like that and admitting that it had all been a total failure.

Being outside for the first time in a long while, I felt unsteady on my feet. But I made it to Jimbocho on the train somehow. Yet the moment I came aboveground from the subway, I felt fierce sunlight bearing down on me. The rainy season had completely given way to summer while I was asleep. Above my head, the sun was glaring down at me like a teenage boy. When I'd quit my job, the real heat of summer still seemed far away. It made me a little sad—even the seasons were betraying me.

This was the first time I'd ever been to Jimbocho. My grandfather's house was in Kunitachi, an hour to the west, so we didn't have much reason to come here.

For a moment, I stood at the traffic signal at an intersection, turning around and around, trying to take everything in.

It all looked so strange.

I saw a main avenue (which my uncle had told me was Yasukuni

Street), and all along it on both sides were rows of bookshops. Everywhere you turned, there was another bookshop.

Now, normally one would be enough for a street. Here, however, the majority of the stores were bookshops. While your eye might have been drawn at first to the bigger ones like Sanseidō and Shosen, what really stood out were the small used bookshops. Seeing them all in a row together had its own subtle impact. On the other side of the street, towards Suidōbashi, there were a few large office buildings, but they only ended up making the place seem even more bizarre.

Still confused, I crossed an intersection that was crowded with salarymen on their lunch break and walked down the street of bookshops. Following my uncle's directions, I left the main road and turned into a little backstreet called Sakura. This brought me to an area of secondhand bookshops.

I murmured to myself, "This is a wonderland of secondhand books."

As I stood there getting broiled in the hot sun, trying to figure out how I was going to find my uncle's store, I noticed a man looking my way, waving his hands in the air. His hair was messy; he was wearing black, thick-framed glasses, and he was so skinny and small that he seemed boyish. He'd thrown on a short-sleeved checked shirt, loose cotton pants, and some sandals. I definitely recognized that look. It was my uncle Satoru.

His whole face lit up as he said, "Hey, Takako, that is you after all."

Up close, I could see my uncle had aged a lot. There was no hiding the deep wrinkles around his eyes. His skin, once as white as some ill-fated damsel in a fairytale, was now marked by a phenomenal number of sunspots. But behind his glasses, you could see that strange, childlike glint in his eye.

"Were you waiting for me out in front of the store all this time?"

"I thought this was around when you'd show up. You know the whole area is just one secondhand bookshop after another, and I figured I can't have you getting lost, right? So I came out to wait for you. All this time I was expecting a schoolgirl in uniform, but at some point, I guess, you must've grown up."

It made sense. The last time I'd seen him I was in my first year of high school. We'd come up to Tokyo for the first anniversary of my grandfather's passing. It had been almost ten years since then. He was still the same though. He might be over forty now, but he still had that same breezy way about him. He was the exact opposite of anyone's idea of a dignified man. Which was something I absolutely couldn't stand about him when I was teenager. I was so sensitive then about gauging the distance between other people and me.

After I stopped staring at my uncle, I turned to look at the storefront.

"So this is the shop my great-grandfather started."

I stared at the shop with its sign that read MORISAKI BOOK-SHOP: SPECIALIZING IN LITERATURE OF THE MODERN ERA and felt a little moved by the sight. Even though I'd never met my great-grandfather, I still thought it was a pretty big deal that my uncle was the third generation in our family to carry on the tradition.

The shop was about thirty years old, but it looked like something from an earlier era. Through the glass doors of the little two-floor wooden building, you could see the books crammed together.

"The original shop was on Suzuran Street back in the Taishō era. Of course, it's gone now, so I guess this is sort of the second Morisaki Bookshop."

"Wow."

"Well, come in, come in."

My uncle practically yanked my luggage out of my hands and ushered me into the shop. The instant I stepped inside I was hit by a musty smell.

I accidentally said the word "musty" out loud.

My uncle laughed and corrected me. "Do me a favor and try to imagine it as the dampness after a morning rain."

Everywhere you looked there were books. In this small room that barely saw the sun, everything seemed suffused with the scent of the Shōwa era. Paperbacks and hardcovers were packed tightly on the well-organized bookshelves. The larger collections of complete works were piled up in stacks along the wall. Even the area behind the little counter with the register was full of books. If there were ever a big earthquake, it would undoubtedly all fall down, and you'd be buried beneath an avalanche of books.

"How many books do you have here?" I asked, half in shock.

"I'd say roughly about six thousand."

"Six thousand!" I shrieked.

"This place is small, so that's pretty much the limit."

"What does that mean, 'specializing in literature of the modern era'?"

"We concentrate on modern Japanese authors. Come here. Look."

At my uncle's urging, I scanned the spines of the books lined up on the shelves. There were authors whose names I recognized like Ryūnosuke Akutagawa, Sōseki Natsume, Ōgai Mori, but mostly it was authors I'd never heard of before. And the ones I'd heard of, I only knew from what I'd read in class in high school.

"So, um, you collect books from all these authors?" I said.

My uncle laughed. "Most of the bookshops around here deal

primarily in one specific field or type of book. There are stores for scholarly books. There are stores that only handle scripts for plays. There are also some more unusual shops that only deal in stuff like old postcards and photographs. This neighborhood has the largest concentration of secondhand bookshops in the world."

"In the world?"

"Yeah. Because back in the Meiji era at the end of the nineteenth century and the beginning of the twentieth, the neighborhood was a center of culture, and it was loved by cultured people and writers. The reason there are so many bookstores is that they built a lot of schools in the neighborhood in that era, which meant there were suddenly all these stores selling scholarly books."

"It goes that far back?"

"Oh yeah, and that history continues uninterrupted to the present here. Writers like Ōgai Mori and Jun'ichirō Tanizaki wrote novels set here. Now, lots of tourists from overseas come."

He was talking about it with so much pride it was like it all belonged to him.

"I've been living in Tokyo, but I didn't have the slightest idea about this place," I said, frankly impressed. Honestly, that response from my uncle to my little question impressed me too. For someone everyone in my family thought was just drifting aimlessly, someone who never looked for a real job, he seemed to know a lot. It reminded me that back when I would go see him when I was young, his room was always filled with difficult books of history and philosophy.

"Next time, you should wander around a bit, check out the area. There are lots of interesting places. Let's leave it till another day though. Let me show you to your room first. The second floor is buried in books from the rest of the collection, but the room is big."

When we peeked into the room on the second floor, I almost fainted on the spot. This "collection" he'd mentioned turned out to be towering stacks of books all over the room. There wasn't anywhere to step inside. It was a scene straight out of a sci-fi movie set in a city of the not-so-distant future. An ancient air conditioner was running full blast, but one by one drops of sweat appeared on my skin. I could hear the piercing call of a cicada somewhere in the distance.

I turned to my uncle standing next to me and gave him an icy glare. What was he talking about when he said he was getting ready for me? There wasn't enough space for a mouse to stretch its legs in that room.

"Damn, I'd meant to organize things in there before you got here, but . . ." he said, rubbing the back of his head apologetically. "You see, I threw my back out three days ago. It's the bookseller's destiny, I'm afraid. But I did move half of the books over to the empty room next door. So if you just toss the remaining ones in there too, you should be right at home."

At that moment, we heard the sound of the glass door downstairs opening, and my uncle said, "Sorry about that," and ran back downstairs.

I looked around the room and sighed. "Toss" them in there, he said. Easy for him to say. I felt like I'd been duped. But I'd already broken the lease for my apartment, and I didn't have anywhere else to live. I prepared myself for the worst and started cleaning up the room.

For the entire day, I waged a war against those books. I was heaving huge piles into the room next door, dripping with sweat. But if I got even the slightest bit careless, my Towers of Babel would collapse, struck down by an angry God. Little by little, my intense hatred for those books grew stronger. Nevertheless, by evening, I'd somehow succeed in clearing out the majority of books into the empty room. I rescued the little table that had been buried in the avalanche. In the room next door, the books were piled to the ceiling. I was a little worried that the floor might collapse. But it seemed like a sturdy enough building, so I told myself it would be okay. Then I took out the vacuum and sucked up all the dust and bits of trash that had been floating above the ground like evil spirits. Once I had wiped down the walls and tatami mats with a dust cloth, the room started to look like someplace a human being might actually inhabit.

I was standing in the entrance to the room with my hands on my hips, surveying my work with some measure of satisfaction, when my uncle closed up the shop and came upstairs to see me.

"Whoa, you really cleaned things up. Amazing," he said. "Takako, I swear if you'd been born in England in the latter half of the nineteenth century, you could have been a brilliant maid." He went on saying more ridiculous things like that to me.

Oh God, I thought, *I'm going to have to get along with this person.*

"I'm tired and I'm going to bed," I said.

"Definitely, take it easy, get all the rest you need. Tomorrow morning you can help me out though, right?"

Once my uncle had left the shop, I got right into the bath, and then crawled into my musty-smelling futon without even drying my hair.

When I turned off the lights, the room suddenly fell completely silent. It was like all those books were absorbing the sound.

I looked up at the dim ceiling in a daze and started feeling hopeless. *Can I really stay here for a while? I don't see myself getting used to this.* But it only lasted a moment. One second later, I was snoring.

In my dream, I was an android maid living in a city in the not-so-distant future. In that neighborhood, all the buildings were made of used books.

When I opened my eyes the next morning, I had no idea where I was. I looked over at the alarm clock beside me. The time read 10:22.

All of a sudden, I came back to reality. "Ah!" I yelled and jumped out of bed. The store opens at ten. Before I went to bed I set my alarm for eight, but at some point it must have been turned off. *Who on earth played this cruel trick on me?* The culprit, of course, was me.

What a mess! I'd always been good at waking up on time. I'd been proud of the fact that in my three years at the company I was never once late. But here I was in my pajamas, with total bed head, hurrying down the stairs, rushing to push up the heavy metal shutter out front. As I did, the summer light poured into the room. All the stores facing the street were already open. I was clearly getting a late start.

What could I do? For about a half hour, I just sat stupidly at the counter in my pajamas, half-panicked. But to my surprise, no one came in.

Later on, it didn't seem that anyone was going to show up. There were some people walking down the street, but they walked right by. Feeling like an idiot, I casually went upstairs and changed my clothes, brushed my hair, and even put on a little makeup, and then came down again.

At around noon, people started to trickle in. But for the most part, they only bought the cheap fifty-yen or one-hundred-yen paperbacks. I found myself worrying whether the shop was going to make it. After stifling about thirty yawns, I dozed off a couple of times.

Around one, a middle-aged man turned up. He was short and stout and spectacularly bald. As soon as he saw me sitting behind the counter, he did a double take. "What? Where's Satoru—more importantly, who are you? Did they hire a girl to work part-time? But this place can't afford to hire anyone, can it?"

He hit me with one question after another. How could I describe him? He was the kind of middle-aged man who didn't hold anything back.

"Um, my uncle will be coming in around two. I'm his niece, Takako. I'm sort of part-time, I suppose. I'm working for room and board. As for the shop's financial situation, I'm afraid I'm not familiar with the details."

As I ran through my replies, the man studied me carefully with a look of deep interest.

"Oh wow," he said. "How did I not know that all this time Satoru had a cute, young niece."

I flashed a sweet smile. It was lucky for me he hadn't seen my shameful appearance this morning. Maybe he was a sweet old guy after all. He seemed pleasant enough, and what's more, he had good taste.

"So I was thinking about reading Naoya Shiga again. It's been a while. You know how my wife threw out most of mine a while ago."

He wandered around the bookshelves as he talked. How should I know what happened with his wife? I just met him today.

"Where are they again?"

"Where are what?"

"The Naoya Shiga books."

"Ah, well, um, they're probably somewhere around there."

The man suddenly gave me a stern look, as if he were trying to evaluate me.

"Are you a reader?"

"Definitely not."

In the instant I answered, my middle-aged companion transformed into a demon. His eyes lit up as he glared at me.

That is when his diatribe began. *Good grief.* "Young people today, they don't read books anymore. They just play computer games. It's hopeless. And even if they do read books, it's just manga or these shallow little stories on their cell phones. Even my son, he's almost thirty and he still just plays video games all the time. Is that okay? You think so? Absolutely not. They're only seeing the surface of things. And if you don't want to be a shallow person, then you should try reading some of the wonderful books in this place."

The man went on and on talking like this. When he finally went home, it was almost an hour later. In the end, his monologue went on so long that he left without buying anything. I was getting exhausted too. When my uncle showed up a half hour later, for a moment, he seemed like my savior.

"How was your first day? Any trouble?" he said. As he asked the question, he went straight to check the account ledger for the day.

"No," I said wearily. "But a little after noon, a guy came in. It was as if his head was a dandelion and all the fuzz blew away except for the sides. He talked a lot."

"Ah, that's Sabu. He's been a regular here for about twenty years."

I laughed in spite of myself. The name Sabu fit him perfectly.

"That guy, what can I say, he loves the great writers of Japanese literature from the bottom of his heart. But he's a talker. I get trapped sometimes too. But if you make a little tea, and nod and say 'oh' and 'ah' a little bit, he goes home."

Ah, I thought, there's a lot to the service industry. Even the notion of a regular customer seemed like a rare thing these days.

"By the way, Uncle . . ." I said, remembering my biggest question of the day.

"What is it?"

"Is the shop okay? There aren't that many customers. And the people who buy books only buy the cheap ones . . ."

My uncle laughed, sounding apparently happy.

"That's true. These days secondhand books don't sell well. Back when my father was young, the secondhand bookshops did incredible business. But the situation is different now. I mean the publishing industry wasn't like it is now, and there was no television. However, we started selling online six years ago. And sometimes we sell a sought-after book that goes for a lot of money. We're making it work somehow. And we have a good number of regular customers like Sabu, who have been with us since my father's time. Takako, don't you go to secondhand bookshops?"

"I go to BookOff sometimes. I can read manga there."

"These days it's just big chains like that. But in those places you're never going to find a book written by a writer from decades ago. There's no demand for it. Still, there are a lot of people in this world who love old books. There are even some girls your age. For people like that, this place is heaven. And I happen to be one of those people."

"I remember your room used to be filled with books. How long ago did you take over the store?"

"It was right after my father died. So almost ten years? But compared to the other shop owners around here, I'm just a spring chicken. They've all been running their bookshops for thirty, forty years."

"Wow. That's amazing. It's almost beyond comprehension."

"Takako, you should try to read some. You can read any of the books here," he said, smiling.

I just laughed.

3

I didn't oversleep again after that day, and somehow figured out what to do in the store. Fortunately, business was mostly slow until the afternoon. I would sit at the counter in the back and zone out. My routine didn't change much once I'd settled in. I would open up first thing in the morning, tend the store until my uncle arrived and relieved me of duty. Then I would trudge upstairs, bury myself in the covers of my futon, and sleep.

My room contained only the absolute bare necessities. I'm sure it wouldn't have looked like much of a life to anyone else, but it suited me. Honestly, in my frame of mind, I was ready to leave behind the things of this world.

My uncle Satoru would appear after noon, dressed in the slouchy, loose clothes that would never have been allowed at a normal company. When he came in, he would first check the account ledger, and then the online orders, before getting on the phone to chat about something or other for work.

I could hear him complaining to the person on the other end of the phone, saying, "Nah, no way" or "That's pretty harsh, isn't it?" or "If we don't make it through this . . ." He might have been complaining about the situation the business was in, and yet something about the tone of his voice always seemed happy.

What I didn't expect about the used-book business was how big the network was. According to my uncle, the network of booksellers and your personal relationships were a big part of making sure you could bring in new inventory and keep the store from running out of books. A specialty store like the Morisaki Bookshop couldn't maintain its inventory just by buying books that customers came in to sell. The periodic auctions that the bookstore union organized were crucial for stores to get more used books.

"Even though we think of it as an independent business, what matters in the industry more than anything are the relationships you have with people. I guess that's probably true of the world in general," he said, looking rather pleased with himself.

There was still a considerable gap, however, between the man proclaiming this to me and the image I had in my mind of a secondhand bookshop owner that came from my grandfather. My grandfather was hard-headed and inflexible, a man of few words. At family get-togethers, he sat imposingly at the center of the group, surrounded by all of our relatives. As a child I was secretly afraid of him, and my grandmother would always laugh and say, "He's an old used bookseller. That's just the way he is."

But compared to him, my uncle was as flexible and indecisive as a jellyfish. I'd never spent so much time with him before, but the more I did, the more I was surprised by how wishy-washy he was. I even got the wild idea that my aunt Momoko had run off because she'd gotten sick of it. And yet in spite of all that, the regular customers kept coming, ready to chitchat.

The two of us didn't talk much aside from work, but after about a week had passed, my uncle couldn't take it any longer. "Takako," he said with an amazed look on his face, "all you do is sleep. You're a sleep monster."

"I must be going through a sleepy phase," I replied coldly. My uncle was just itching to interfere in my life, but I refused to let him draw me out.

"At twenty-five?"

"That's right. It's like they say, 'a sleeping child is a growing child.'"

"But you have so much time. Why don't you try going for a walk? There are lots of interesting places. Listen, I've been coming here since I was a kid and I've never gotten tired of it."

"I'm okay. I'd rather sleep."

I could tell my uncle wasn't finished talking, but I put an end to the conversation. After that, no matter what he said, I wasn't going to reply. I was as silent as a stone. Deep down, I was sulking.

Of course, my uncle must have heard everything from my mother, so he more or less knew what was going on in my life. And yet despite that, he was just casually bringing up the subject without any consideration. It made me angry.

Even our regular customer Sabu seemed to know all about my life. He came in one day and said, "Oh, if it isn't the sleep monster, Takako."

"Who told you that?" I said, indignantly. But of course, it could only have been my uncle, the person I was really angry with.

"That you regularly sleep fifteen hours and you're still sleepy?"

"I don't sleep fifteen hours. More like thirteen."

When I corrected him, Sabu shook his head in amazement.

"When I was in my twenties, I couldn't spare that much time for sleep. I was always reading."

"When I decide to sleep, I sleep."

"You're stubborn, just like your uncle."

"That's absurd. How could you compare me to that fool?"

"You also have his peculiar sense of humor," Sabu said and giggled.

"I'm not like him. Please don't lump us together."

"No, no. Don't underestimate him," Sabu said, suddenly turning serious. "That man might be a nincompoop, but he's also this shop's savior."

"Savior?" I replied, my eyes getting wide.

"That's right. Ask him sometime." As he spoke, Sabu gave me a knowing look. Then to show off a bit, he said, "Adios," gave a little wave goodbye, and left the store.

Who cares, I thought. I have zero interest in whether my uncle thinks he's a savior or not. All I want is to go back upstairs and get under the covers and sleep.

Still, even I was amazed at how sleepy I was. I told Sabu that I was sleeping thirteen hours a day, but on days when the shop was closed, I slept all day long. I slept and slept and wished I could sleep forever. In my dreams, I didn't have to think of those awful things. My dreams were like the finest, sweetest honey. And I was like a honeybee, flying in search of more.

In contrast, there was nothing good about the hours I was awake. Even though I hated him, I was constantly thinking of Hideaki. The way he laughed. The way he touched my hair. I like everything about him: the way he was a little self-centered, the way he had a complex about being tone deaf, the way he cried so easily. I knew I was being an idiot, but when he and I were together, I truly was happy, and those memories were engraved into the cells of my brain so deeply I couldn't erase them.

Sometimes I even imagined that the words he said to me the last time were all lies. That he was just teasing me. "It's all fake," he'd tell me. He'd just wanted to play a little joke on me. And, of course, that wasn't true. If it had been true, I wouldn't be here.

So to put it out of my mind, and stop remembering what happened, I went on sleeping, perhaps out of stubbornness, perhaps for some other reason.

The time passed by so quickly that I could never catch up.

4

"Takako, you still up?"

One night at the end of summer, my uncle called out to me from the other side of the sliding door. When I looked at the clock, I saw it was eight o'clock—closing time for the bookshop.

"I'm sleeping," I said from under the covers.

"Come on. People who are sleeping can't answer back like that."

"But I am sleeping. Because I'm a—what'd you call me?—a sleep monster, remember?"

I heard him laugh through the door.

"Are you angry?" he said. "I talked to Sabu."

"I am angry. You said I was like a monster."

"Well, I was worried about you, so I talked to him. He's worried about you too. Come on, don't you want to go outside? There's a place I want to take you. How about it?"

"I'm fine," I replied, facing the sliding door.

But my uncle persisted. "Trust me, you won't regret it. And then I promise I won't interfere anymore with your sleeping."

"For real?" I asked warily.

"Pinky swear. If I'm lying, you can hit me three hundred times."

"That's a promise." When I glared at him through the little gap in the sliding door, I saw him smiling and nodding.

"I promise."

The place he wanted to take me was just a stone's throw from the Morisaki Bookshop.

"We're here!" he said, coming to a halt in front of a storefront on a little backstreet. It was an old wooden coffee shop that I didn't think I'd ever noticed before. An extremely elegant, middle-aged man with a mustache seemed to be the man in charge.

The name of the coffee shop, Saveur, lit up by the sign, seemed to float above the dark haze.

"This is my spot," he said. As soon as my uncle heaved open the heavy door, we could smell the rich aroma of coffee.

The man pouring boiling water into a special siphon placed on the counter greeted us as we came in.

"Hey, this is my niece, Takako."

I took a seat next to my uncle at the small counter and gave a quick bow.

Even without the mustache, the owner's slender, refined face would have been quite dignified. He was probably in his late forties. I wished my uncle, who looked like a kid no matter how old he got, would follow his example.

"A blend for me. How about you, Takako?"

"Um, me too."

I turned and looked around inside. It felt so peaceful there. The interior was lit by soft lanterns. Gentle piano music was playing. The blackened brick wall was covered with doodles and graffiti from past customers. All of it fit together beautifully and matched the warm, soothing ambience of the coffee shop. It's so nice here, I thought. For the first time in a long time, I felt joy well up inside me. And I felt a little bit better, a little less tired.

"This place has been around for fifty years," my uncle explained. "In the old days, a lot of famous people used to come here."

"Wow. I'm sure it wasn't easy to create an atmosphere like this," I said, nodding deeply. "It's so calming."

Around five minutes later, a waitress brought us our coffee.

"Good evening, Mr. Morisaki."

"Hey, Tomo, this is my niece, Takako."

"Nice to meet you," I said, bowing.

Tomo smiled and said hello.

"Tomo's one of our regular customers," my uncle said. "She's a true reader."

"Oh, I'm nothing special," she said, smiling shyly. She was about my age, maybe a little younger. She had fair skin and round, full cheeks. There was something gentle about her way of speaking. And she looked cute in her black apron. I had a feeling we might get along. My mood brightened.

"What's the deal, Takako? You prefer girls? There are young guys here too." My uncle waved to the other end of the counter. "Hey, Takano!"

A tall, thin young man promptly popped his head through a gap in the curtain from the kitchen.

"Takano! Why don't you take my niece out on a date sometime?"

"Hey!" I shouted and slapped my uncle's hand.

Takano seemed pretty shy. That's all it took for his face to turn completely red.

"Takano has been training here so he can open his own café someday. But all he does is screw up, so the owner's constantly yelling at him." My uncle looked genuinely happy as he said the part about being yelled at.

"Let's not start tarnishing his reputation," the owner interjected.

I felt bad for Takano, but he looked so unsteady on his feet that you could knock him over with a little push. He ended up inadvertently confirming what my uncle had said.

My uncle was still in a good mood afterward. A middle-aged woman sitting nearby called out, "Hey, Satoru!"

"Oh, Mrs. Shibamoto!" he said and went over to her with his tail wagging. Then someone else at another table called out his name, and he quickly moved over to them.

At the bookshop, my uncle kept things more under control, but take one step outside and he was totally different. I sighed, feeling like a dog owner being dragged around by her pet.

"Satoru's a popular guy around here." The café owner laughed wryly. When he smiled, the wrinkles around his eyes made him look kind.

"He's very friendly, if nothing else," I said, sarcastically. "But this truly is the first time I've ever had coffee this good. And I love the feel of this place. It's wonderful."

The owner gave a soft laugh. "Thank you very much. When young people come here for the first time, they see it with fresh eyes. That means a lot to me. It's Takako, right? Are you new to the area?"

"This is my first time. I just started living at my uncle's store."

"At the Morisaki Bookshop? That's a great spot. I really hope you enjoy life in Jimbocho."

I made a face and groaned a little.

"What's wrong?"

"My uncle says the same thing."

"That makes sense. No one loves this neighborhood more than your uncle."

I groaned again. "I'm not sure I get it. But I wasn't lying when I said your café was wonderful. I definitely want to come back."

"Anytime," he said and gave me a big smile.

We *stayed so* long at the café that when we left it was late in the evening. My uncle and I strolled around the neighborhood, just wandering. The night breeze was cool against my face. It already felt like autumn.

My uncle seemed drunk from the one beer he'd ordered. He walked ahead of me, stumbling a little and mumbling about what a nice night it was.

I realized then that it was the first time we'd gone for a walk together like this since my childhood. Back then, we would walk all day long near my grandfather's house, hand in hand, pretending we were exploring. Why was that so much fun? I was always giggling with excitement.

In those days my uncle always seemed more like a sweet older brother. I guess it's natural for an only child, especially one like me, so wrapped up in her own thoughts, to be so excited to be spending time with someone like that.

As my mind drifted back to that time, vivid memories returned to me . . . the two of us in his messy little room, him playing Beatles songs terribly on the guitar, and both of us singing . . . or spending hours reading Osamu Tezuka and Shotaro Ishinomori, totally engrossed in manga.

These memories made me start to feel a little bit of that same closeness to my uncle again as he walked ahead of me.

"Uncle Satoru?" His back was to me when I called out to him.

"Yeah?" My uncle turned and stared at me with those boyish eyes.

"What were you doing when you were my age?"

"I guess I just read all the time."

"That's all?" I felt a little disappointed. "That doesn't seem that very different from now."

"That plus traveling."

"Traveling?"

"Yeah, I would work a little here in Japan, save up some money, that kind of thing. Then I'd backpack around. I went to all kinds of places—Thailand, Laos, Vietnam, India, Nepal. I even went across Europe."

The idea that my uncle had been so adventurous amazed me.

"What made you want to do that? Didn't you think about getting a regular job?"

"Hmmm . . ." He folded his arms and spoke slowly, as if he was thinking back on that period of his life. "The short version is I wanted to see the whole world for myself. I wanted to see the whole range of possibilities. Your life is yours. It doesn't belong to anyone else. I wanted to know what it would mean to live life on my own terms."

I found myself nodding, but it seemed like a bit of a contradiction to escape Japan and go off in search of the possibilities for your life only to end up running the bookstore.

Still, listening to him talk, I realized just how different he was from the image of him I'd been holding on to since childhood. Now that I'm an adult, I think I can understand a little bit of what he felt then. In college, I used to dream about living a life that felt true to my own values, my own sense of things. Of course, when it came time to act on that in the real world, I found I just didn't have the courage.

That might have been the secret to why he was able to be so wild and free.

I felt a little jealous of him.

"Well, I guess I spent my twenties drifting around like that. My father was always getting angry at me. And then one day in the midst of all this, he dropped dead. And I ended up taking over the store for him."

"Do you regret it?"

"Not at all," he said, smiling. "There's no job that suits me better than this one. For someone who loves books, there's no place more wonderful than here. I'm proud to have a shop here. I can't thank my father and grandfather enough really."

"That's great."

"What is?" My uncle looked at me with a confused expression.

"That you're doing what you want, and you're making a living at it."

"That's not really true. I resisted it a lot in the beginning. I mean taking over the store from my father wasn't exactly what I dreamt of doing when I was young. Even now I still go back and forth all the time. But, I don't know, maybe it takes a long time to figure out what you're truly searching for. Maybe you spend your whole life just to figure out a small part of it."

"I don't know. I think maybe I've been wasting my time, just doing nothing."

"I don't think so. It's important to stand still sometimes. Think of it as a little rest in the long journey of your life. This is your harbor. And your boat is just dropping anchor here for a little while. And after you're well rested, you can set sail again."

"You're saying that now, but then you complain when I'm sleeping," I said spitefully.

He laughed. "Human beings are full of contradictions."

I was pouting without realizing it. Especially this guy, I thought.

"So, when you were traveling around and reading all those books, you must have learned a lot, right?"

"It's funny. No matter where you go, or how many books you read, you still know nothing, you haven't seen anything. And that's life. We live our lives trying to find our way. It's like that Santōka Taneda poem, the one that goes, 'On and on, in and in, and still the blue-green mountains.'"

"Uncle?" I thought that this might be my opportunity to ask the question I'd been wanting to ask him all along.

"Yeah?"

"Why did Aunt Momoko leave?"

"Hmmm . . . She and I have the same way of looking at things. It's what brought us together, and I think it's also the reason we split up. We met in the middle of the journey and we fell in love. But that doesn't mean we'll always be traveling together. At some point, everyone has to find their safe harbor. I'd always thought we'd make it to the end together. Unfortunately, that's not how it turned out."

"What was it like . . . when it happened? Were you sad?"

He looked up at the thick clouds covering the sky. "Of course, it was sad, but . . ."

"But?"

"But, no matter where she is and what she's doing now, I want her to be happy."

"Still . . ." I couldn't understand how he could feel that way. "Didn't she dump you and leave?"

"But Momoko's still the one woman in my life that I've truly loved. That fact will never change. And the memories I have of our time together, they're all still here in my heart. So, in that sense, I'm still in love with her."

I wanted to ask him why, but there was something so sad about the look of him from behind, so small under the streetlight, that I decided I couldn't say anything more.

That night, for some reason, I couldn't get to sleep. I felt strangely agitated. Even in the middle of the night, I was still tossing and turning. I remained there on my futon for a long time, struggling. All of these thoughts were swirling together inside my head, filling it until I thought it might explode. They kept going around and around, these painful memories of the past, of my old life. They commandeered my mind.

This is terrible, I thought. I sat up suddenly. If I don't do something, I said to myself, I'm going to suffocate here. I thought I could maybe watch TV, but then I remembered that would mean rearranging those stacks of books again first. It was three in the morning. Nothing was open outside no matter where you went.

As I stared into the darkness, I wished I had a book to read... It would've at least been a way to pass the time.

That's when it hit me. Isn't this a bookstore? I was practically drowning in books. I'd completely forgotten their original purpose because up till then I'd only seen them as a hostile presence in the room.

I turned on the light and started rummaging around, searching for an interesting book. But I had absolutely no idea how to judge which ones might be interesting. They all just looked like musty old books. I was sure though that my uncle could have easily picked out some that he loved.

At a loss, I stood in front of a mountain-sized stack of books and closed my eyes. Then I reached out my hand and pulled out the first book that I touched. It was titled *Until the Death of the Girl*. The author was Saisei Murō. I had heard his name before in my modern lit class back in high school, but that was all I knew.

So there in that dim room, with only the light of a little lamp near my pillow, I burrowed under my covers and began to read. My hope was that the book would be boring enough that I would fall right asleep. But a funny thing happened. An hour later, I was totally absorbed in it. Sure, there were some passages where the writing was difficult, but the subject of the book was human psychology, which is universal.

The story centers around a man trying to start his life in Nezu. After spending his childhood in Kanazawa, he moves to Tokyo to follow his dream and become a poet. There he gets entangled in a relationship with a woman who is the lover of a friend and his half-sister. He's struggling in poverty with no way to support himself in Tokyo when he meets the girl in the title by chance. It's through his relationship with her that he starts to heal his wounded heart, however briefly.

The main character has grown up in difficult circumstances and has survived a depressing youth, but somehow the whole story is suffused with this quiet tenderness.

Little by little, I felt something wash over me, a feeling of peace that words can't express. If I had to explain it, I'd say it could only have come from the writer's fervent love for life.

When I looked up, I realized the night was fading, and the day was beginning to dawn. I read on, turning one page after another.

That day, when Uncle Satoru came around, I was still feeling excited.

Usually I hardly greeted him, so when I leapt to my feet, he looked back at me with wonder.

I had *Until the Death of the Girl* in my hand. "This book was good," I told him.

How did he react? All of a sudden, my uncle's face lit up—just like a kid who had gotten a wonderful birthday present.

"Really? You liked it?" My uncle was as excited as if it had happened to him.

"Yeah, it was amazing," I said. "I don't know how to describe it. It hit home." I was frustrated that I couldn't come up with a better word. "It hit home" couldn't begin to describe the complex things happening inside me.

"No way! It means so much to me to hear you say that. I'm overjoyed. But going straight to Murō Saisei, that's jumping into the deep end."

My uncle was so profoundly happy that it somehow made me happy too.

We talked about the book for a while. It was a joy to feel connected to someone I'd felt I had so little in common with. It thrilled me even if it was just with someone like my uncle—no, it thrilled me even more because it was someone like him.

It was as if, without realizing it, I had opened a door I had never known existed. That's exactly what it felt like.

From that moment on, I read relentlessly, one book after another. It was as if a love of reading had been sleeping somewhere deep inside me all this time, and then it suddenly sprang to life.

I read slowly, savoring each book one by one. I had all the time in the world then. And there was no danger I'd run out of books, no matter how much I read.

Kafū Nagai, Jun'ichirō Tanizaki, Osamu Dazai, Haruo Satō, Ryūnosuke Akutagawa, Kōji Uno . . . I read them voraciously, the authors whose names I knew but hadn't read, the ones whose names I'd never even heard of, any book that seemed interesting. And yet for all I read, I found book after book that I still wanted to read.

I'd never experienced anything like this before. It made me feel like I had been wasting my life until this moment.

I decided to stop sleeping all the time. It no longer seemed necessary. Instead of taking refuge in sleep after my uncle took over for me at the bookshop, I went to my room or to a café to read.

These old books held more history within their covers than

I'd ever imagined. That wasn't limited to the content of the book itself. In each volume, I discovered traces of the years that had gone by.

For example, on a page of Motojirō Kajii's *Landscapes of the Heart*, I came across this passage:

The act of seeing is no small thing. To see something is to be possessed by it. Sometimes it carries off a part of you, sometimes it's your whole soul.

At some point in the past, someone reading this book had felt moved to take a pen and draw a line under these words. It made me happy to think that because I had been moved by that same passage too, I was now connected to that stranger.

Another time, I happened to find a pressed flower someone had left as a bookmark. As I inhaled the scent of the long-ago-faded flower, I wondered about the person who had put it there. Who in the world was she? When did she live? What was she feeling?

It's only in secondhand books that you can savor encounters like this, connections that transcend time. And that's how I learned to love the secondhand bookstore that handled these books, our Morisaki Bookshop. I realized how precious a chance I'd been given, to be a part of that little place, where you can feel the quiet flow of time.

As a result, I became pretty knowledgeable about the writers we carried. Before I knew it, I had become close with our regulars too. When Sabu realized something was a little different about me, he revised his earlier impression of me. "Hey, Takako," he said, "you're getting into it, aren't you?"

There was one more change: I started taking walks around

the neighborhood. It was right about the time when the weather had turned properly cool, the perfect season for walking around.

Day by day, the leaves of the trees along the streets turned to gold. It delighted me to see how well the changing colors matched the slow transformation happening inside me.

As I walked around, I saw the neighborhood so differently from when I first arrived in Jimbocho. Now, the whole place felt like the setting for an adventure. It was exciting. In any case, there were so many places I wanted to stop and check out all along the avenues and backstreets. It had such a strong downtown feeling, this little section of secondhand bookstores and coffee shops and foreign bars. And yet despite all that, there was nothing about its atmosphere that was chaotic in a way I couldn't stand. The whole neighborhood felt distinctly calm.

This is where I finally realized that even though we call them all "bookstores," each store has its own totally distinct flavor.

They're divided by their various specialties: some sell only novels, some only foreign literature, or historical novels. There were even shops that dealt only in film magazines, or children's books, or Edo-era texts bound in the traditional style. There were all kinds of store owners too. Some were stubborn old guys like my uncle, but there were also younger ones with gentler dispositions. I stopped by the welcome center one day, and they told me there were actually more than 170 bookstores here. Like my uncle said, it really was the world's greatest neighborhood for bookstores.

When at last I was tired from walking, I would stop at a coffee shop to rest. The warm coffee was perfect for the chilly season. Drinking a cup at the end of my walk, I felt relaxed to my core.

I spent day after day this way as we went deeper into autumn. I have no doubt that my new routine helped brighten my mood.

Things were still knotted up inside me, but it felt like the more I walked, the more they loosened up.

Perhaps, as a result, it was at that time that I started to get to know more people around the neighborhood. I became a regular at the Saveur coffee shop and started to get very close with the owner and the staff, especially with Tomo, the waitress.

Tomo was a first-year grad student in Japanese literature who was working at the Saveur in her free time. And sometimes she came to the Morisaki Bookshop as a customer. Two years younger than I was, she looked quiet and reserved, but deep down she was fiercely passionate. As you might expect of a grad student in literature, she had an incomparable love of writers. That wealth of knowledge was one of the things I admired about her.

Around this time, Tomo started coming by the store on her way home from work, even when she wasn't looking to buy anything, and the two of us would go to my room on the second floor and have tea together, surrounded by books.

The first time she came into my room, she lit up. "This place is amazing. It's like a dream."

"Really? It's so small—and there's no gas range." Since I was the one actually living there, I gave her my candid opinion. At least when it came to convenience, the place really had nothing to recommend it.

"Are those things really that important?" Tomo said, looking like I was the one who didn't get it. "Not a single thing here is superfluous. You reach out your hand and the books are right there. Isn't that wonderful?"

"I guess so."

"It's true," she said as she brought her face close to mine. Her eyes shone.

I looked around the room again. It was strange—somehow

her excitement about my room transformed the place from being dull into something wonderful. She suggested that we could make the room even nicer by buying some flowers at the corner florist. We arranged cosmos stems in a vase and placed it on the low table. The room felt so much brighter afterward. From that point on, I always decorated that spot with an arrangement of seasonal flowers.

One day as we were really becoming close, we were drinking tea together and I suddenly decided to ask her something.

"Tomo, how did you get so into books?"

She answered me in that same gentle voice. "That's a good question. When I was in middle school, I was painfully shy. I had this fear of telling people what I thought. And because of that there were just these terrible feelings rumbling around inside me. I was carrying around this awful shame. That's when I read the copy of Osamu Dazai's *Schoolgirl*. That's how it started for me. Now I'm basically totally addicted to reading."

"I think every serious reader at some point in their life encounters a book like that. And they never forget the experience," I said with admiration.

"Here's hoping we both encounter some wonderful books in the future," Tomo said with a smile.

"I hope so," I said, agreeing with all my heart.

Afterward, something else happened connected to Tomo.

Early one afternoon when I was tending the shop by myself, Takano, who worked at the Saveur, came by. I hadn't had many chances to talk to him because he worked in the kitchen, but it was hard to miss his lanky figure inside the shop.

I noticed him right away and said hello.

Takano bowed and greeted me, but he seemed restless as he wandered the shop looking around.

What an odd guy, I thought. "Anything in particular you're looking for today?" I asked.

"No, I'm, um . . . not . . ." he muttered incoherently.

What's going on with this guy? I wondered. His face was all red. He was acting just like a little boy in front of the girl he had a crush on. That's when it hit me. What if he was interested in me? I remembered that when my uncle had told him to take me out on a date, he'd gotten extremely embarrassed. As I thought it through, I found myself suddenly getting nervous too.

The awkward silence inside the shop dragged on for a while. The air seemed to get so thick with it that it was getting harder to breathe.

When I couldn't bear it any longer, I opened my mouth to say something, but at that very moment, he said in a loud voice, "Um!"

I braced myself automatically. I assumed he was about to confess his love for me, and so my mind was racing, wondering how I could delicately turn him down.

But what he actually said next wasn't what I was expecting at all.

"Does Miss Aihara come here a lot?" Takano's face turned bright red as he spoke.

"By Miss Aihara, you mean Tomo?"

"That's right."

"She often pops in during her lunch break from the coffee shop."

"What do you two talk about?"

At this point, my fever broke, and my anxiety subsided.

"Wait, do you have a crush on Tomo?" I asked.

"No, it's not that. It's just . . ."

"It's fine. I mean Tomo is really cute. But since you two work together, I'd think you might know her better than I do."

"No. I'm in the kitchen. She's in the dining area. And I'm terrible at talking to people."

"So it seems. You really are shy, aren't you?"

"Does she have a boyfriend?"

The tone of his voice as Takano asked the question suggested this was a matter of the greatest urgency.

"Well, now that you mention it, I've never asked her. But Tomo is a really cute, likable girl. I wouldn't be surprised if she did have a boyfriend."

"Would you be able to casually ask her for me?"

"Why would I be the one to ask her? Why don't you ask her yourself?"

"You two are good friends, Takako. You could ask her in a way that felt natural, right? And besides, I've never talked like that to a girl before."

"You're talking to me right now," I said, rather taken aback. Didn't I count as a woman? But Takano didn't seem to notice my reaction.

"I'm not asking you to do this for nothing. If you agree to help, anytime you come into the coffee shop, I'll pay for your coffee refills.

And with that, I wrote off all of his many offenses. My face lit up. "Really?" I asked. "In that case, I'll come every day."

"Every day? That might be a bit much . . ."

"Why do you sound so stingy? You'll be getting close to the woman you've been longing for, all for the mere price of a cup of coffee!"

"Ah . . ." Takano nodded reluctantly in approval. "But please promise me you won't mention a word of any of this to her."

"Understood," I told him, thumping my chest.

And that's how Takano and I entered into our secret agreement.

I learned that he had secretly been in love with her for half a year already. But in all that time, apparently, he hadn't done more than say hello to her. He'd spent the whole time off in the shadows thinking to himself how wonderful she was. That might sound weird, but you could also see it as innocent.

Having taken on this role, I wanted to try to make things work between them if at all possible. Tomo might think it was none of my business, but Takano seemed like a respectable young man, albeit rather shy and awkward. If I gave them a chance, I thought, it might not be a total bust.

So I worked hard, not for the free coffee, but for the good of those two young people. The first step was to gather some information on the sly. I came to learn that there was no boyfriend at present, and, it seemed, there was no one in particular that she had on her mind. Her favorite color was Prussian blue. Her favorite animal, the dormouse. And her favorite neighborhood was, naturally, Jimbocho. All of this seemed perfectly in line with what I knew of her, but it felt a little bit creepy that Tomo didn't know what was really going on.

Having obtained this new information, I proceeded to the Saveur, where I passed it along to Takano over a cup of free coffee. I leaned over the counter and whispered, "It looks like Tomo's favorite animal is the dormouse."

"That . . . that's amazing," Takano whispered back. Unfortunately, this led to the surprisingly nosy owner starting the false rumor among the regular customers that Takano and I were together.

What's more, all my hard work on behalf of our young couple proved totally useless. Takano, whose role was crucial, was not making any attempt to start a conversation with Tomo, which meant we were making no progress at all. He'd let out a victory cry when he learned she didn't have a boyfriend, but at this rate, it was going to take a decade before he could even start making small talk with her. It would all come to nothing.

I was getting impatient myself. There had to be some way to get these two talking. I thought of everything.

And then good news arrived from an unexpected source.

One afternoon, when Tomo and I were enjoying a quiet cup of tea, she told me about the used book festival.

"Used book festival? What's that?" I said, dumbfounded.

"You don't know about the festival, Takako? Every year in the fall, all the used bookstores in the area set up an outdoor bargain book market. So many people come, the whole neighborhood feels crowded and lively. It's incredible."

"Oh wow. That sounds fun."

"Your uncle's doing it too, of course."

"Really?"

"Yeah, all the stores join in."

I felt embarrassed that my uncle had never said a word about this major event. I vowed solemnly to exact my revenge on him later.

"I'm thinking about going this year," she said. "Do you want to walk around together?"

At that moment, I had a flash of inspiration. "Yes. Let's go. Let's go," I said, jumping at her offer. There might be a way to take advantage of this. I should tell Takano.

5

The Kanda Used Book Festival took place over the course of a week in late October. And for that week, carts and bookshelves, crammed with used books, crowded the streets in an open-air flea market.

The festival was such a success that it surprised me. Book lovers of all ages flocked to the neighborhood. Maybe because it was a once-a-year event, but the turnout went far beyond my expectations. You could feel the energy on Yasukuni and Sakura Streets. This old sepia-toned neighborhood of secondhand bookshops was now buzzing with activity before noon. It was a pretty spectacular sight.

Our Morisaki Bookshop joined in too, of course. My uncle and I brought out the cart with all the used books we'd set aside over the previous few days. To our delight, we had twice as many customers as usual come to the shop. There was even a brave soul who was so worried he'd miss out on the sale that he bought a whole cardboard box of our bargain books.

As expected, my festival-loving uncle was very much in his element. Apparently, he'd been coming to the festival almost every year since he was a kid. Thanks to that, he could feel his body start to ache in anticipation when that time of year came around.

"After this, it'll get cold, and the number of people coming to the store will decrease significantly," he said. "We need to make enough money now to get us through." It was rare for my uncle to talk like a businessman, but despite what he said, when I lost sight of him for a moment, he was off visiting other shops. Of course, it was up to me to bring him back.

On the evening of the third day, I ended work early with my uncle's permission and went out with Tomo to have a look around the rest of the festival. And who should appear then, apparently by accident, but Takano—just as we'd planned.

"Oh, what a surprise," he said.

"Oh, wow, it really is," I replied. We were lousy actors putting on an obvious charade, but Tomo was so innocent that she didn't seem to notice at all.

And, with that, one of us said, "The three of us should walk around together."

In front of Tomo, Takano was stiff and tense at first. I whispered to him discreetly, "What are you doing? You look like RoboCop."

"I've forgotten how to walk," he replied. Even his voice sounded robotic. Tomo overheard him and burst out laughing.

Why was it that all the excitement in the neighborhood seemed to lift our spirits as we walked around? The two of them were waltzing around with such animated expressions on their faces that they looked like a couple. Though at least in Takano's case, there was another major reason for this. When Tomo spoke to him, he looked ecstatic, like he was running through a field of flowers. The look on his face was so funny that I struggled not to burst out laughing.

We bumped into Sabu as we were rummaging through the books at the special booth set up at the main Jimbocho intersection. Sabu was with his wife, and he was holding so many paper bags that he could barely carry them in his hands. Sabu's wife looked so elegant in her perfectly matched kimono that I thought she might be too good for him. But seeing the two of them side by side, I could sense that they had the kind of bond that can only come from years spent together in good times and in bad. The feeling was overwhelming.

"It looks like you've bought quite a lot again," I said to Sabu when I saw all the bags he was holding.

"He has," his wife said mournfully, giving Sabu a little push from the side. "He keeps on buying more books. Our house is overrun with them right now. Would you mind coming by one day and buying all of them?"

"Oh no, please not that," Sabu said, panicking. "Didn't I down-size a bit the other day?" He put his hands together, begging her.

Even after they walked away, we couldn't stop laughing.

The crowds on Yasukuni Street didn't go away once it got dark. We were still happily walking around. We were on a shop-ping spree, buying all the books we could get our hands on. "There's an interesting shop over here," Tomo said, and took us to Kintoto Books, which sold grade-school textbooks from the Taishō era, in the early twentieth century. On a whim, I bought a Japanese textbook that cost two thousand yen. The language in it was so old that it ended up feeling surprisingly fresh.

In the evening as all the stores started to close, we went to the Western-style restaurant inside Sanseidō and ate dinner. By this point, Takano was pretty relaxed. He no longer seemed to see himself in a field of flowers every time he was in front of Tomo. It turned out he knew a lot about foreign literature. While we ate, he spoke so easily about the charms of Faulkner, Capote, and Updike that you never would have believed how awkward he'd been earlier. Tomo and I were both properly impressed.

In the end, it turned out to be a fulfilling and exciting day. Afterward, Takano thanked me and said how incredibly grateful he was, but I didn't see any reason to thank me, because I was the one who enjoyed it the most.

6

On the last night of the festival, after we closed the shop, I was sitting alone in my room in a daze. Outside the window, the streets were so quiet and still that the crowds of the past week already seemed like a dream. As I lay on my futon, the ticking of my alarm clock seemed too loud. I was staring up at the ceiling when I felt that strange uneasy feeling return, that loneliness I'd felt when I first arrived here.

Suddenly, there was a knock at the door. I felt my shoulders trembling. As I turned timidly toward it, I saw in the narrow opening at the edge of the sliding door an eye glaring back at me.

"Aahhhh!" I turned pale and shrieked like a heroine in a horror movie.

"Oh, did I surprise you?" a strange, high-pitched voice said. And then a shaggy head popped into view.

I heaved a sigh of relief.

"Please don't surprise me like that, Uncle."

"Sorry, sorry." He put down the plastic bag he'd been holding in both hands and said, "Mind if I come in for a second?" as he walked into the room. He took out some bottles of alcohol and juice and set them up on the little dining table. He'd even brought potato chips and shredded squid snacks.

"Didn't you go to the end-of-festival wrap party?" I asked.

"I just went to say hello and then I came back. Besides, I'd rather have a wrap party with just the two of us," he said with a smile like a mischievous child.

"Now that you mention it, we've never had a drink together."

"Well, okay, then. Let's do it." My uncle spread out all the contents of his plastic bag and we had our little wrap party. We sipped our sake, listening to the faint chirping of crickets through the open window. The quiet night enveloped us. Time passed so slowly that it felt like it had come to a halt.

My uncle stretched his legs comfortably as he leaned back against the bookshelf.

"Takako, it looks like you've totally gotten used to life here," he said.

"I think so too. At first I wasn't so sure it would work out, but somehow it has. I'm fully enjoying this little vacation from my life," I said with a little laugh.

"I'm glad to hear it."

"But I'm frustrated too."

"About what?"

"You knew from the beginning that I'd totally love it here."

"Don't feel bad about that. It makes me very happy that you like it. If you want, you know, you can stay here forever."

Hearing my uncle's kind words, I felt a little twinge in my heart.

"Why are you so good to me though? I know I'm your niece, but we hadn't seen each other in so long."

"Because I love you, Takako." He said it without any hint of embarrassment. He seemed almost distracted. "I know, for you, I might be some relative you don't know that well, but for me it's different. For me, you're an angel."

I almost spit out my beer.

No one had ever said anything like that to me before—no man, no woman had ever talked to me like that before.

"That's right. An angel. You're the person who saved me."

"Saved you?" I asked, understanding him less and less.

I had no memory of having ever done anything for him.

"That's right. You saved me. That's just my way of thinking of it. But I'm sure it won't be a very interesting story to you. Let's drop the subject."

"No, I want to hear it," I said sincerely.

My uncle stared at me for a moment and then asked if I promised I wouldn't laugh.

I nodded in agreement, and my uncle started speaking slowly, as if he were remembering something from long ago.

"It started in my late teens. I was feeling depressed. I couldn't see the value of life anymore. I couldn't seem to fit in, at home or at school. I just withdrew into myself and closed everything else out. I was overly self-conscious, I had too many ideals and ambitions for one person, and because of that, I ended up without a single one I could hold on to. I was an empty person. That's what I was. It seemed like there was absolutely nowhere I belonged in this world."

I'd never had the slightest inkling that my uncle had felt this way. But I also had no idea what on earth this had to do with me being an angel.

"You were born right around that time. I first met you when my sister brought you back home to introduce my father and everyone to his new granddaughter. The instant I saw you, so tiny wrapped up in your blanket, sleeping so peacefully, I thought I might cry. How can I put it? I could feel the mystery of life filling my heart. The idea of this child growing up, experiencing so many things for the first time, absorbing so much—all of it brought me as much joy as if it were happening to me.

"All of a sudden, I felt as if my twisted heart was being filled with warm light. It was still blurry, but I could feel a sense of purpose growing within me. That's when I made my decision. It was time to stop shutting myself up in a cage. It was time to get moving, to look around, and learn what I could from it all. Time to go in search of a place where I belonged, a place where I could say with confidence that I felt right. All the trips I went on, all the books I read, were the consequences of that decision. In other words, Takako, meeting you led me to a kind of epiphany."

"An epiphany . . . That's amazing."

"So, that's what I mean when I say you're the one who saved me. That's why I'll do anything for you."

My uncle said this so earnestly that I didn't know how to respond. I felt embarrassed by how childish I'd been, getting angry at him, and feeling sorry for myself. To think that all this time he'd cared so much about me. I felt like I finally understood the reason that he'd been so kind to me when I was little. I was an idiot. At the time I thought it was my natural right to be treated so kindly.

The joy of realizing that someone loved me that much made my heart want to burst. I tried to make a joke to hold back the tears welling up in my eyes. "Uncle," I said, "that's not exactly dialogue you should deliver while you're eating shredded squid."

My uncle laughed out loud.

"So did you end up finding the place you belonged?"

"Well, I guess you might say that. But it took me many years to get there." My uncle nodded quietly. "This is it. Our little, run-down Morisaki Bookshop. I had so many aspirations. I flew all over the world only to end up back at the place I'd known every bit of since I was a child. Hilarious, isn't it? After all that time, I came back here. That's when I finally realized it wasn't just a question of where I was. It was about something inside me. No matter where I went, no matter who I was with, if I could be honest with myself, then that was where I belonged. By the time I realized that, half my life was over. So I went back to my favorite harbor, and I decided to drop anchor. For me, this is a sacred place. It's where I feel most at ease."

"That reminds me," I said. "A long time ago, Sabu told me that you were the store's savior."

He laughed. "Its savior? That's a pretty big exaggeration. Basically, when my father fell ill, the business was on the brink—all I did was take over and keep it going. At first, my father was pretty strongly opposed to me taking over the shop. It was a tough time in the used book business, after all, and I was this irresponsible guy. But I got down on my knees and pleaded with him to entrust the shop to me."

"So that's how it happened."

"I mean I couldn't sit back and let it all fall apart, could I? This was where I spent most of my childhood. I would sit at the counter next to my father, quietly reading books like *Hans Christian Andersen's Fairy Tales*, and from time to time, he would stroke my head firmly with his giant hand. I was truly happy then. It felt like if this place was gone, then all of my memories would disappear too. I couldn't handle that."

I felt absolutely bowled over by what my uncle was telling me.

I'd thought I knew—or at least I'd meant to find out—what my relationship with my uncle was all about. Didn't I realize that he had his own private worries and pain? Didn't I see that his heart had been crying out for far longer than mine had? Why didn't I see how much was going on inside him?

Maybe the reason my uncle was always clowning around in front of people was to hide what he was feeling from them. The effort must have been excruciating. To look at him, they'd never realize what he felt inside . . .

The thought of it made my heart ache.

"I wish this place could have meant as much to Momoko too. She left just as I was trying so hard to rebuild the business. Right up until the end, I still had no sense what she was feeling beneath the surface."

"Uncle."

"Yes?"

"I love this shop. I really do."

I'd meant to say something more clever, but that was all that came out of my mouth. It was true, though, and I felt it sincerely.

"Thank you. This shop might not be indispensable for most people, but if it matters that much to even just one other person, then I feel I can keep it going for decades. It's like the line from Naoe Kinoshita in *Confessions of a Husband*, 'My boat travels lightly, drifting aimlessly at the mercy of the current.' That's how I want to live my life with this shop," my uncle said, and then he smiled without saying any more.

From that night, I started to think more seriously about my own life. I'd found a warm, calm place to stay here, but I couldn't remain dependent on others forever. If I did, I would never grow up. My heart would always be weak. I was convinced that if I didn't leave, I would never be able to start over.

But the moment I thought that, my fears came rushing back. The thought of leaving frightened me. *Just let me stay a little longer.* In my heart I was still dependent on others.

In the end, I hesitated, and, for a long time afterward, I went on living on the second floor of the Morisaki Bookshop.

Maybe I was waiting for some kind of cue. Then one day, suddenly, it arrived.

7

The call came on the second of January.

Instead of going home for the holidays, I spent the period around New Year's Day hanging around the bookshop. With the store closed until the fifth and my uncle off on a trip to the hot springs with his friends from the booksellers' association, I was all by myself.

Over the holiday, Jimbocho was a ghost town. Since there weren't any homes in the area, and the restaurants and companies were closed for the holidays, there was really no one around. There weren't even many cars driving down Yasukuni Street.

On New Year's Eve, Tomo and I went to visit the Yushima Tenjin Shrine, but besides that, my calendar was basically blank. So on New Year's Day and the day after, I got up early and strolled around the neighborhood. It felt great to walk around the deserted city. Even the air seemed much clearer. With my scarf fluttering in the wind, I made my way at random, stopping again and again to take another deep breath.

When I came home in the evening on the second, there was a blinking light on the cell phone that I'd left in the room. I'd already deleted the number from my phone, but I recognized it as soon as I saw it in my missed calls. At that moment, all of the good feelings of the day magically vanished. I felt my chest tighten. My finger trembled as I tapped the button and listened to the message.

"Hey, Takako, it's been a while. You good? I've got zero plans at the moment. You want to come out? If you call me, I can be right over."

I pressed delete before I'd heard the whole message. But it was too late. That awful feeling was already spreading rapidly through my heart. It happened so quickly. And now I would never get rid of that feeling.

When the shop reopened after the holidays, the pain in my heart only got worse. I can't put it into words exactly, but it was like there was this thing that was heavy and cold and it was starting to close around my heart. It made me realize once again that none of those things had ever been resolved. I had just tossed it all aside, waiting for my memories to fade away over time. But even though six months had gone by, just hearing his voice for a moment had left me all churned up inside. I understood at last that none of my problems had been solved. The trouble was still there.

"Takako, is there something you need to get off your chest? If something's going on, talk to me." Around the end of January as we were closing up the shop, my uncle suddenly said this to me.

I was flustered. "How did you know?"

"What do you mean? It's obvious just looking at you. Your uncle's not blind," he said, almost sulking.

It was just childish. I'd been acting like everything was normal, but my uncle saw through the whole thing.

"You seemed like you were doing really well, so I wasn't worried about you before. But lately, you just seem really off. When I try to talk to you, it's like you're not there."

"That's true, I guess . . ."

"Yes, it's true. Well, I might not be up to the challenge, but if you talk to me you might feel a little better."

I hadn't planned on telling anyone about it, but hearing what my uncle said, I realized I was wrong. I'd wanted someone to ask me about it. I'd wanted someone to console me. I'd wanted someone to take care of me. It amazed me how utterly pathetic I was, but my uncle's words had wiped out my defenses.

As we sat together in my room drinking, I told him the whole story. Outside a cold winter rain started to fall. We could hear the patter of raindrops hitting the window.

"It's not a big deal," I said to preface the story, and as I told him what happened, I realized that it actually wasn't a big deal after all. I'd lost my boyfriend and I'd lost my job. That's it. Midway through the story, it all seemed so insignificant that I couldn't help but laugh. I fought through it and finished the story, and once I did, I felt a little bit better.

The whole time my uncle just listened without uttering a word, as he drank his whisky with unusual speed. Even when I finally finished my story after an hour of halting and stuttering, he didn't say anything for a long time. He stared at the glass in his hand like he was thinking of something.

Then, at last, he drained the remaining alcohol from his glass and said decisively, "All right, let's go make him apologize. We're going to make him say, 'I'm sorry I hurt you. I'm a terrible person.'"

I was dumbfounded. This was a totally unexpected development.

"What? Now? It's already eleven."

"Doesn't matter." As he said this, my uncle got up and started to go outside. I grabbed hold of his arm in a panic.

"It's okay. I was being stupid. I just wanted to tell someone what happened. You're drunk, aren't you?"

"Nah, I'm not drunk. Well, maybe a little. But that's beside the point. Aren't you mad, Takako? He took advantage of you."

"Yeah, I'm mad. I've been getting madder and madder, and I'm still mad.

"That's why we're going. You need to get this off your chest. If not, the ghost of this thing will haunt you forever."

"Yes, but I'll be even more embarrassed if it turns into me acting like a little kid trying to bring in my parents when I get in a fight," I said, on the verge of tears.

"There's nothing to be embarrassed about!" My uncle shouted in a voice that seemed shockingly loud coming from someone so small. The sound of his voice reverberated in the little room. "There's nothing to be embarrassed about. You are my niece, and you matter to me. I already told you, didn't I? I really love you. So I can't allow this guy to get away with that. It's my own ego. I can't let it go."

"You keep contradicting yourself. And, in the end, it just comes down to your ego."

"That's why I'm going to get this off my chest. Even if you don't come with me, I'm still going. Tell me the address. I'm going to give him a beating."

A beating? This conversation was suddenly heading in a dangerous direction.

"Wa-wait a second. That's not going to end well. Someone will call the police. And he was on the rugby team in high school and college. If a string bean like you tries to beat him up, you'll end up getting beat up ten times worse."

"Th-that doesn't faze me," my uncle said, but he started to back away a little.

"Come on. Let's not do anything foolish. Let's go back to drinking," I said, forcing a smile as I tried to smooth things over.

"Don't run away from it, Takako," my uncle said, turning back to me with a terrible seriousness. "I'm with you. Don't run away."

My uncle looked at me fiercely. I could see the intensity in his eyes. For a few seconds, we just stared at each other.

He was right. I couldn't run away. If I did, nothing would change. Wasn't that obvious?

I bit down hard on my tongue.

"Okay, I get it. Let's go, Uncle."

My uncle nodded firmly.

By the time we arrived in front of his apartment, after forty minutes in a taxi, the rain was growing more and more intense. We got drenched as we ran to the entrance without an umbrella.

"This is it?"

My uncle had stopped in front of the door with the number 204 on it.

"Definitely," I replied. Old memories were stirring inside me.

Thinking back, I probably only came here two times while we were together. When we met at someone's place, it was always mine. The fact that I was only now realizing there was something weird about this arrangement proved how slow I was.

Raindrops dripping from his hair, my uncle rang the doorbell without a moment's hesitation. My whole body was trembling from the cold and the stress. I felt nauseous too. Whatever assertiveness I'd felt when I said "I get it" faded away quickly once I was standing in front of Hideaki's place.

As I stared at the metal door waiting for a response, deep down I thought about how much better I would feel if we just left and pretended nothing ever happened. But it was already too late. We heard someone rummaging around on the other side of the door, then the click of the door unlocking, after which the door opened about the width of a finger.

A low, familiar voice said, "Who is it?"

My uncle immediately grabbed the door and forced it open.

Hideaki was standing stock-still in the entrance, wearing a

tracksuit, his mouth open in shock. He had probably just fallen asleep. His hair was messy and you could see the imprint of his pillow on his cheek. But those solid, well-defined shoulders and almond-shaped eyes were just as I remembered them. It made sense, of course. It's not as if ten years had passed. In that moment, I felt that stabbing pain in my chest return.

Hideaki looked back and forth at the two of us, wide-eyed with surprise, then turned to my uncle and asked, "Who are you?"

"I'm Takako's uncle."

"Huh?"

"I'm her uncle Satoru. Her mom is my older sister."

"No, I get that part. I mean what are you doing here?"

"Oh, I wouldn't be here without a reason. Do we look like we're here to ask you to subscribe to a newspaper?"

"No, I mean, tell me what business you have here," Hideaki said, sounding a little exasperated.

I was watching the back-and-forth between them anxiously. My uncle was being extremely aggressive that night.

"You want to know why we're here? We're here because you did something terrible to her. Don't act like you have no idea what I'm talking about."

"Eh?" The volume of Hideaki's voice went up a level. But my uncle wasn't the least bit daunted.

"You toyed with her emotions so mercilessly that you drove her to quit her job. Don't you feel anything? Don't you feel any remorse for hurting someone so badly?"

"Hey, hey. I hurt her? Is that what she said?"

"That's right."

"Are you stupid? Maybe it's because you're her uncle, I don't know, but you think you can just swallow everything this woman says? It's obvious she's lying. She's the one who pushed herself on me!"

"How would she benefit from lying? Isn't it your fault that she quit her job, and that she's still suffering?"

"She probably quit because she felt like it."

My uncle let out a big sigh when he heard what Hideaki said. "It's no use, Takako. This guy's rotten to the core."

"Hey, old man, watch what you say."

Hideaki came forward into the hall, glaring at my uncle. My uncle was short, and Hideaki was so tall that there was an almost twenty-centimeter difference in height between them. So even though my uncle was glaring back at Hideaki, the impact was, unfortunately, limited.

"Is something wrong?"

A woman in pajamas poked her head out from inside the apartment. It was his fiancée, Murano.

Things had gone from bad to worse. Standing there might be embarrassing, it might be unbearable, but there was no way out now.

"Takako?" Murano said. When she noticed me, she frowned and said, "What on earth happened? You're all wet."

"She showed up out of nowhere. Isn't that right, Takako? Have you gone crazy? What were you thinking of showing up in the middle of the night with this old man in tow?"

"Tell him, Takako."

"Umm . . ."

Frightened, I looked and saw everyone was staring at me.

How had I ended up here?

I felt pierced by their glances. I wanted to disappear in a puff of smoke. They were all waiting silently for me to say something.

I ransacked my brain for something to say that might somehow bring the situation to a peaceful end.

I was just in the neighborhood and thought I'd drop by . . . I was hoping he'd return a book I'd lent him . . . I wanted to congratulate you on your engagement . . . No. That was all wrong. What I wanted to say was something else entirely. Why was I here? To get something off my chest. If I just told them what they wanted to hear, that wouldn't fix anything.

I told my heart to brace itself.

"I . . ."

Everyone's attention was focused on my mouth. I took a deep breath. My uncle was looking at me with encouragement. Tears formed in my eyes. And at that moment I could feel all of the emotions that had been building in my chest welling up within me. There was no time to think—suddenly, the words came pouring out of my mouth in a torrent.

"I came because I want you to apologize! You might have just been playing around, but it wasn't like that for me. I really loved you. I am a person. I have feelings. You might look at me and see just a woman you can take advantage of, but I think about things, I breathe, I cry. Do you know how much you hurt me? I . . . I . . ."

After that, I was at a loss for words. I was also sopping wet from head to toe from the rain and the tears and my runny nose. But after all this time, I had finally been able to say the words I'd wanted to say that night in the restaurant.

"Well said, Takako," my uncle said, putting his arm around me and drawing me close to him.

"What are you going to do? She just told you honestly how she feels. You have to respond."

Hideaki hung his head for a long time, saying nothing. Finally, he muttered quietly, "This is ridiculous. I don't have time to hang around with people like you who have nothing to do. I'm going to bed. Unless you want me to call the police, you'd better go home."

After he said this, he quietly closed the door. We could hear the lock click on the inside of the door. Then it was quiet in the hall.

"Hey!"

My uncle stared at the door with the intensity of a bullfighter. Then he banged on it loudly with his fists. I held on to him desperately from behind.

"That's enough, Uncle."

"But Takako."

"It was enough. Really. I feel better, maybe better than I've felt in my whole life up till now. It's amazing. This might be the first time I've ever raised my voice and told another person what I really felt," I said, and then burst out laughing at my uncle with my face covered in tears and snot.

"If you say so, Takako . . ." my uncle mumbled, seeming a little dissatisfied.

"It's really okay now."

"Let's go home then, shall we? At this rate, we'll both catch a cold."

Facing the door, I murmured a final goodbye to the place, and then I left it all behind.

In the taxi on the way home, we barely said anything. My uncle, having exhausted all his energy, lay slumped in the back seat. I sat beside him, set free at last from my anxieties, lost in my own thoughts.

It wasn't solely Hideaki's fault. I'd known that from the beginning. I was half to blame for the way things turned out. It was my carelessness and my lack of will that made the situation possible.

But I'd just needed to say what I was feeling, no matter what.

Even if someone told me I was being selfish, I had to share what I was thinking. I'd been suffering because I was too weak to do that. Maybe Hideaki never believed he had any reason to be blamed, and he felt caught off guard by my reaction, but I still needed to vent what I was feeling to him. If not, I couldn't move on. No matter how much time passed, I'd still be stuck. If my uncle hadn't given me the chance, I would've just been left holding on to these feelings forever.

I turned the words around inside my mind, trying to express how grateful I was to my uncle. But nothing came out. In the end, the only thing I could come up with was just one word. So I said it to him sincerely.

"Thanks . . ."

My uncle smiled and pulled me by the shoulder closer to him. Sensing the warmth of his body next to mine, I felt a wave of relief well up from deep within me.

I was protected. There was someone who worried about me, who got angry because what happened to me mattered as much as if it had happened to him.

For a long time, I'd let myself feel like I was totally alone in this big world, but all along there was someone close by, thinking about me, looking out for me. That made me immensely happy.

The taxi we were riding in drove silently across the rainy, neon-streaked city.

8

It was right after that that I decided to leave the shop. As strange as it might sound, that event gave me the boost I needed. All my troubles had vanished, and my body felt light. At last I was ready to leave.

I found a new place where I could live starting in March. It was pretty far away from the shop, but it was the best I could do. I still had a lot of questions about what I was going to do next. For the time being, however, I'd gotten a part-time position at a little design firm through my old job.

When I told my uncle I intended to leave, he seemed quite surprised. "You don't have to rush into any decisions," he said in a panic.

But I had already made my decision.

"I've been enjoying this little vacation from my life for a long time already. If I don't go now to look for the place where I belong, I might end up never finding it."

My uncle listened to me, but he didn't say anything else.

The month before I moved to my new place, I savored my last days at the Morisaki Bookshop. I worked diligently and spent my free time reading lots of books. Out of gratitude, I also did a deep clean of the shop and the second floor. And I even carefully organized the collection of books that was crammed haphazardly into the spare room on the day I arrived.

I let the regular customers and everyone at the Saveur know that I was leaving. They were all sorry to see me go. It almost made me cry to discover they cared so much about me. Sabu went so far as to say that I should marry his son and join his family. And it seemed like he was actually going to bring him by to set us up.

Takano and Tomo held a little going-away party for me. We gathered around a hotpot in my room on the second floor of the shop and celebrated late into the night. Tomo told me how sad she was that her book-loving friend wouldn't be around anymore. "Next year," she said, "let's go to the festival together again, okay?"

That night Takano whispered to me that he'd taken Tomo to the movies in Shibuya a bit earlier. They didn't seem to be a couple yet, but, given where Takano had started, this sounded like substantial progress. I was so happy to hear it, I actually said, "Not bad!" and slapped him as hard as I could on his slender back.

It was after this that Murano, Hideaki's fiancée, contacted me unexpectedly, and we met up at the coffee shop to talk. My biggest worry about that night was that we'd ended up being terribly rude to her as well. I headed to the place we'd agreed upon, planning to offer my sincere apology. But once we were face to face, she was the one bowing deeply to apologize to me. She said she'd had her suspicions about his behavior earlier on, but after my unusual appearance that night, everything clicked for her. She questioned him again and again until he finally confessed. Until that night, she said, she never would have guessed that I was the other woman.

I kept trying earnestly to apologize to her. I said, "I'm to blame too," but she just shook her head. She said the wedding was off now. When I heard that, I rushed to apologize again, but she said firmly, "It's not your fault, Takako."

That guilty feeling stayed with me though. When I told my uncle the next day what had happened, he said, "She's right. Isn't it better to find out now instead of after they're married when it's too late?" My uncle might be biased since he despised Hideaki, but when I realized he had a point, I felt a weight being lifted off my shoulders.

My uncle and I spent my last night at the shop drinking coffee together on the veranda on the second floor, staring up at the dark winter sky.

He gave me a giant stack of old books to remember my days at the bookshop. He said they were all books that had made a deep impression on him when he was young. Peeking into the heavy paper bag, I saw he'd filled it with books by some pretty serious writers, people like Takehiko Fukunaga and Kazuo Ozaki.

We spent our last night together feeling really at ease with one another. I'll never forget what my uncle said to me then.

"There's one thing I want you to promise me," he said first as a preamble. Then he said, "Don't be afraid to love someone. When you fall in love, I want you to fall in love all the way. Even if it ends in heartache, please don't live a lonely life without love. I've been so worried that because of what happened you'll give up on falling in love. Love is wonderful. I don't want you to forget that. Those memories of people you love, they never disappear. They go on warming your heart as long as you live. When you get old like me, you'll understand. How about it—can you promise me?"

"I get it. I promise," I said. "I think this place taught me that. So you don't have to worry."

"In that case, you'll be alright, no matter where you go."

"Thank you, Uncle."

The day of my departure, I stood in the morning light, staring at the Morisaki Bookshop. Such a tiny old wooden building. I lived here, I thought, but I could hardly believe it.

I remained where I was for a while, my breath turning white in the cold air. The street was enveloped in soft morning light. None of the stores had opened yet, and everything around seemed so profoundly peaceful and quiet.

I stood up straight, faced the shop, and bowed deeply. I vowed never to forget what my life at the bookshop had given me.

My uncle took the trouble to see me off despite how early it was. I thanked him from the bottom of my heart.

He had become an enormously important part of my life. It's funny. I never would've imagined things turning out this way when I first arrived here.

As we said goodbye, my uncle's manly attitude of the night before suddenly disappeared and he let himself sob like a child in front of everyone.

"I can't take it. Please don't go, Takako," he said, holding my hand so tightly I thought he might never let go.

"I can come back and see you anytime," I said. It seemed backward, but I was now consoling him.

"You take care of yourself for me, will you? And I'll look after the shop, no matter what."

It felt like if I stayed there a second longer, I'd lose my nerve to leave. So I quickly said goodbye to my uncle, who was still trying to hold on to me, and walked away down the street.

I kept on moving, making it to the end of Sakura Street without looking back. As I was walking, the memories came rushing back, and tears filled my eyes. But I somehow held on and walked to the end of the street.

Then on a hunch I stopped and snuck a look behind me. I saw my uncle standing right in the middle of the street waving to me, looking so small in the distance. Seeing him like that, I couldn't hold on any longer. I burst into tears and started to sob.

I waved back to him with my face crumpled, and tears came pouring down my cheeks.

In response, my uncle waved back even more enthusiastically. I could see the morning light shining behind him.

I shouted, "Take care!" turned around, and walked into the crowds of Yasukuni Street.

Seeing me sobbing as I marched down the street, the people I passed must have surely thought there was something wrong with this weird woman. But I didn't care in the slightest. After all, I was crying because I wanted to cry, and these were the happiest tears I'd ever known.

In the brisk early morning air, I sensed a faint sign of the spring to come. I looked straight ahead and kept going.

Part Two

Momoko Returns

1

"Takako, it's been so long! I feel like I've been away for a hundred years."

That's how my aunt Momoko greeted me when she saw me in front of the Morisaki Bookshop. She let out a loud laugh. She had a voice that carried, and you could hear it reverberating down the little street of bookstores.

It was true. She had come back. Now that she was standing in front of me, it finally felt real. Uncle Satoru had told me she was back and so I knew this, at least, in my head. But until I actually saw her, I didn't really believe it. If a friend had told me they'd seen a ghost, I would've felt the same way.

But Momoko was really there. And she was incredibly cheerful. What was she so cheerful about? Was this the behavior of someone who suddenly reappeared after disappearing for five years? Uncle Satoru, on the other hand, was standing there looking like a dog who had just eaten something rotten. Shouldn't it have been the other way around?

"You look like you've seen a ghost," she said to me, acting offended. "That's a little harsh." I hadn't said a word to her this whole time.

I almost told her I would've been less surprised if I had seen a ghost, but somehow I held back and managed to say, "You look great." It had been more than ten years since we'd seen each other.

When Momoko was young, she was quite pretty. Maybe not drop-dead gorgeous, but there was a quiet beauty to her that caught your eye in an odd way. Like a stone you see glittering on the beach that's not worth much on the market, but there's still something about the way it shines. When I was a child and I saw her at family gatherings, I was always impressed by the way she sat so properly, tucked away in the farthest corner, as if she were trying not to stand out (Momoko is pretty small in stature). There was something almost mystical about her.

Despite the years, Momoko was still beautiful. She wore a simple outfit—a brown sweater with blue jeans—and barely any makeup. And yet with her perfect posture, her expressive face, and her brisk way of talking, she still seemed young. Rather than getting older, she looked more like she'd shed anything that was unnecessary.

In any case, this woman who was bursting with energy didn't look at all like someone who had run off and suddenly come home. My uncle, on the other hand, with his hunched posture, shabby clothes, and messy hair, was looking awfully old.

"Takako, you look just like your mother," Momoko said, narrowing her eyes and squinting at me. "At your grandfather's funeral, you were in high school. It seems like that was just yesterday."

And that's how my uncle Satoru, my aunt Momoko, and I were all reunited on a bright and clear autumn evening, in front of the Morisaki Bookshop.

2

"She's back."

Two days earlier, my uncle had called. He sounded agitated. It had already been a year and a half since I'd left the Morisaki Bookshop.

After my long vacation there had ended, I started working at a small design firm. Three months ago, they'd promoted me from part-time to full-time, which meant that my days were slightly busier, so it had been about a couple of months since I'd stopped by for a visit.

So when my uncle called me, I'd assumed he was just going to ask me to come see him. But hearing how upset he sounded, I knew something big had happened.

On the phone, my uncle described the situation in so much detail that I started to get impatient. To briefly summarize our two-hour conversation, this is what happened.

On that particular day, my uncle had been working in his shop in Jimbocho from the morning to the evening, as usual. At lunch, he'd sold some rare volumes of Ōgai Mori and Sakunosuke Oda, a pretty good haul for the day, so he was in a particularly good mood at the start of the evening. He was whistling as he closed up the shop when he heard someone quietly open the front door and come inside.

He thought, "Oh no, a customer at this hour?" But he had his back to the door and was focused on closing for the day.

The customer didn't seem to be coming any farther inside. They were just standing there in front of the door, almost like they were holding their breath. How odd. My uncle started to get suspicious and turned around. Then he heard the customer mutter something. Hearing that voice was such a shock that my uncle said it felt like "getting hit over the head ten thousand times."

At first, he thought he must be wrong, but he knew there was no way that could be true. It was impossible for him not to recognize that voice—as impossible as squeezing a hundred people into the Morisaki Bookshop.

While my uncle was still frozen with his back to her, unable to move, the customer repeated what she'd said a little more clearly, "Satoru . . ."

He took a deep breath and turned at last to see the owner of that voice. Suddenly, the familiar interior of the store receded into the distance, and there, in focus in the center of his field of view, was a single figure: his wife, who had left him five years earlier without so much as a word, until this moment. He couldn't look away from her. He felt like he was dreaming. He'd had dreams like this hundreds of times before. But in those dreams, his wife had never felt this real. It was definitely Momoko standing there, looking almost exactly the way she did before she left.

After a long silence, Momoko quietly smiled and said, "I'm home."

She said it exactly as if she'd just come back from a short walk. Her only luggage was a little bag she held in one hand.

My uncle stared at her for a long time before he finally replied, "Welcome back."

Without saying anything more, Momoko went up quietly to the room on the second floor. She'd been living on the second floor of the bookshop ever since . . .

"Wait, wait, wait a second." I had been listening patiently on the phone, but at this point he had gone past the limits of my endurance.

"What!? What's all this *'I'm home!' 'Welcome back!'* What do you mean she moved in? It sounds like a ghost story."

"But it's all true, Takako," my uncle replied earnestly.

"If that's true, then you're both weird. Why did Momoko suddenly come back? And why did you just welcome her in without getting upset?"

"I don't understand it myself," my uncle said, sounding bewildered. He seemed deeply affected by what he'd told me. "But it happened so naturally."

I was now too flabbergasted to speak. Granted, my uncle was a pretty unusual person, but the way they both were acting flew in the face of common sense.

"And after that did she happen to tell you anything more?" I asked him in all seriousness.

My uncle replied nonchalantly, "Yeah, I don't know. It's kind of hard to ask about it."

"Well, in that case, why don't you take her back to the house in Kunitachi and ask her about it the right way?"

"She doesn't like it there. She says it's hard to relax. She likes it better on the second floor of the shop. Listen, Takako, I don't have the slightest idea how women's emotions work. Why do *you* think she came back?"

I could hear how perplexed he was at the other end of the

receiver. But I replied coldly, "How should I know? She's your wife. Shouldn't you know her better than anyone else?"

"I thought I knew her better than anyone else, but now everything's screwed up. I'm groping around in the dark. You're a girl. There's got to be some kind of mutual understanding you share as women, right?"

"We have the same gender, but I think we might be entirely different species," I said. My uncle was quiet for a long time, then he just said, "But, Takako . . . do you think . . . she's going to leave again?"

Hearing the urgency in my uncle's voice made me change my mind a tiny bit. I could still see how sad and lonely he'd looked from behind as he walked wearily up the road that night I asked him about Momoko. He still loved her, no matter what. And he was still in pain. I never wanted to see him like that again if there was anything I could do about it.

"You don't want her to go?"

"I don't know. Before, I used to think that as long as she was happy where she was, I was fine with that. But now she's back, my feelings are starting to change. But that doesn't mean that I want her to be unhappy. Ah, I'm such a jerk."

Good grief. We weren't going to make any progress this way. I gave up and asked him, "So, what do you want to ask me?"

"Huh? How did you know I wanted to ask you something?"

"I know. How much time have we spent together?"

"Ah, Takako, there's no more wonderful niece in this world. I owe you."

It was mostly what I expected, but my uncle wanted me to find out what Momoko was really thinking. Why had she come back now? And what did she plan to do next? He said that five years ago she'd left behind a two-line note: "I'm fine. Please don't look for me." She didn't really take any bags with her. Since he hadn't noticed any signs or advance warning that this was going to happen, he had no idea what was going to happen now.

He had mixed feelings about it, but after a lot of worrying, he ended up following the instructions in her note and didn't look for her. He said he never even put in a missing person's report to the police. "We were never blessed with children of our own," he said, "and she took a liking to you, Takako. That's why I think you're the one she'll talk to." He added, "Thanks in advance!" at the end before he hung up.

Aunt Momoko had taken a liking to me? Even though we'd barely ever talked? It seemed pretty doubtful. People tend to find it embarrassing when an outsider intrudes on their marital problems. But after hearing him pleading with me, there was no way I could turn down my uncle. After all, I owed him everything.

3

"Let's go inside," Momoko said. "We've got a lot to talk about."

At Momoko's urging, the three of us stopped standing in front of the shop and went in. I hadn't set foot inside the store in two months.

As usual, the shop was overflowing with books. When you walked, the wooden floorboards creaked beneath your feet. Dust drifted back and forth in the soft light of the setting sun streaming through the window. I took a deep breath and filled my lungs with that familiar scent.

I remembered the first time I walked into the shop—how my uncle laughed with embarrassment when I winced and said, "It smells musty." Strange that now I loved that musty scent of old books so much I couldn't get enough of it.

The three of us gathered around the counter, eating sweet taiyaki cakes. I had picked them up on the way as a little gift. Twice while we were eating, customers came into the shop. They looked rather startled to see us huddled together like a bunch of mice, and bought their books. Momoko handled the customers for my uncle, talking to them in a friendly way. After so many years as the wife of a bookseller, she had plenty of experience.

After we went inside, Momoko still did nearly all of the talking. But it was impossible to follow the way she veered from one thing to the next. She was like a plane in a tailspin.

"Takako, you lived here once? That's just like me now, isn't it?

The AC doesn't work at all so summer here must've been hot. Oh, the sweet filling in this taiyaki cake goes all the way through! It's so good. Where'd you buy it? This neighborhood has changed since the old days. There are more fancy stores. Ugh, saying 'fancy' makes me sound so middle-aged, doesn't it?"

As she bounced from topic to topic, Momoko also, for some reason, occasionally reached out and pinched my uncle's cheeks. She had pinched him so many times that both of his cheeks were already bright red.

It seemed so strange and surprising to me that I interrupted her and said, "Um, why were you just pinching his cheek?"

"Oh, was I pinching them?" Momoko asked, looking surprised.

"You definitely were."

"It's just an old habit of mine, pinching people. When I feel close to someone, I just find myself pinching them. Maybe it's a way of showing affection. But wasn't Satoru's face kind of cute when I was pinching him?"

As she said this, Momoko pinched both of my uncle's cheeks firmly, moving them up and down and side to side, as if this were some punishment in a children's game. My uncle's face looked so incredibly miserable. It wasn't especially cute.

"Quit it . . ." My uncle cried out in pain, but he let her do it. He seemed used to it. You could hear in his voice that he had half resigned himself to it. His reaction made Momoko burst out laughing. Finally, she let him go. It seemed like Momoko had a hidden sadistic streak.

"Aren't you embarrassed to do that in front of Takako?"

"What's the big deal? She's not a total stranger. She's our niece."

"We're supposed to be adults. What about our dignity?" my uncle asked.

"Since when did you have any dignity?" Momoko hit back.

If she and I become close, am I going to end up getting pinched too? As I watched them banter, I shuddered at the thought.

Then Momoko jumped to another topic.

She suddenly grabbed hold of both my hands and fixed her gaze on me.

"But I'm so happy to see you. I used to think about you sometimes, you know. I'd wonder what had become of my sweet little niece. After all, you seemed like such a lovely young woman when you were in high school, so quiet and composed. And you looked so cute in your pageboy haircut."

"Is that what you thought of me? I really wasn't anything like that." I was at a loss for words. Back then I was at the peak of puberty; I always felt like I was about to be crushed under the weight of all my frustrations, all these feelings I couldn't express to others or process internally. I was in agony. It's hard to believe that someone could have seen me so differently. The only reason I was so well-behaved at family gatherings was simply to avoid drawing any attention to myself.

People's impressions really aren't very reliable, are they? That's what crossed my mind as Momoko was staring at me with a twinkle in her eye. I was wrong about so many things when it came to my uncle too. In the end, it doesn't matter if you're related by blood or if you spend years together in the same class at school or the same office; unless you really come face to face, you never really know someone at all. It was like that with Hideaki too. I couldn't avoid the fact that I bore a lot of responsibility for what happened. It made me start thinking about all that again.

"So, Aunt Momoko, I get the sense that maybe my old image

of you was pretty far off too," I countered with a touch of irony. But Momoko gave a hearty laugh as if she didn't mind at all.

"Well, at those family gatherings, I was playing the good girl too. Don't you think a lot of the people in that family are a bit stiff? My father-in-law was definitely one of them. Come on, his facial expression never changed. You'd think he was wearing a Noh mask. Plus the fact that we'd run off and gotten married. Those family get-togethers were unbearable. When we showed up, everything got so tense. That's why I was always tucked away in a corner, trying not to be noticed."

"So that's what it was like. And you still got married?"

"Well, we were living together at the time, so they still saw us as suspect. We met in Paris and fell in love, and as soon as we came back to Japan, they added my name to the family register. We just got caught up in the momentum, I guess."

"Pa-Paris?" I cried. "Why Paris?"

"You didn't know? I happened to be living in Paris then. He was traveling around on the cheap, and we used to run into each other sometimes at the used book stalls at the flea market. You'd think a guy from a family that owns a used bookshop wouldn't need to go to bookshops when he was off traveling. Not this guy. Plus he had this bushy beard and dressed in rags, so he looked like a beggar."

"That way you don't end up getting targeted by pickpockets and muggers," my uncle tried to explain, but Momoko didn't pay him any attention.

"But once I started talking to him, he turned out to be a pretty interesting guy. A little dark, maybe, and not sure what to do with himself. The kind of person who needed looking after. Then I ended up thinking I might hang out with him a little bit . . ."

"Oh, really?"

At some point, I started to catch on to Momoko's rapid narration. So the two of them met while my uncle was dealing with his issues by traveling around the world. Still, Paris was romantic. But what I couldn't understand most of all was why Momoko was in Paris. I tried asking her, but she only said, "Oh, I was young, you know," and did her best to dodge the question.

This woman is full of mysteries, I thought.

"Anyway, that's how we met. We came back to Japan, got married, and everyone gave us the cold shoulder, but then his father fell ill, and Satoru decided to take over for him. After that we worked together desperately to show them all up."

"It never occurred to me to try and show them up," my uncle interjected.

"Liar! You had all sorts of issues about your father! I figured that much out."

My uncle did not make a sound. He just sat there looking dejected. She was his wife, but he didn't seem to be much of a match for her. It was the first time I'd ever seen him like that; it was so funny I almost burst out laughing a few times.

And yet if you looked at it objectively, they actually seemed like a genuinely happy couple. As funny as it sounds, I even felt a little jealous of their relationship. The intimacy between them made them seem less like a married couple and more like old friends or comrades. It definitely put me at ease.

After a while, my uncle left, mumbling an excuse about how the store was busy, and Momoko pulled me upstairs to the room on the second floor. She suddenly leaned in close like she wanted to share something in secret.

"That's why I want us to be friends, Takako."

She took my hand and fixed her gaze on me again. Her hands were so small, I thought, like a child's.

"Ah . . ."

"It's not fair that you're only close with Satoru. I want you and I to be close too. Does that sound good to you?"

"Ah . . . yes . . ." I nodded to her, but in my head I grumbled, *This isn't going to be easy.*

4

When night fell, I fought off Momoko's attempts to make me stay longer, said goodbye, and left the bookshop.

I wandered along the narrow backstreets on my way to the train station. The night was cool, with just a slight chill in the air. As I passed beneath the streetlights, the shadows I cast on the asphalt grew longer.

As I reached the Saveur, my feet stopped on their own. Seeing the orange light of its sign shining in the lonely street at night, I was like Pavlov's dog—it triggered a sudden urge to drink coffee. When I looked at my watch, it was just a little after eight. I opened the door. It was like something was pulling me inside.

The coffee shop was as lively as it always was, even at this time of night. From the entrance, I could hear the sound of gentle piano music mixed with the lively conversations of the other customers.

Then I spotted a familiar figure sitting at the counter. Seeing that short and stout body and smooth bald head from behind, I knew it could only be Sabu. He was deep in conversation with the owner about something or other. When he noticed me, he waved and called for me to come over and sit beside him.

The owner greeted me with his usual smile as I sat down next to Sabu. "Hey, Takako, it's good to see you back."

Just as I was about to smile at him, Sabu cut in, saying, "Takako, you've got to smile more. Try to be a little friendly. That's why you're not popular with the guys."

I told him it was none of his business.

Sabu giggled as if something were funny. "But you came at the right moment," he said. "We were just talking about all of you. Momoko came back, right? Satoru's playing it cool—why didn't he tell me about it?" You could hear the obvious curiosity in his voice.

"Sabu, let's not pry too much," the owner said, reprimanding him.

"Why? What's the big deal? Besides, aren't you the one who told me about it? You said Momoko had come back," Sabu said, pretending to sulk. There's absolutely nothing cute about an old man pretending to sulk. The only cute thing at the Saveur was my friend Tomo, who used to work here part-time. Unfortunately, she'd finished grad school and gotten a job, so she was no longer at the coffee shop. From what I heard, however, she and Takano were keeping up their "friendship."

Sabu was still complaining as the owner gently placed my coffee in front of me.

"Last night, Sabu wandered in, and I let it slip," the owner said, sounding apologetic. His eyes, on the other hand, showed he was curious to know more.

"The two of you both knew Momoko before, right?"

"Naturally. How many years do you think I've been hanging around this neighborhood?" Sabu said, sounding quite proud of himself.

"Mr. Morisaki was married before? It doesn't fit my image of him." At some point, Takano had come out of the kitchen carrying plates and towels in both hands, and he eagerly joined the conversation.

"That's right," Sabu said. "You never knew. He's really sort of a widower, isn't he? But when he was young, those two used to make out in front of everyone. It was quite a show, wasn't it?"

"There was a bit of that, I guess," the owner said. "At any rate, Momoko is still beautiful, isn't she? When she came in, she said, 'It makes me so happy to have your coffee after all this time.' She looked like she was doing really well."

"Oh, you're a soft touch. She just wanted to flatter you. If you ask me, she suddenly comes home after being missing for years, she'd better have more than a few jokes. Satoru should run her off straight away. If my wife tried that, I'd knock her down." As he talked, Sabu worked himself up to such a state of excitement that his face turned all red like an octopus.

"Hold on now, Sabu. You sound so aggressive. But whenever your wife tries to make you get rid of some books, aren't you the one begging her in tears?"

When we heard that, Takano and I both burst out laughing.

"Hey, shut up! What are you laughing about, Takano? Get back to work!"

"Sorry, sorry." Takano fled to the back in a hurry as Sabu threw a towel at him.

"If you're ticked off, don't take it out on my staff," the owner said with an exasperated look on his face.

"Aren't you the one who normally bullies him?"

"That I do out of love. Love," the owner said earnestly, "whereas the feeling your wife inspires in you is . . . fear."

"You've always been a real jerk, haven't you? Fine. I'm angry. I'm pissed. Okay. How about I have some stern words with Momoko for Satoru. We know that nincompoop will never be able to say anything."

"Hey now, stop butting into other people's business."

The owner was chiding Sabu, even though he was the one who got Sabu riled up in the first place.

Wow. This neighborhood definitely attracts its share of weirdos.

The thought made me smile, but then Sabu took aim at me. "Takako, quit smirking there by yourself. It's unpleasant."

Right after this, there was another little development at the Saveur. Around nine, Sabu stopped making a fuss and went home (probably because if he didn't get back early his wife would've let him have it), so I moved to sit at a table. As the night wore on, there were only a few customers left. I ordered another coffee, and promptly took the book I'd been reading from my bag and opened it up to my page. Then I noticed something. There was someone I recognized sitting by the window.

He was a slim man in his late twenties. He wore a pale blue shirt with gray pants. His hair was cut short and neatly trimmed. There was nothing flashy about him, but there was something appealing about how neat he was. He was staring out the window absentmindedly, with a half-read paperback lying facedown on the table. He looked as if he were waiting for someone.

Who was he? As I stared at him, thinking this over, he suddenly turned to me as if he'd noticed I was looking at him.

When our eyes met, we both looked surprised. He looked at me and then at the paperback I was holding, then again back and forth, as if he were comparing the two, then he nodded as if he'd understood, and quietly said, "Hello."

Hearing his voice, I finally remembered where I'd met him before. How could I have forgotten? He was someone I'd dealt with many times at the Morisaki Bookshop. Because we were inundated with extremely idiosyncratic regulars—with Sabu chief among them—it was harder for someone a bit more withdrawn like him to make a strong impression. So it just took me a moment to remember him. I was flustered as I returned his greeting, embarrassed about having stared at him so shamelessly.

"Nice to see you. It's been a while," I said, and quickly bowed, but he smiled and said, "Oh, there's no need to be so formal." He had a nice smile that put you at ease.

Right at that moment, the waitress arrived at my table, carrying my coffee on her tray. She was standing directly between the two of us and seemed confused about what to do in the situation. I got caught up in it too and started feeling flustered.

Seeing this, he shyly offered an invitation. "Would you like to sit here?"

"Would you by any chance be waiting for someone?" I asked hesitantly.

"Not especially at the moment," he replied.

Hearing this, the waitress regained her confidence and her smile. "In that case, here it is," she said, quickly placing my coffee in front of his seat.

To which I responded, "I guess I'll sit here then," as I moved to the seat across from him.

In times like this, I tend to get sort of carried away. *He had just been kind enough to invite me over. It wasn't that he especially wanted to talk to me. Now I was interrupting his alone time.* Once I started thinking this way, I felt I needed to apologize.

When I reached my new seat, the waitress told us to take our time, then she bowed and left us. We watched her walk away before we turned to face each other again.

Silence.

Well, this is awkward, I thought as I shifted in my seat. Then he started to laugh to himself quietly. I stared at him blankly.

"Sorry," he said, "this sort of feels like a setup for an arranged marriage."

The smile on his face won me over and I burst out laughing.

"We haven't properly introduced ourselves," he said, clearing his throat. "My name is Akira—Akira Wada." He said he worked at a publishing company nearby that mostly dealt in textbooks and teaching materials.

When I introduced myself, he said, "That's right, Takako! I remember the cheerful owner of the shop was always yelling out 'Takako! Takako!' in a loud voice." He nodded again and again as he laughed.

My face turned red. "Ah, that would be my uncle," I murmured.

"Really, your uncle? It must be great to have a relative who runs a used bookshop," Wada exclaimed, sounding genuinely jealous. "But you're no longer working at the shop?"

"Yeah, for one reason or another, I ended up staying there for a while and working at the shop in exchange for room and board. I guess you could say I was there long enough to recharge my batteries."

"Recharge your batteries? At the shop?"

"Yes."

"I like that, recharge your batteries," Wada exclaimed again. "But to get to do it at a used bookshop, now that sounds luxurious. Oh man, I'm jealous." Then he went on what was almost a little monologue about how if it had been him, he would've never left, he would've just kept on recharging his batteries forever.

Somehow the idea of living at a used bookshop seemed to ignite something within him. He was turning out to be a surprisingly humorous guy.

"Oh, how's your girlfriend doing?" I asked. "I used to see you together a lot." He was still oohing and aahing about living in a bookstore when I remembered her.

Wada used to come to the shop by himself for the most part, but occasionally he brought a girl with him. She was slim and tall like him, and the two of them looked good together. But she didn't seem especially interested in books. Wada would be carefully examining the books with this earnest expression on his face while she was off on her own looking bored. When she finally got tired of waiting for him, she'd get miffed and say, "Still not done yet?" and he would desperately apologize, "Sorry, just a little longer!" Sabu used to say, "Going to a used bookshop as a couple is a preposterous idea," but watching the back-and-forth between them gave you a sense of how close they were. I thought it was charming.

"Oh, I remember those days." The tone of his voice dropped in response to my question. "I'm afraid I've been dumped," he added and laughed dryly. Then he got a rather distant look in his eye.

"I'm sorry!" I apologized right away. I was ready to throw myself at his feet.

"No, no, I don't mind at all," Wada said, trying not to make a big deal of it, but still with that distant look in his eye.

So in our first talk, I'd gone and stepped on a landmine. I was in a colossal panic. I was searching desperately for a new topic to talk about when my gaze stopped at the book lying on the table.

"What is it you're reading there?"

"Ah, it's a book called *Up the Hill*. Actually, I think I got it from the hundred-yen section at Morisaki Bookshop."

Wada picked up the book and showed it to me. I secretly breathed a sigh of relief that we'd moved on from the last topic.

"Oh? I don't know it. Is it a good book?"

"It's hard to say, actually. It's kind of one of those tragic love stories. The author is a guy who had this one book and ended up dying in obscurity. When you read it, the writing can be clumsy, and there are a lot of places where it feels like it's missing something. But there's something about it that fascinates me. I've read it around five times already."

As he talked, he was staring at the oil painting of a road in the hills on the book jacket. There was something tender in the loving way he looked at the book that ended up making me want to read it.

"Really? Five times? Maybe I should check it out."

"I'm not sure I can really recommend it. What are you reading, Takako?"

When I took the book out of my bag, he said, "Oh, Taruho Inagaki? He's great." He looked at me with a glint in his eye.

I guess I should've known from how often he came to the store that he knew much more about books than I did.

"Even though I worked at a bookshop, I don't know all that much about books. I feel like I've barely scratched the surface."

"I don't think it really matters whether you know a lot about books or not. That said, I don't know that much myself. But I think what matters far more with a book is how it affects you."

"You think so? My uncle always says something like that."

"You were always behind the counter in the back, lost in your book. It used to make me curious about what on earth you could be reading."

"Really? I'm so sorry. I was a terrible employee."

"No, that's not what I meant," Wada said, and he looked at me like he was trying to remember something. "You just fit in so well in the store that I wanted to let you be. It was almost like that moment when you're watching a butterfly coming out of its chrysalis, and you're holding your breath, and you want to keep on watching . . . I guess you left a big impression on me. That's why when I saw you there a second ago with a book in your hand, I remembered you right away. I said, 'It's the woman from that bookshop.'"

The thought of being seen like that by someone I didn't know left me feeling terribly embarrassed. But, in those days, I really was like a butterfly waiting patiently to come out of its chrysalis. As I turned page after page, I was waiting for my chance to take flight. So it might not be out of the question that Wada could sense that when he looked at me. I'm not entirely sure though that I've learned to fly that well.

"If I'd never gone to the shop, I'd still be living my life in a daze. I met so many people there, and I learned so many things, and, of course, there were all of the books I discovered. I feel like I finally learned to see something a tiny bit valuable within myself. That's why I know that I'll never forget the days I spent at the book-shop." Although this was the first time I'd ever really spoken to him, the words came pouring out of my mouth with such force I couldn't help myself.

Wada nodded along as he listened with a look of admiration on his face. "To think that all that drama was going on while I knew nothing about it. Man, oh man." He might have been seri-ous, but his way of putting it was oddly funny.

It was also strange—it felt like we'd been friends forever, like I could talk to him for hours. When Wada seemed like he was listening to me seriously, he'd come out with something funny and make me laugh.

That's how we ended up talking for such a long time. When I happened to glance at the clock on the wall, it was already almost eleven o'clock. "Oh, they'll be closing soon," I said, surprised.

"What?" Wada looked caught off guard as well.

His home was nearby, so Wada was going to stay till they closed. I decided to leave a little ahead of him.

"I'm here most nights. We should talk again sometime," he said, smiling as we said goodbye.

After I'd finished paying at the register near the entrance,

I noticed the owner was furtively glancing at me from behind the counter. I had a pretty good idea what he was thinking, so I glared at him, until he made a show of muttering aloud, "I'm busy, busy, busy," and retreating to the back.

Once I'd gone outside, I could see Wada through the window of the Saveur, sitting there with his chin resting in his hand, staring out. I bowed to him, thinking he might be looking at me, but he didn't seem to notice. I turned and started walking to the station. My body felt strangely light, like my feet were floating above the ground.

How weird, I muttered to myself.

When I looked up, I saw the nearly full moon, missing just a sliver on the left, floating in the night sky.

5

"Let's go on a trip together, just the two of us."

When Momoko sprung this question on me, it was about two weeks after I'd seen her for the first time in years.

"There's a really great spot in Okutama," she said, with a glint in her eye.

I nodded, feeling a bit cornered.

"There's a huge mountain, and on the peak is a historic shrine. The scenery is wonderful, and the air is so pure. It's amazing. There's a lovely inn on the mountain, where we can stay and take it easy for a bit. A girls' trip. What do you think?"

When I tried to imagine just the two of us going on a trip together, I started to feel a little uneasy. But she was holding my hands in hers, squeezing them tight, and I could see in her eyes that she was waiting for me to say yes. I had the overwhelming feeling that I was being pressured into it.

In the two weeks between our reunion and this invitation, I'd been visiting the bookshop fairly often. Of course, I was there to spy on Momoko for my uncle. He and I often crossed paths as he was leaving work, but Momoko was always in the room on the second floor.

Whenever I visited, Momoko was very happy to see me. And she always treated me to a home-cooked meal. When I lived there, the kitchen on the second floor had felt too small, so I never felt much like cooking there, but Momoko made all kinds of things.

She simmered hijiki seaweed, beef with tofu, octopus and daikon. She fried horse mackerel nanbanzuke-style, grilled pike mackerel in salt, made miso soup with daikon greens, radishes, and fried tofu. I was so starved for the taste of home cooking that I basically started coming just for the food. When I called her at lunch from the office, Momoko would act like a new bride, always asking, "What do you feel like eating today?" To which I'd respond by blithely requesting whatever I was in the mood for.

At first, Momoko kept saying it was her treat, so I didn't ask, but after a while, I insisted on splitting the cost and paying for half the groceries.

"Okey dokey," she said, happy to oblige.

"Momoko, everything you make is delicious," I said, and I meant it. I was eating my way through some of the dishes she had spread out on the little dining table as usual.

"Well, you always eat with such enthusiasm. You make it look delicious," Momoko said as she proceeded to devour twice as much as what I ate. I could never figure out how she managed to fit so much food in her tiny frame.

"But it really is delicious," I said, crunching on a pickled radish.

"Don't you cook?"

"I cook a little, but just things like pasta. Never anything like this."

"Well, then what'll you do when you have a boyfriend?"

"You think it'll be a problem?"

It's true that I didn't have much experience regaling my boyfriends with my cooking. The idea of cooking for someone made me so embarrassed that I'd avoided it up to this point. Anyway, it's not like I had much experience with relationships in the first place.

"Men are simple. It doesn't matter who they are. You can always seduce them with food." She laughed and said, "I'll teach you. You just try to remember." I wasn't sure I had a sense of how men felt. In fact, it seemed more like the person Momoko was winning over was me.

Of course, I didn't forget my uncle's request entirely. I tried to get her to talk. But Momoko always managed to evade my questions. When I asked her something in earnest, she'd just say, "Oh, I don't know." No matter how I tried to pin her down, she'd wriggle away like an eel. She was already someone who seemed to jump from one topic to another without rhyme or reason, so she'd always end up going off on a tangent. And once the food was spread out in front of me, I would fall into a trance and completely forget to ask about anything else. That's basically how it went every time, so I didn't really make much progress.

Nevertheless, I was able to learn a few things about her. (When Momoko got drunk, she tended to let her guard down and tell me more, so I often urged her to keep drinking.) She lost her parents early on and was raised by her aunt and uncle in Niigata. After middle school, she worked at a small factory, then left for Tokyo on her own at twenty-one, where, among other things, she fell in love with an up-and-coming photographer ("Is that for real?" I couldn't help asking).

Momoko lived for a time in Paris because her boyfriend had gone over for work, and she chased after him. She decided on her own to go without talking with her boyfriend. A bold move, but very Momoko.

"I was young, you know. I was just a girl who didn't know anything, and he was all I thought of. Later I found out that he had a wife and kids back in Japan. That's why it ended. The idea that to have the family I'd always wanted I'd have to destroy someone else's . . . It was just too much." Momoko stared off into the distance as she told me the story.

She couldn't see any future in their relationship, and, in the end, it all fell apart. She was brokenhearted. That's when she happened to meet my uncle Satoru. At first, she saw him as someone who needed looking after. She helped him take care of a few things, and before she knew it, they'd fallen in love.

"I never knew about any of that," I said, impressed by how much history they shared.

"My past makes Satoru jealous. So he doesn't like to talk about it much," Momoko said with a shrug.

Meanwhile, Momoko sussed out the real reason for my frequent visits. It happened one night once it had become perfectly routine for us to eat together. In between sips of sake, Momoko grinned to herself and suddenly said, "Satoru asked you to do this, right, Takako?"

"Huh? What do you mean?" I said, privately panicking as I attempted to keep up the charade. But it was no use. Momoko looked exceptionally happy as she reached over and pinched my cheek.

"I understand what he's thinking. But Takako, deep down, do I make you uncomfortable?"

My heart was racing as she pinched my cheek as hard as she liked. Somehow she had seen through the whole thing. It was true that there was a little part of me that didn't really love being with her. I definitely didn't dislike her, but if someone asked, I'd have been hard-pressed to say that I loved her. That's how it felt. If someone asked about her cooking, on the other hand, I would've answered right away that I loved it.

To be honest, I found her a tough person to figure out. My uncle was similar in that sense. There was something I couldn't grasp about him, but she was different. It felt like no matter how many times I talked to her, I could never close the gap between us. Sometimes it felt like we were standing on opposite sides of a river, talking to one another from across an enormous divide.

"It's okay, because I love you, Takako. And I think it's cute how honest you are. You can't tell a lie. It makes me wish I had a beautiful soul like that."

"I definitely do not have a beautiful soul."

I felt like she might be making fun of me, and I was a little offended.

But Momoko said she really meant it. "I just lie all the time," she said, sounding lonely somehow. For a moment, she hung her head.

Her facial expression revealed something in that instant that was not lost on me. I felt like it was the first time I had gotten close to what Momoko was really feeling.

But it only lasted an instant.

Immediately afterward, her face lit up, and she became her normal self again and changed the subject. Which is when she proposed her idea: "Hey, how about going on a trip together? It's too early for the fall foliage, but that means that there won't be many people and we can take our time. Are you busy at work?" She kept going on and on like this as she put pressure on me.

"No, it's a relatively flexible company."

"So, we're good?"

"Um, well . . ."

At first, I thought I would try to say no, but for some reason the expression I'd seen on her face had left me worried. So in the end, I agreed. "Let's do it."

I can't quite explain why, but I sensed something then. It wasn't exactly a premonition—nothing as grandiose as that. It was something I couldn't put into words, but I definitely felt it when I saw her face, like it was a sign I shouldn't ignore.

I saw Wada two more times at the Saveur before our conversation about the trip. Both times, I was stopping by the coffee shop on my way home from seeing Momoko, and he was there. He'd said he came often, and it seemed to be true. He was sitting at the same seat by the window when I saw him, staring out the window as he had before.

I wasn't entirely sure myself whether or not I went there because I wanted to see Wada. I don't think I went to the coffee shop expecting anything in particular. But when I walked in and I caught sight of Wada from behind, I heard myself say, "Oh."

I said hello, and his shoulders trembled like I'd woken him up from a dream. He stared at me for about five seconds as if he were verifying something about me, then he smiled and said hello.

He seemed to be asking me to join him, so I took a seat across from him and we talked. It was just small talk, nothing special, but just talking together made me feel strangely at ease. One time we even left together before the coffee shop closed and went on a little walk to the Imperial Palace.

"See you soon."

"Bye."

That's how we said goodbye, even though we didn't have each other's contact info, and there was no guarantee that we'd ever meet again.

After that night, I went to the coffee shop a third time, but Wada wasn't there. I knew there was no reason for me to expect him to be around, but I still somehow felt let down. I felt like I'd come for no reason. But I persuaded myself that it would actually be weirder if he were there all the time.

That night, I took a seat at the counter and tried subtly asking the owner about Wada.

He'd seen me talking to him, so of course he remembered him.

"He's a bit of a quiet customer. These days, as soon as it gets dark, he comes in. But I don't remember if he used to come before too."

"He isn't quiet. He's reserved." I said, gently correcting the owner.

"Oh, forgive me. He does seem like the type who tends to stay a while."

Then Takano joined in from across the room to offer an absurd suggestion. "Isn't he coming to see Takako? From back here, they do kind of look good together."

I stared at him with my mouth hanging wide open for a second, and then I furiously denied everything. "That's ridiculous!"

"Aw, come on, don't be mad."

"You'd better stop butting in!" the owner said, running him off.

Takano yelled, "Sorry!" as he fled the room.

As I lifted the coffee cup to my lips, I thought about what Takano had said one more time. *That can't be, can it?* And I told myself again that Takano had to be wrong.

But . . . but what if it was true?

Wada was a great guy. He was friendly and polite, and he had a good sense of humor. And he knew a lot about books, of course, too. He wasn't always boasting about himself or laughing crudely at his own jokes. With his personality, I'm sure lots of women were attracted to him.

Well, what about me?

Just as I was contemplating the question, I realized the owner was staring at me again.

"You should work on your habit of watching people so intensely. Especially when it comes to girls. They'll resent you," I said coldly.

The owner laughed his high-pitched laugh as he hurried after Takano and disappeared into the back of the coffee shop.

I had lost my urge to think through the question, so instead I took out the book Wada had told me about, *Up the Hill*, and gave it a try. When I was visiting Momoko earlier, I'd come across it by chance on one of the shelves at the bookshop around closing time.

When he saw the book in my hand, my uncle took it upon himself to tell me, "It's nothing special."

"I don't mind," I said. I handed my uncle one hundred yen and bought the book.

It's a short novel, about two hundred pages long. That night, first at the Saveur and then back at home before bed, I read the whole thing.

It was a sad story, just as Wada had said.

The story is set in Tokyo, during the period when the country was rebuilding after the war. The main character is an unsuccessful writer named Matsugorō Ida. He meets a beautiful woman who works at a "modern" café up the hill. For him, it's love at first sight. At first, she doesn't take him seriously, but Matsugorō keeps going to the café every day, and, after he confesses his love to her, he and the cheerful Ukiyō become a couple. But just when you think the happy days might last forever, Ukiyō is forced to marry the son of a wealthy man to pay off her father's debts. With barely any prospects for his own future, Matsugorō has no way to stop the wedding.

Matsugorō keeps on writing novels through his loneliness and despair. His sole motivation is the idea that if he becomes famous and makes a name for himself in the world, he might be able to get Ukiyō back. Finally, when he's in his late thirties, Matsugorō's dream comes true, and he finds success as a novelist. But that's when he discovers the awful truth: Ukiyō has succumbed to an epidemic and is no longer in this world.

From that time on, Matsugorō spends his days drowning himself in alcohol, women, and then drugs. His dissipated life leaves his body battered. But he never lets himself forget Ukiyō, not even for a moment, and he keeps going to the café where they first met every day. Then, one day, on his way home from the café, he collapses, coughing up blood. As he loses consciousness, all that remains in his heart is his memory of Ukiyō.

Matsugorō's painful, single-minded obsession hit home for me. After I finished the book, my heart fell silent. Tears ran down my cheeks and dropped onto the book, leaving little stains on the pages.

Under the covers of my futon, as I drifted off to sleep, I found myself thinking that Wada had a pretty romantic side.

In my dream that night, I was the woman who ran the café in the novel, and I was shaking Ukiyō by the shoulders, doing my best to persuade her to go out with Matsugorō.

6

"Why do you have to go on a trip with her?"

The night before we were to leave, I got a call from my uncle. I was working at the office, the last person still there. He said he'd just heard from Momoko about the trip. "I asked you to find out what was going on with her," he said, sounding disconcerted, "but you didn't have to go this far."

"It just sort of happened as we were talking," I responded vaguely. I wasn't feeling able at that particular moment to explain exactly how it happened.

"Knowing her, I bet she just forced you to go along with her," my uncle said, sounding worried.

"No, it wasn't like that."

"I don't know," my uncle said, still worrying.

"I'll bring you home a present," I said cheerfully.

"If you're okay with it, Takako, that's good enough for me, I guess," he said, reluctantly conceding. "By the way, Sabu keeps storming into the shop and saying he wants to see Momoko. What the hell's going on?"

I remembered the little drama at the Saveur and laughed out loud.

"He seems to want to have a word with her."

"What?" I could hear my uncle's astonishment on the other end of the phone. "Momoko will roll right over him, and then she'll flatter him and he'll end up going home happy. She's weirdly good at dealing with guys like him."

I could see the whole scene vividly in my mind.

"I think you're right."

"No doubt about it. But Momoko mostly goes out around lunchtime, so she isn't here when Sabu comes, which makes him angry."

"Is that right?"

"And even if I subtly try to ask her where she's going, she won't tell me."

It was my turn to be astonished. "Because she's not a child," I said. "As long as she comes back afterward, does it really matter?"

"I guess that's true . . . Anyway, you don't have to go on this trip if you don't want to. I don't know why she asked you . . ." he went on muttering and then he finally hung up.

That night, after finishing work, I decided to drop by the Saveur again. By the time I left the office, it was already after nine, and I didn't feel like going home, so I ended up there. The place was still crowded. Wada's usual spot by the window was occupied by two girls.

I found a seat at a table and read slowly from the book I bought for my trip—*Friendship* by Saneatsu Mushanokōji—but I couldn't really concentrate. Although I didn't mean to, every time someone came into the coffee shop, I'd find myself looking toward the door, thinking it might be Wada.

I had only managed to make it through about twenty pages when Wada showed up for real. I greeted him with a slight bow, feeling flustered, and he came slowly over to where I was sitting. Seeing him from that distance, I got a strange feeling. He seemed less lively than usual.

I waited until he had taken a seat before I asked any questions. "Have you been busy at work?"

"No, on the contrary, things have been slow." Wada smiled as he said it, but his face showed how tired he was.

We both fell silent for a moment. Normally, I wouldn't worry about a moment of silence between us, but for some reason, I felt a heaviness in the air. I thought of what Takano had said, and then it got even harder to make conversation.

"That reminds me . . ." I said with a smile, remembering something good to tell him. "I read *Up the Hill.*"

But Wada didn't seem to take much of an interest. "Oh, is that right?" he mumbled. I'd selfishly expected he would be happy to hear this. I felt dejected that my expectations were so far off the mark.

"The story is a bit of a cliché, don't you think?" Wada said with a touch of irony.

"No way. I loved the book."

"But the whole idea of waiting for someone you love till the day you die. That kind of thing never happens in the real world."

"Is that right?"

"At least that's what I think. Instead, the person you love just comes out and tells you you're being creepy."

"Huh?" I had no idea what he was talking about. But Wada went on speaking in fits and starts.

"When she and I first met, I brought her here. She liked the place, so after that day, she and I came here a lot. That's why I told her I'm still waiting for her here. 'If you change your mind,' I said, 'come look for me here.' Well, the day before yesterday, she sends me an email making herself perfectly clear: 'You're being creepy. Stop.'"

At this point, I'd heard enough to understand what he'd meant earlier. *So that's what's been going on. If only he'd told me sooner. No, but why would he tell me?*

He'd been waiting all this time—waiting for the beautiful woman he used to bring to the bookshop. He was just like Matsugorō waiting for Ukiyō. Or rather, was that why he transferred all those emotions to the novel and kept reading it over and over?

Oh, what the hell. I kept repeating the words to myself again and again. It's not that I was particularly sad. Somehow deep down I'd always had the feeling that he didn't think of me like that. I just felt like a complete idiot for letting myself get so worked up over everything.

What about the weird way we could talk and talk? Or the way we felt like old friends? None of that was real. Wada was kind enough to listen to me, and I took advantage of that and talked about myself. That's what really made me feel good. I felt so guilty when I finally realized this.

"I'm sorry. It's not a very interesting story," Wada said apologetically, perhaps because he'd noticed that I'd been looking down all this time.

I shook my head. "No, I'm the one who should apologize."

"What? Why should you apologize, Takako?" Wada seemed surprised.

"Just because."

"Huh?"

I really wanted to apologize more, but I also didn't want him to think I was weird, so I held back. I've got to change the subject, I thought, but I also felt the urge to ask more bubbling up inside me.

"You loved her, didn't you?" I blurted out, and then immediately regretted it.

Wada smiled a little.

"I hate to admit how childish the whole thing was. But, you know, I can understand it too. At first, she and I didn't seem to have anything in common. There was no way for things to work out between us. But it's like I was stubborn about it. I fell in love with her. And for some reason I could never just see that we were too different and we'd be better off ending things. I've always thought of myself as a rather sober person, but I discovered I have a passionate side. It came as a bit of a surprise."

He could've skipped the analysis at this point. I guess he was a little weird after all.

"I think you're a good person," I said, trying to cheer him up. I wish I could've come up with something better to say, but nothing else came to mind. I meant it sincerely though. Wada was a really good person.

"Thank you. If you say so, I must be a decent human being. That much is true," he said, laughing softly. "But I got told, 'You're a good person, but you're not interesting.'"

"Don't you think she was being a bit cruel?" I said. I was getting a little angry at this woman. I felt like she couldn't recognize the goodness in him.

"No," Wada said. "Because I agree with her. So much so that I was actually impressed by how well she'd hit the nail on the head. But this is a boring subject, let's drop it." Wada tried to change the subject and get me to open up by asking how I'd been recently. But I was still feeling hurt, and I couldn't contribute to the conversation.

"Sorry, I've got an early start tomorrow . . ." The conversation never seemed to get any more cheerful. I kept it going a little longer and then I excused myself and got up.

"Oh really?" Wada looked at me a little blankly.

When I tried to leave, the owner called out from near the door. "Are you going home, Takako?"

"Yes" was all I said before I walked out.

I was in a dark mood. The owner must've realized it too. I didn't feel much like coming back for a while.

As I walked, I felt more and more depressed. I must've sighed about thirty times. By the time I realized that I'd forgotten my book on the table, I was already on the train home.

7

I met up with Momoko at Shinjuku Station at ten.

It was cloudy, but according to the weather forecast on TV, the sky was going to clear up in the afternoon.

I was using up my vacation days to go on this trip, so before I left home, I tried to give myself a pep talk: *Don't let last night drag you down.*

Momoko showed up at the jam-packed south entrance of Shinjuku Station, carrying so little—just a backpack that could've been mistaken for a child's—you would've never guessed she was leaving on a trip. Her hair was tied back in a bun, and she wore a green hoodie and black tracksuit pants. She was so small that from a distance, she looked like a schoolgirl on a field trip.

When Momoko saw my outfit, she furrowed her brow. "Oh my," she said, "you're not dressed like someone who's going to the mountains, are you?" This was my first trip in a long time, and I was decked out in a dress I'd just bought on sale.

"I did put on sneakers though," I said, trying to explain myself. "And I have some proper hiking clothes in my bag."

"You didn't need to pack so much," Momoko said.

That shut me up. I was embarrassed by how much I'd been looking forward to the trip. Perhaps to make up for what she'd said, Momoko added, "I guess that's just what it's like being young. You're always carrying around a lot of luggage."

"And when you're old, you have less?" I countered.

"It's fine for you, Takako. I just don't like anything weighing me down," she said dryly.

"That makes sense," I said, convinced.

"Anyway, thank you for coming. Here's to a good three-day trip," Momoko said. She straightened her posture and bowed theatrically.

"I should be the one thanking you," I said, bowing.

We took the Chūō line from Shinjuku, and changed to the Ōme line at Tachikawa Station. In the roughly five years since I'd moved to Tokyo, this was my first time heading that way. The train cars on the Ōme line were fairly empty. Sitting in the seats across from us was a high school student, a bit of a bad boy type, who looked like he'd overslept. He sat there with a sullen expression on his face, restlessly tapping his foot. He looked angry at the whole world.

Momoko took her seat and stared out the window, humming to herself. The night before I'd been up till dawn, thinking of one thing or another, none of it very interesting. Once I settled in on the train, I was asleep before I knew it.

When I woke up a little while later, the bad boy high schooler was long gone. He'd probably gone to school angry.

I glanced out the window, and I saw that at some point the clouds had disappeared and blue sky now stretched into the distance. There were far fewer houses and buildings, and the mountains in the distance beyond the farmland and rice paddies were growing bigger and bigger.

"Amazing," I said, rubbing my eyes.

"Just wait till you see what's next," Momoko said with a grin.

We got off the train at a little station called Mitake. The mountains were right in front of us now, with the blue sky behind them, and in the center of it all was an enormous mountain that towered over everything else. It was a majestic, massive mountain—it was not going to budge one bit. The leaves hadn't really started to change color yet for fall, so the mountain was still a deep green. Somewhere up there was the inn we were heading to.

"We're not far from the center of the city, but it feels like we've gone a really long way," I muttered, looking at the scenery in front of me. I took a deep breath and filled my lungs with fresh, clean air. It was impressive to see how much nature was still left within the city limits.

"It only took a few decades for the city to fill up with all those buildings," Momoko said.

It made me think of the short story "Musashino" in one of Doppo Kunikida's books. At the beginning of the twentieth century, when Doppo was alive, the area around Musashino was still so wild you could lose yourself inside it. These days it's just another neighborhood in Tokyo. The times change so quickly. It was enough to leave you dizzy.

At the little stop in front of the station, we caught a bus that took us on the highway to the starting point of the funicular, halfway up the mountain. By the time we got to the bus stop, two tour groups that had probably arrived on the same train as us had already taken their seats. Both were groups of elderly men and women. It was a mystery though what had brought them all here together. We gave a quick bow and sat down next to them. The oldest-looking woman in the group smiled and said, "On a little mother-daughter trip?"

"Yes," Momoko said, smiling back.

We're not mother and daughter, I thought, but it was too

much trouble to explain our relationship, so I nodded and let the expression on my face say, *That's my mom, and I'm her daughter.*

As soon as we got on the bus, three grade-school-age boys started talking to us. They were apparently quite used to tourists because they didn't seem the slightest bit shy. Momoko seemed to like kids. She gave them a big smile and started happily chatting with them. "What grade are you guys in?" she asked.

"First!" they answered in unison, full of enthusiasm.

They told us their families ran inns up on the mountain, so they had to come down the mountain every day to go to school.

"That must be hard," I said, which was probably what tourists always said to them.

"I suppose," one replied, sounding quite grown-up. It was like he was saying, "Oh, *now* you tell me."

"Come on, come on!" they shouted. Letting the kids lead us, we got off the bus and climbed the mountain road to the funicular station. The kids were running fast, and I quickly ended up a little out of breath as I brought up the rear. Momoko turned around and looked at me.

"Takako, you know the real climbing doesn't start until after the funicular. If you're already tired, I don't know what we're going to do with you," she teased.

The kids burst out laughing. "Lady, you're never going to make it. This is what happens when you grow up in the city," one said, and they laughed again.

"Actually, I grew up way out in the country in Kyushu," I said, trying to argue the point from the back, but they were going so quickly and I had fallen so far behind that no one seemed to hear me. Why was Momoko in such great shape? The age difference between us was enough for people to mistake us for mother and daughter. I was starting to regret that I hadn't packed lighter.

When I finally made it to the base of the funicular, Momoko handed me a bottle of tea she'd bought at a gift shop. "Here you go," she said.

I accepted gratefully and gulped it all down.

The funicular took us up the mountain like the tracks were running along a stream. It dropped us off just before the summit. Then we waved goodbye to the kids and began to trudge uphill again. We'd already made it to nearly one thousand meters above sea level. It was hard to believe that just an hour ago we'd been at the foot of the mountain.

Along the narrow road that led to the peak were signs with advertisements and directions for each inn. "Our inn is the farthest, so it's going to take forty minutes," Momoko said casually.

"What?" I whined.

"But the view is incredible," she said, and pinched my cheek.

More stairs and steep slopes followed. There was only one little store and a single rest stop. Everything else was either a mountain inn or a private residence. Each time someone coming down from the peak passed us, they greeted us with a cheerful "Hello!"

And each time, Momoko and I answered back enthusiastically, "Hello!"

The overwhelming majority of the people we saw were elderly, but there were some young couples and large groups of what looked like college students. I felt a tiny bit relieved to see that most of the young people were dressed in normal clothes like I was.

Finally, the inn we'd been looking for came into view. At this point, I was completely out of breath. Momoko seemed to be feeling the strain a bit too. "We made it. We made it," she said, sighing as she wiped the sweat from her forehead with a towel.

The wooden building looked pretty worn down. It had three floors that seemed to be joined to a private home. The back of the building was right up against the cliff. In the large yard out front, someone had left out a tractor, a rusty bicycle, and some logs. The place had a very lived-in look. To put it nicely, I guess you could call it unpretentious. To put it not so nicely, it was a dump. But I had trouble imagining Momoko staying at some neat little inn. So I took one look and thought, This looks great.

"Is anyone there?" Momoko opened the door and yelled inside. After a moment, we heard the sound of someone running down the hall, and a young girl appeared.

She was dressed in loose jeans and a sweatshirt that was clearly too big for her. She looked about twenty years old.

The girl looked at Momoko and spoke so bluntly you never would've guessed she was talking to a guest. "Hey, is that Momoko?"

"It's been a while, Haru. How've you been?" Momoko replied.

"Who's this? She your daughter? Wait, you have children?"

"I'm her niece, Takako," I said, introducing myself to Haru before Momoko could tell another person I was her daughter.

Haru might be a little bit rough around the edges, but she didn't seem particularly mean-spirited.

"Nice to meet you," she said, and gave a quick bow in my direction.

We heard footsteps from inside again. This time a woman in her fifties came slowly walking toward us, dressed in an apron coverall and a headscarf.

"Ah, Momoko, you're early," the woman said with a friendly smile. She had a brisk way of talking, but you could sense that she was someone who liked taking care of people.

"It's nice to see you again," Momoko said, and bowed properly. I realized the woman in the apron was the innkeeper.

"Hey, Momoko," Haru said, "you gonna work here again?"

"No, Haru. Momoko came as a guest today."

"Oh no, really?"

Seeing me marvel at this back-and-forth, Momoko whispered in my ear. "When I left Satoru's, I moved up here for a little while and the innkeeper gave me a job."

"So that's what happened?" I said, raising my voice in surprise.

"Basically," she replied nonchalantly.

The innkeeper led us to our room. It was only just after 2 p.m., so we were the first guests of the day. The inside of the building was just as messy as the outside. There was stuff everywhere. In the hallway, someone had left an empty aquarium, a huge pile of magazines, an old TV, and an acoustic guitar. When I snuck a peek at the kitchen next to the entryway, it looked pretty chaotic. Same for the toilets, the washroom, and the bath. It felt more like a boardinghouse than an inn. During summer vacation, it was probably filled with students. I don't know whether the other inns on the mountain were similar, but in this inn, the atmosphere was extremely casual.

She led us to a room at the far corner because it had the best view. It was about ten tatami mats large, the perfect size for the two of us.

Outside the window, we were surrounded by dense green foliage. The trees swayed gently in the breeze. Now and then we heard a bird call that might have been a thrush. The mountains in the distance were shrouded in mist. Up above, drifting slowly across the aqua-blue sky, was a group of little, dappled clouds that looked like a school of fish. As I stared at the view, I felt myself losing all sense of time.

I sat by the window for a while, gazing at the scenery. Beside me, Momoko was unusually quiet as she looked at the view, perhaps overcome by the same emotions. I tried to imagine what it must've been like to live and work in a place like this. I surprised myself when I realized I might enjoy it.

Then there was a forceful knocking at the door, and Haru came in. "It's already getting really cold at night," she said, carrying a heavy-looking stove in both hands. She put it down with a thud in a corner of the room.

"Thanks," I said.

"Yup, enjoy!" she replied on her way out, sounding more like a waitress at a bar.

"Momoko, how long did you work here?" I asked.

She cocked her head to one side to think. Then she said, "About three years, I guess."

"What did you do after that?"

"Well, all sorts of stuff. People can live anywhere if they put their mind to it."

That was definitely true in her case. She seemed fierce enough to live anywhere.

"Well," she said, jumping to her feet. "Shall we go out for a bit before dinner?"

We were going to leave the real hiking for the next day, and so we decided to pay our respects to the shrine up the mountain. Momoko said the shrine was just a stone's throw from the inn, and it would take us less than five minutes to get there. When we passed the little corner with its modest gift shop and restaurant, the large torii gate of the shrine appeared before us. We gave a quick bow at the gate and followed a group of people onto the grounds.

The shrine was much nicer than I expected it to be. We passed one sanctuary and treasure hall after another. On the path leading to the main shrine, countless stone monuments crowded side by side. I read a sign that explained its history, and it said the original shrine had been constructed in this location more than 1,200 years ago in the Nara period. From the Middle Ages, the site was considered one of the sacred mountains in the region. Worshippers had flocked to the mountain for centuries.

I was shocked to discover that it had been around for so long. For hundreds of years, so many had made the same trek to visit this shrine. There was no transportation then, so the walk must've taken days or even weeks. It must've meant even more to them than it did to us today. I felt humbled by my lack of faith.

We climbed the steep stone steps to get to the main shrine. There were bright purple blossoms in the wild gentian growing along the route. The stairs seemed to go on forever, and we struggled to make it up to the shrine. The other tourists were breathing hard as they climbed the steps. When we finally stood in front of the hall of worship, I struggled to catch my breath again.

I somehow pulled myself together, and we threw our coins into the collection box and pressed our hands together in prayer.

I looked over at Momoko when I was done, but she was still praying. The expression on her face was extremely serious.

When she opened her eyes again, I asked, "What are you praying for?"

"Nothing."

"But it looked like you were praying with such intensity."

"A shrine isn't where you pray for something. It's a place for you to express gratitude. It's for you to tell the gods, 'Thank you for always watching over me.'"

"Oh, I just asked for something, um, fervently."

"What did you ask for?"

"You know, good health, and that I don't go broke."

Momoko laughed, saying that sounded a lot like me. We did a loop around the grounds of the shrine to look around. Then she said, "When I first left Satoru, I wandered to this shrine. That's how I ended up asking if I could stay at that inn. I didn't have anyone else to turn to, so I asked the innkeeper if I could move in and work there. It turned out that she was actually short-handed at the time. She had just lost her husband, and she didn't have Haru yet. But even so, for her to hire a strange middle-aged woman . . . It was really generous of her."

She likes to talk about herself in the third person, I thought, weirdly impressed.

Before we left, we stood together and bowed again. The main shrine was shining beautifully in the setting sun. Then we went back down the steep path to the inn.

I took a bath to wash away all the sweat. While I was lying around on my futon waiting for Momoko to finish her bath, I was overcome by drowsiness again. When Momoko shook me awake, it was already well past dinnertime.

While I was in dreamland, two other groups of guests had come to the hotel. We all met in the dining hall. One group was composed of three generations of the same family. The other was a pair of middle-aged men. The men were already a little drunk. When we came into the room, they greeted us by shouting, "Sorry, we started without you!" Their voices were ridiculously loud.

There was so much to eat at dinner that it was overwhelming. The innkeeper kept bringing one thing after another. Simmered dishes, fermented soybeans, pickled scallions, kimchi—there were so many different little sides. She even made a hot pot and tempura.

The most delicious dish of all was the ayu sweetfish grilled with miso. After eating that with rice and miso soup, I was full, so I gave my hot pot and tempura to the men. Thanks to the relaxed atmosphere at the inn, there was an unusually festive feeling in the dining hall. The men were both interested in mountain climbing, and they had been to this mountain many times. As blind drunk as they were, they still took the time to tell us all their recommendations for places to visit. I would've liked to have seen the spots where the violets and false anemones grew, but it was too late in the year.

The family said they'd come for a little trip, just to be together as a family before the grandson's wedding. The grandmother was now somewhere between eighty-seven and eighty-nine. (The question of her exact age provoked a brief dispute.) They had to push her wheelchair the whole way from the funicular station to the inn.

"This is my last trip," the grandmother murmured.

"What! You're still so young. You've still got time for lots of trips!" Momoko insisted, looking quite happy.

Later, after the two other groups went upstairs, Momoko launched into a nonstop conversation with the innkeeper, so I went up to the room ahead of her.

When I got back to our room, I thought about what Momoko had been like all day, and came to the conclusion that all my worries about the trip had been in my head. She seemed so happy. She was the same cheerful person she always was. She'd probably just been nostalgic for the place where she used to work.

I'd come all this way with the wrong idea. Just like with

Hideaki. I was someone who took a long time to figure things out. But maybe it didn't matter. I was enjoying myself. That's what I thought as I waited for Momoko.

When Momoko came back to the room, she said, "We've got an early start tomorrow. Let's go to bed," and quickly got under the covers.

But having foolishly taken two naps that day, I couldn't fall asleep.

Momoko was asleep within three minutes of getting into bed. I could hear her breathing peacefully (with the occasional bout of snoring).

As I lay there, I was sorry I'd forgotten my book at the Saveur—not that those regrets did me any good now. Then, at the same moment, Wada's face appeared in my mind.

I wonder what he's doing right now. Probably sleeping. And here I am spending a sleepless night in a strange place. We might not be far from home, but I feel lonely. I really miss him. It wouldn't have killed me to have asked him for his number. Now I might never see him again. He doesn't have any more reason to go to the coffee shop. It hurts to realize that it might be too late now for anything but regret.

The more I thought about it, the more awake I felt, so I quietly snuck out of the room. The whole inn was asleep. But then I saw a light coming from the sliding door of the little room at the end of the hall. Tiptoeing over and sneaking a peek inside, I saw Haru sitting with her legs crossed in front of a desk, scowling at the computer screen. She had the same intense expression on her face that Momoko had when she was praying at the temple.

When I tried to tiptoe away, she noticed me and called out absentmindedly "What's up? Something happen?"

"I just couldn't sleep," I said.

"In that case, maybe you should go for a walk. It's a clear night, the stars should be pretty." She gestured toward the entrance with her chin.

"Maybe I will," I said.

As I was about to walk out the door, I heard, "Wait a sec. It's pitch black out there and it's dangerous for a girl to be all alone." Haru came after me with a flashlight in her hand.

We quietly opened the front door and went into the yard.

Because of the high altitude, we could see our breath even though it was still only the middle of October. When I looked up at the sky, the stars seemed so much closer than usual. There were winter constellations that we wouldn't have seen in the city. Across from the cliffs, they were twinkling over the rolling mountains.

We walked slowly together toward the shrine. Everyone was asleep. There wasn't a single room with a light on. The only noise was the satisfying clip-clop sound of our sandals.

"I'm sorry I dragged you along on this."

"No worries. I was just looking at something online." Haru took a cigarette from her pocket, put it in her mouth, and lit it. Then she stood there looking out at the darkness, exhaling smoke.

"When did you start working here, Haru?"

"Since I graduated high school. The boss is one of my relatives."

"Is that right?"

"Pretty much everybody here's like that. They run the inn with their families and relatives. Beyond that, the local high school kids come to work part-time when they're on break. People like Momoko are pretty unusual."

"Is the job fun?"

"Hard to say. This is the only job I've ever had. It gets pretty busy when the students are here. But this time of year can be a little lonely. Why are you traveling together? You don't seem that close." Haru asked the question without seeming to have any special interest in the answer.

"I don't really know. Before we left, I had the feeling there was something she wanted to tell me, but now it seems like that was just in my head."

"Hmmm . . . Now that you mention it though, back when she was working here, she was in a much darker mood. Seeing her again now, I was kind of surprised to see how cheerful she was."

"Really?"

"Yeah. In her later days here, she was more upbeat, maybe, but when I first started here, she hardly ever talked. She kinda scared me."

I tried to envision Momoko being like that, but I really couldn't do it.

"I don't get it, I guess," she said, and threw her cigarette in the ashtray that had been installed right in front of the torii gate of the shrine.

A shooting star streaked across the night sky and disappeared. At which point, Haru let out a single, massive sneeze.

"Should we head back?" I asked.

Haru sniffled and said, "Sure."

8

The next morning, I couldn't seem to muster the energy to get out from under the covers of my futon. I just lay there dawdling. Momoko tried to rip the covers off me a few times, but I held on tight and fought her tooth and nail.

It was after nine when I finally got up, washed my face, and wandered the inn in search of her.

"She's got to be in the yard," the innkeeper told me, trying to keep from laughing.

When I went outside, I saw Momoko standing in the middle of the yard, drenched in morning light. She was still wearing her yukata from last night, but she was in a funny pose.

"What're you doing?" I asked.

"Tai Chi," she said. She told me it had been a morning routine for years. "It's really good for your health. Plus it makes you feel good. You want to try it with me, sleepyhead?"

Was she doing it every morning at the bookshop? I'm sure the sight of a middle-aged woman doing Tai Chi in front of a second-hand bookstore surprised the businessmen on their way to work. Just imagining it made me almost burst out laughing.

After finishing breakfast, Momoko and I finally left for our hike. Today I was fully prepared, wearing clothes it was much easier to move in. All of the other guests seemed to have started off long before us. When I told Momoko we still had plenty of time, she turned and gave me an icy glare.

As we left the inn, the innkeeper called after us, "See you soon!"

If you went over two mountains on the trail, you'd make it to an overlook with an amazing view. That's where we were headed.

It was nice and cold in the mountains. We were surrounded by cedars, some of them five times my size. When I stopped to have a look at the pretty wildflowers growing here and there along the way, Momoko would point at each and tell me its name. She had only lived here for a few years, but still she knew quite a lot about life here. I, on the other hand, had not been hiking since a summer program in grade school. It was fun to walk in the mountains with such a knowledgeable guide. I didn't have to worry about getting lost. Feeling a little better, I started to hum a song we sang on the weekend trip, "The Bear in the Woods."

But this was only at the very beginning of the hike. After that, I wasn't singing songs anymore. The path, which was flat and wide at first, gradually grew narrower and steeper. It's like it was telling me, "This mountain doesn't mess around." Soon it was hard to find your footing, and I was afraid that if I stopped paying attention for a moment, my feet would slip. One minute, I was blithely singing, "And this is what the bear said!" The next, I felt like I was trapped in a bottomless pit, too uncoordinated to find my way out.

But Momoko didn't seem to think the path was bad at all. She kept going, nimbly making her way, showing no mercy. When the distance between us grew too wide, she would stop and wait for me to catch up.

"Hey, um, Miss Mountain Guide, can we slow down a bit?" I grumbled, around the time we had just passed the gigantic boulder known as Tengu Rock, because it looked a little like that mythical creature with the long nose.

"I wonder whose fault it is that we don't have much time? If we don't hurry now, the sun will set on our way home. And it gets pitch black at night in the mountains, you know," Momoko said curtly.

I didn't have a response for that.

"We'll take a little break a little farther ahead. Keep it up a bit longer," Momoko said to encourage me. Then she walked on briskly.

It was after midday when we finally took a brief rest beside a clear mountain stream. We divided up the onigiri the innkeeper had packed for us, so we each had two. Listening to the soothing sound of water in the dappled light that streamed through the trees eased my weariness a little. I took several deep breaths of that pure mountain air, trying to catch my breath. Momoko still seemed perfectly well composed. She had a placid expression on her face as she bit into her onigiri.

"Momoko, you're really in good shape."

"Takako, as young as you are, you really have no endurance."

I laughed, and teased her a little. "Momoko, you'll probably be in great shape even when you're that old lady's age."

Momoko laughed. "Honestly, it doesn't look like it's going to turn out that way. I'm sick. And pretty soon I'll start to fall apart."

"What?" I said.

"Okay, break's over. Just a little farther to go," she said, sounding all fired up as she walked away.

Sick? How could Momoko be sick? She doesn't look sick at all . . .

Momoko turned back and saw me still standing there. "If you don't get a move on," she called, "I'll leave you behind!" She looked so small at this distance from behind. I rushed to chase after her.

After that, we devoted our attention to hiking and hardly exchanged a word.

At one point, we went down a rugged slope that was just bare rock, then circled halfway around the mountain, and went up another slope. We went up and down, again and again, on our route. My poor feet were screaming in pain.

Then, all of sudden, the sky opened up before us, and the summit came into view. On the peak, the viewing platform looked sort of like a flan resting on a plate. There were a few pines scattered around an expanse of reddish-brown earth. Ahead of us was the steep drop-off of the cliff. The only other visitor was a middle-aged man, sitting on a bench mounted right next to the edge of the cliff. Everything around was quiet and calm. We sat down together on the bench across from the man. The gentle breeze, coming straight at us, began to cool our burning muscles.

The view from the mountaintop was definitely impressive. We were surrounded by green as far as the eye could see. Everywhere you looked there were mountain peaks pressing up against each other. And the sky felt unbelievably close. So endless and clear. If I stared at it too long, I felt like it might swallow me whole.

When I squinted, I could just make out the city of Tokyo. It was so small it looked like a little speck in the distance. I tried to imagine that tomorrow I'd be back living my life again in that little speck, but here on the mountain I couldn't believe that life was real. Wouldn't it be better to just stay here and live like this? It felt like it. I wondered if Momoko had the same thoughts the first time she came here.

"Hey, Momoko?"

"Yeah?"

"What made you decide to leave Satoru?"

I wasn't asking because my uncle wanted me to. I just wanted to ask her. And this time I hoped Momoko would actually answer me. All of a sudden it felt like she would.

"Hmmm . . ." she nodded slightly, staring straight ahead. As I waited for her to say something, I stared straight ahead like her, not saying a word. A swallow flew across the sky above us without making a sound.

"I told you about the person I was in love with a long time ago, right?" she said, still facing forward.

"Yeah."

"Well, when I was with him, I got pregnant. I'd always wanted a family so badly, so when I found out I was unbelievably happy. He didn't share my joy at all though. Well, that's because he already had a wife and kid back in Japan. I found that out afterward."

A strong gust of wind blew in and swirled up a cloud of sand. A moment later, everything fell silent again.

"If I'd been stronger, I might have been able to save the baby at least. But I wasn't. I didn't have the confidence to find happiness by causing someone else so much pain, or the courage to pay that price and go on living. Afterward, I regretted it so much I wanted to die. But, by that point, it was too late." She sighed a little and smiled faintly.

"Then I met Satoru and we got married. Satoru was desperate to have kids too. But somehow we were never blessed with them. Ten years passed and then we were given a child at last. Satoru was happy too. I was so happy I cried. But before the baby was born, it died inside me. I felt like I was being punished. And I was being punished because back then I had let my baby die. I felt like I didn't deserve to give birth now. Satoru tried his best to comfort me. I'm sure it was hard for him too. He's so ridiculously kind. You already know that though, right, Takako?"

I nodded.

"After that, I managed to get back on my feet somehow, and

the two of us worked hard together to revive the Morisaki Bookshop. Satoru was careful not to say another word about the baby. And then he became more and more absorbed by running the bookshop. I liked the shop, and I liked to think that I could love Satoru the way he loved me. But that wasn't enough. No matter how much time passed, the sadness never went away. I was carrying this feeling around—like there was a gaping hole left open inside me. And instead of disappearing, the emptiness inside me seemed to grow day by day. I started to think that being with him when I was feeling this way was almost a betrayal. Then I woke up one day and realized how far I'd let things go." Momoko let out a long sigh. It was like she'd been holding her breath until she finished telling me the story. "If he wants to look down on me for doing something so selfish, what can I say? I can't argue with him. That's why I've been afraid to talk to him about it. I mean you seem pretty shocked."

How could I possibly respond? I had no idea what to say. There's probably no way at this point in my life for me to imagine the pain she felt. I could understand only the intensity of feeling. In the face of something like that, any easy words I might offer seemed meaningless. I could only sit there beside her, shaking my head in silence.

After a while, Momoko got slowly to her feet. "Sorry to bore you with all this. Let's hurry back."

That's when I noticed the light was starting to fade on the mountain ridge across from us.

On the way home from the summit, Momoko moved so quickly that she ended up ahead of me again. I had so much on my mind that I was lost in my own thoughts the whole way. Thanks to which, I lost my footing a few times and fell hard on my butt.

By the time we got back to the inn, I was exhausted. It was already fairly dark outside, and at some point it had even started to drizzle. There was still an hour before dinnertime, so we went straight to the bath.

I soaked for a long time in the hot water, staring up at the ceiling in a daze. It had been a really long day. When I looked out the window, the view was already giving way to a deep darkness. The milky white steam rising from the bath drifted outside like it was being swallowed up by the night.

The clatter of a door being flung open caught me by surprise. When I looked over, I saw Momoko standing there in the steamy haze, totally naked. Now that she'd stripped off her clothes, she looked even smaller than usual.

"Can I come in?"

"Um ... sure ... please," I started to say, but she came in without waiting for my reply.

"You're so young, Takako. Your skin's so nice and fresh," she said, having a look at me in the bath.

I automatically turned my back to her. "I'm not that young," I said.

"Oh, you've still got a lot ahead of you. I mean look at that gorgeous curve from your neck to your chest. As you get older, your age tends to show there. But your skin is still so nice and smooth. I'm jealous," she said, eyeing me with a little smirk.

"This totally counts as sexual harassment," I said.

"Oh, don't worry, Takako," she said, laughing loudly. The sound of her laughter reverberated pleasantly inside the walls of the bathhouse.

When she first walked in, I'd noticed the fairly painful-looking scar from her operation running vertically about ten centimeters down her stomach. Although she hadn't made any attempt to hide it, I still felt like I'd seen something I shouldn't have. I looked away. It made me think of what she'd said earlier in the day about what had happened to her and about the emptiness she felt inside. It felt hard to talk, like I had something stuck in my throat.

After she was done washing, Momoko got into the water beside me and closed her eyes contentedly. "Ah," she said, "that feels so good."

As I looked at her face in profile, I felt a strange impulse to take her in my arms and hug her. "What's that?" I said, pointing out the window. The moment she was distracted, I leapt. But Momoko must have sensed me coming because she nimbly eluded me.

"What? What're you doing?" she shrieked.

"Nothing," I laughed, splashing as I came closer, slowly but steadily backing her into one end of the bath, like a border collie running down a wayward sheep.

"What is it, Takako? You've got a crazy look in your eye."

Ignoring the sound of fear in her voice, I pounced. Then I closed my eyes and held on tight. Her shoulders felt very small and very warm.

"Wait a . . . what are you . . ." She fought me off frantically. Water was splashing everywhere. Waves spread over the surface of the bath. But I didn't loosen my grip.

Finally, she seemed to understand and gave in. Her body relaxed, and she let her head rest on my shoulder.

"I give up. I didn't know that's what you wanted, Takako," she said as she leaned on me.

"You weren't paying attention."

We both let out a laugh, but we stayed like that for a long time, at one end of the big bath, holding each other.

9

Our second night was much quieter than the first. The guests we'd met the night before had already gone back down the mountain. In their place were a man and a woman who seemed to have just arrived that day. The couple talked quietly to each other through dinner. I found myself hating them. Why did they have to come to a boarding house like this place? They ought to be at one of those hot spring inns where they could do what they wanted and keep their relationship a secret.

The innkeeper came in carrying a serving tray and discreetly turned on the fairly ancient television in the middle of the room. I think there was something wrong with the volume, because the sound of people laughing on screen would suddenly cut out, disappearing inside the cathode-ray tube of the TV. When that happened, the room seemed even more silent than before. I found the way the sound cut out weirdly scary, and eventually I got up, went over to the TV, and turned it off.

We went back to our room and lay under the covers of our futons, side by side. Once we turned off the lights, it felt terribly quiet. The rain seemed to have stopped too. We could no longer hear the sound of rain falling in the distance.

"Let's not rush to leave in the morning," Momoko said quietly.

"That sounds good," I said, but my mind was elsewhere. I was staring up at the ceiling in the dark. Momoko had told me before that she couldn't sleep if there was even a small light on, so it was pitch black in the room. And yet as I lay there with my eyes open, gradually getting used to the dark, I could make out the silhouettes of things in the room, however dimly.

A moment later, I called out softly to Momoko, whom I knew had to be right next to me though I couldn't see her. "Are you awake?"

"Yeah?" She answered right away as if she was awake too.

"Can we talk for a second?" I asked in a quiet voice, still staring at the ceiling.

"Sure. I kind of feel like talking too."

"It's about what you said this afternoon . . ."

"What were we talking about?"

"Being sick . . ."

"Oh yeah." She had paused for a moment before she answered.

"Is it—is it really bad?" I asked the question in one breath like I was reading a line from a script. My voice sounded so helpless in the dark.

"Yeah. If you think of it like that, it's pretty bad. But if you think about it another way, it's not so bad."

"What do you mean?"

"Hmmm . . ." Momoko drew out the sound until it became a groan. "What I mean is, you know how there are people who die unexpectedly in an accident or from a sudden illness, and they never get the chance to say goodbye to anyone? Well, maybe, compared to them, I'm really fortunate. I still have time for all that."

"You mean . . ."

"Nah, it's nothing to get so worried about. It's not like I'm about to die right now or anything. A little while ago, I went into the hospital and they removed my uterus and did a bunch of other things, and now I'm going regularly to the hospital, and they're figuring out my prognosis. I think it's just something I have to keep an eye on for the next few years."

"And is that why you went back to my uncle?"

"It's not like I decided to come back as soon as I found out I was sick. The thought didn't even occur to me at first. But then I had this dream one day when I was in the hospital and feeling pretty depressed."

"A dream?"

I rolled over to face Momoko in the dark. But it was too dark to see the expression on her face.

"In the dream I was on a boat that was right about to leave the harbor. No, actually, I think I might've been the boat. Anyway, I was paddling out toward the horizon. I could see all the way out there in the distance. I knew for certain that once I got there, I was never coming back. When I turned around, I saw a man standing in the harbor, waving at me. I could tell at a glance that it was Satoru. I had this feeling deep down that we would never see each other again, so I tried with all my might to wave back at him. But my boat was too fast—Satoru grew smaller and smaller as I left him behind. Before I knew it, I'd lost sight of him, and I was alone, drifting across the ocean. That was the dream." I could hear Momoko rustling her covers as she turned to face me. Then she laughed for a moment.

"It's embarrassing, but when I woke up from that dream in my room at the hospital, I started crying, and I cried so much I couldn't believe it. I mean I knew it was just a dream. But the tears kept coming, one after another. In the end, I was sobbing. I can't even remember the last time I cried before this. That's how rarely I cry, but that day I was just a total mess. I was so, so sad. It was unbearable. And then I knew I wanted to see Satoru again, no matter what. It's weird, don't you think?"

"I don't think so." When I tried to imagine how lonely she must have felt then, I kept shaking my head. I couldn't see her going through something like that.

"It's definitely weird," Momoko declared. "But that's why I came back, even though I still felt ashamed."

"So that's what happened . . . but you're still not planning on talking to my uncle about your illness?"

"Nope. Not planning on it," she replied flatly.

"Why not?"

"At this point, I don't want to be a burden to him now."

"He's much stronger than you give him credit for."

"You're right. Of course he can handle it. That's not the issue. It's about his feelings. I can't do that to him. It wouldn't be fair after everything that's happened."

"But if you don't try to tell him—" Momoko interrupted me before I could say, "you'll never know."

"I made my decision the moment I decided to come see him."

"But . . . but . . . then you told me." I realized my voice was getting louder.

"I guess I wanted to tell someone after all," Momoko said softly. "I just wanted to open up to someone . . . about leaving . . . about getting sick. And I knew that if I asked you not to tell Satoru, that you would keep my secret."

"That's not . . ." I said, my voice breaking as I started to cry. "That's not fair."

"You're right. It's not fair. I'm sorry, Takako. It made me so happy when you hugged me in the bath. I was truly happy. You're a really kind girl. That's why Satoru and I love you so much."

I buried myself in the covers as tears ran down my cheeks. I kept repeating the words over and over again. *It's not fair . . . It's not fair.* Momoko kept saying she was sorry. But I went on repeating the phrase dozens of times. And I kept on going until, at some point, I cried myself out and fell asleep.

The next morning under an overcast sky, the innkeeper and Haru saw us off. Just as she had when we arrived, Momoko stood in the entryway and bowed formally to the innkeeper. The innkeeper laughed as she tried to get her to stop, but Momoko persisted. "See ya!" Haru said casually and waved goodbye.

Momoko was back to her usual cheerful self in the morning. On our descent, she talked cheerfully. "Oh look, the lilies are blooming . . . The leaves are starting to show some color over there." When I replied, I tried my best to be as cheerful as I could. I didn't know what else to do.

We parted ways at Shinjuku Station that evening. With the crowds teeming around her, Momoko stood in front of the turnstile and bowed deeply to me. "Thank you, Takako," she said. "I had a really good time." The smile on her face was almost dazzling. Looking back at her, I took a risk and asked, "What are you going to do now?"

"I'm going back to the bookshop."

"No, that's not what I mean. I mean after that."

Momoko said, "Hmmm . . ." and folded her arms. "I'll figure something out." That was all she said. Then she turned briskly on her heels and disappeared into the crowd.

I stood there staring, even after I lost sight of her small figure in the crowd. I tried to imagine what might happen next, but the feelings it stirred up in me were more than I could bear.

10

Uncle Satoru called two days later, sometime before noon. When I saw his number show up on my cell phone, I could already imagine what had happened.

"Sorry to bother you at work," he said in a low monotone as soon as I picked up. "There's a letter waiting for you when you come by the shop ..."

So that's what happened. I let out a long sigh. I shouldn't have let her go off like that. Yet even if I had known that this was going to happen, what on earth could I have done?

Momoko didn't play fair. I knew that. As I squeezed my cell phone in my hand, I could feel the anger welling up inside me.

"Takako?" I hadn't said anything for so long that my uncle called out to me, starting to doubt I was still there.

"I'm coming right over."

"What about work?" my uncle was asking when I hung up.

It's not fair. It's not fair. I kept repeating the words over and over again in my head as the train carried me to Jimbocho. *It's not fair. This isn't how adults act.* I could understand some of what she was feeling. To be missing in action for five whole years, and then suddenly return only to say you're sick. I could see how you might hesitate to say something. But if she really still loved my uncle, then that was all the more reason to tell him. And what was going to happen to my uncle once she'd left him again? It had been hard enough for him the last time she left without saying anything.

I was on my uncle's side. Just as he had been on my side all this time. And that's why I couldn't forgive Momoko for disappearing again. The anger kept welling up inside me. I couldn't contain it. I was so angry. I was angrier than I'd ever been before. My body was trembling.

When I got to the bookshop, my uncle showed me the note she'd left for me.

It said, "Thank you. Please take care of yourself."

I tore it into little pieces and let them fall on the floor.

My uncle stared at me, dumbfounded.

"It's not fair. It's cowardly. I can't believe her. She only showed me her good side, and then she left. She just ran away."

"Takako?" My uncle was peering at me with a look of concern. "Um, Taka—"

I interrupted my uncle right there, and, with my head held high, announced to the room, "I'm breaking my promise. Actually, it wasn't even a promise. She just told me not to say anything."

"Huh?"

My uncle sat there with his mouth hanging open as I told him the short version of what Momoko said to me that night. I was well aware, of course, that all this would come as a shock, but he had a right to know. And there was no one else who could stop Momoko.

And yet my uncle didn't appear shocked. When I finished telling him, he just gave a little nod and said, "Okay."

"You knew?"

"Not at all."

"But then . . ."

My uncle sighed deeply and tried to sit down and almost fell into his chair. "I knew it would've taken something pretty significant for her to come back. Like I said before, once she makes a decision, she doesn't change her mind. So for her to show up again despite that, well . . . That's why I was afraid to ask too many questions. Which is why I asked you. How stupid am I? I never just talked to her directly, and this is the result," he said. He sounded like he had already given up.

I got up close to him, looked him straight in the eye, and said, "There's still time. But if you let her go now, you truly will never see her again. Even if you don't know how everything will turn out, you can't let her go. Do you understand what I mean? The only person who can stop her is you."

"Okay . . ." That was all he said. His voice lacked any conviction.

"So hurry up and get going!" I said, raising my voice. "Uncle, you remember when you told me not to run away from everything? It's just as bad if you and Momoko do it too. I'll watch the store. You go to her."

"But I don't know where to find her . . ." He still had a look in his eye like he felt powerless to stop her.

"Nothing comes to mind? Some place Momoko would think to go first?" I asked.

He stared at me for a moment, looking dumbfounded.

"Nope."

"It can't be. There's got to be someplace. Momoko's your wife."

"That's true, but I'm telling you . . ."

"Try thinking of a place that's special to her."

My uncle stared at me blankly for a long while, then suddenly he said, "Oh! There is one place. Maybe—no, it's got to be there."

"You've got it?" I asked again.

"I do. I might just make it there in time," he said, nodding forcefully now.

He almost flew out of his chair. "Takako, can I ask you for another favor?"

"Sure."

"I'm not paying you for the hours, right?"

"I know that, you idiot!" I shouted. There was no time for this stupid routine. My uncle finally went running out of the store like I'd given him a kick in the pants.

I hoped that he would be able to stop her this time.

I stood in the doorway of the store and watched as my uncle bolted down Sakura Street. He seemed to get smaller and smaller as he ran. Unfortunately, because of his bad back, the scene was interrupted a few times by him stopping to thump his lower back, but that's how it goes, I guess.

After my uncle disappeared from view, I stood for a while in a daze looking up at the narrow band of sky visible through the gap between the buildings on the block. It was that same aqua-blue autumn sky—with little, dappled clouds drifting slowly across it like a school of fish.

"What happened? The store's open, right?" A middle-aged man had stopped in front of the shop. He gave me a curious glance and then ducked inside.

I followed him in. "Welcome to the Morisaki Bookshop," I said. I'd played my part. Now the rest was up to my uncle.

I sat down at my old spot at the counter and waited for Momoko and my uncle to return.

11

The trees on the street had already dropped the last of their leaves when I saw Wada again.

That night, I stopped by the Saveur for the first time in close to a month. I hadn't felt much like going for a while. Even when I'd passed it on the street, I just walked right by. But as the weather turned colder day by day, I found myself craving their coffee.

I opened the door and said, "Oh."

Wada was sitting at a table in the back. Our eyes met right away. He had noticed me too. I thought, I screwed this up, didn't I, and tried to get away with just a quick hello, but he stood up conscientiously and waited for me to come over.

"Nice to see you," I said, feeling a bit flustered as I sat across from him.

"It's been a while," he replied with his usual cool tone.

The waitress brought over water and asked, "Are you ready to order?"

At the moment, I was still thinking I could just say hi, then change seats and order my coffee. So I said, "Not yet." She nodded and walked away still smiling.

It was a little while before Wada spoke. "How have you been?"

"Um, okay, I guess? And you?" I replied.

"So-so," he said cheerfully and took a sip of his coffee.

Was he still waiting for his ex-girlfriend to show up? But he'd told me himself he was done with that. Just as that thought crossed my mind, Wada suddenly said, "I've been waiting for you." Then he reached into his bag and took out a paperback. I realized it was the Saneatsu Mushanokōji book I'd left behind that night before my trip, *Friendship*. So much had happened, I had completely forgotten about the book.

I would've never dreamt that Wada had it.

"You held on to it all this time for me?" I asked as he handed me the book.

"That night I noticed the book after you'd left. I asked the owner if he would give it to you the next time you came in, but he said he didn't know who you were. He claimed he'd never seen you before."

There was no way the owner didn't know me. We'd seen each other dozens of times. I was basically one of the regulars.

"That's how I ended up holding on to the book. I didn't have a way to contact you, so I've been stopping by from time to time to see if you were here. My timing must've been bad though because I never ran into you. I felt guilty about it, but just waiting got boring so I ended up reading your whole book."

I listened to him tell me all this with my mouth hanging open. And then I saw the owner standing at the counter, and I finally understood what had happened. He was polishing the glasses, pretending not to recognize me. I watched him closely until our eyes met for an instant. *Well, that was dumb. He probably had no idea that Wada was waiting for someone else. He'd gotten all worked up over nothing.*

"I'm so sorry for all this," I said, and bowed to Wada.

"No, honestly it was a nice opportunity for me to read a book that wasn't *Up the Hill*. I should be the one thanking you," he said with a playful laugh.

After this strange twist, I felt like I couldn't hold back any longer. I looked down and felt my shoulders start to tremble.

"Are you okay?" Wada watched me with a worried look on his face. But when he realized that I was just laughing, he started laughing too. Little by little, we were starting to feel comfortable with each other. I realized that in my heart I was genuinely delighted to see him again. It's true. Seeing him made me incredibly happy. It didn't matter what he felt about me. It was pointless to worry about that. There was nothing I could do to change that fact.

"Um," I said, looking up at him again, "I'm glad to see you."

I couldn't leave without thanking the owner. I felt that deeply. Without his help, I really might never have seen Wada again. Even if I ordered a hundred cups of coffee, I would still be in his debt.

"I'm glad to see you too," he said. "I mean if I hadn't, I would've been guilty of larceny, so there's that. No, that's a lie. I wanted to talk to you again." He laughed, scratching the back of his head in embarrassment. I was so embarrassed I couldn't look at him. Instead, I glanced out the window and saw a reflection of the two of us, face to face. Outside, the fierce winter wind was blowing, and it looked awfully cold. I was deeply grateful that the two of us had been able to run into each other again.

"Well, now," Wada said, stretching happily. "Let me pick up the tab today to thank you for lending me the book. That wouldn't bother you, would it?"

I held up a finger and smiled. "Well, okay, maybe just one cup."

"Still being modest?" He pretended to act shocked for a moment, then he turned to our waitress who was walking by and waved her over.

12

The Morisaki Bookshop stands alone at the corner of a street crowded with used bookstores. It's tiny and old and really nothing much to look at. There aren't many customers. And because it has a limited selection, people who aren't interested in its specialty never give it a second glance.

But there are people who love this store. And as long as they're devoted to it, then that's enough. That's what my uncle Satoru, the shop's owner, always says with a smile. And I agree. Because I love the bookshop and its owner.

Today, I'm off from work and on my way to visit Jimbocho for the first time in ages. My uncle called me last week. From the excitement in his voice on the phone, I knew something had happened even without him telling me.

"She said she wanted to see you too. It's been so long," he said. Her condition had been improving, and at the moment, things seemed good. It was a relief to hear that, at least for the time being. And the thought of seeing the two of them after so long made me walk a little more quickly up the busy street.

That day my uncle went running after her, Momoko didn't come back to the bookshop. But my uncle was able to find her. He went to the temple where they'd held the memorial service for their stillborn child. He said that when he found her, it looked like Momoko had been standing by the spring in the back of the temple for a long time. I didn't dare ask for the details of what they said to each other. That's between the two of them. But they couldn't have told each other any lies in that place where their child lay sleeping. For them, what was probably most important was that they each came clean about their feelings. It's possible that somewhere in her heart she wished my uncle had come and found her in that same place when she'd left him five years earlier. "When she saw me coming, she collapsed on the spot. She cried out like a little child and started bawling. In that moment, I loved her from the bottom of my heart. Tears were streaming down my face. I felt like I was finally able to face all the things I hadn't noticed before, all the things I'd turned away from. I took Momoko in my arms, and I said 'Don't go' over and over again. 'I need you.' Before I saw her there I couldn't have said something as simple as that."

When he returned to the shop alone late that night, he talked me through what had happened. Rather than being depressed that she wasn't with him, he seemed quite cheerful. "She promised," he said at the end. "The two of us will talk things over, and then one day she'll come back. She made me a promise."

Then, a whole year later, Momoko returned. She said she'd needed to get her thoughts in order first, otherwise it wouldn't have been fair to him. He told me that's what she'd said when they said goodbye that day. She was as strong-willed as ever.

After crossing the busy road, I go down Sakura Street. On this narrower backstreet, I pass a row of used bookstores, and then I can see my uncle's shop right ahead of me. The door clatters when I fling it open and find Sabu holding court at the counter. "Hey, Takako," he says and waves me over.

"Oh, Sabu, you're here? Where's my uncle?"

"That's not the warm reception I was hoping for from you," he giggled. "He just left on a delivery."

I hear a cheerful voice coming from behind him. Looking around, I see a small woman with short hair sitting behind the counter.

"What happened to your hair?" I say.

Momoko raises her hand and touches the close-cropped hair above her ear. "Oh, I cut it. Honestly, when I first thought about it, I really wanted to get a buzz cut, but Satoru stopped me." She laughs loudly.

"It looks good on you," I say and sit down next to her. It truly does look good on her.

"You think so?" she frowns.

The store around lunchtime is pretty slow as usual. Aside from the fact that Momoko is there, nothing much has changed. And that makes me a tiny bit happy.

"By the way, Takako, what's this about you having a boyfriend?" Momoko asks in her usual abrupt way.

"What? Who'd you hear that from?"

She points a finger at Sabu. "Just now, from him."

"No, I heard it from the owner of the Saveur," he says, and starts giggling again as if something were funny.

"Are you cooking him some of the dishes I taught you?" Momoko asks with a grin.

"No—I mean, yes, but not . . ." I stammer.

That doesn't satisfy Momoko. She keeps interrogating me until I cry, "Come on, isn't that enough?"

At that moment, I hear the sound of the door opening. My uncle is back.

"Oh, Takako, you're early," he says.

The moment he walks in, Momoko says, "Hey, Satoru, did you know Takako has a boyfriend?"

"What? I hadn't heard anything. Is that true? Why didn't you tell me?" He comes over and looks me in the eye. "You know you can discuss it with me, right?"

"That's right," Momoko says, clapping her hands together. "And if Takako marries him, then he can take over the shop. After all, we need to find a successor."

For some reason, the thought of this makes my uncle completely lose it. "That's nothing to joke about," he yells. "Why should I let that guy take over?"

"If you haven't even met him yet, how do you know who he is?" Momoko says coldly.

Sabu giggles. "Well, maybe it's time for me to go home," he says. "See you soon, Momoko." He waves to her and leaves the store in quite a cheery mood. He doesn't say goodbye to my uncle or me.

Once Sabu is gone, I say, "It didn't take long for you to have him wrapped around your finger, did it?" I'm amazed.

"Hey, I didn't mean to. I just talked to him," Momoko says nonchalantly.

"They've been at it all this time. I mean, of course, she won him over. Sabu didn't stand a chance." My uncle says this so matter-of-factly that Momoko and I burst out laughing.

Then Momoko suddenly gets to her feet and turns toward me.

"Momoko Morisaki has returned home and is reporting for duty." She gives a brisk military salute.

I quickly stand up straight.

"Welcome home," I say. "We've been waiting for you. And if you disappear again, I really will be angry with you."

"You're the one who broke your promise. Honestly though, I'm grateful for what you did. Thank you, Takako. Let's be friends again," she says and then she laughs as she pinches my cheek. I'm so used to it at this point that just like my uncle, I cry, "Quit it!" but I'm already starting to give in.

"Maybe I should cook something special tonight for Takako to show my gratitude." Momoko thumps her chest proudly. "Will you come shopping with me?"

"Of course, your cooking is the real reason I came," I say with a smile.

"Takako, before you go," my uncle cuts in, "I was thinking about what we were talking about earlier . . ."

We ignore him and walk out the front door.

Outside, the sky is clear. A few large clouds drift pleasantly overhead. I stretch my arms up high and shut my eyes for a moment. I can feel the warm sunlight pressing on my eyelids.

"Hey, if you don't hurry up, I'm leaving you behind."

I open my eyes when I hear her voice.

Up the street, Momoko turns back to look at me. The sun glints off her new short hair and she smiles.

"Come on, come on," she says, waving to me. And then she dashes ahead.

For a moment, I watch her from behind as she walks away. Then I run down the street after her.

Translator's Note

When Satoshi Yagisawa's novel debuted in Japan, it won the Chiyoda Prize, named after the district that is home to Tokyo's beloved Jimbocho neighborhood of bookshops. In the course of the story, he catalogs the many pleasures of reading: the joy of discovering a new author; the hedonism of staying up too late to finish a book; the surreptitious thrill of getting to know someone by reading their favorite novel; and the freedom of walking into a bookstore and scanning the titles, waiting for something to catch your eye.

Any reader who goes looking for all the books mentioned in these pages might not find everything, but that's to be expected, especially in little secondhand places like the Morisaki Bookshop. As far as I know, *Until the Death of the Girl*, the book by Saisei Murō that sparks Takako's passion for reading in chapter 4, has not been translated into English—*yet*. But the book that played the same role for her friend Tomo, Osamu Dazai's *Schoolgirl*, is available in a recent translation by Allison Markin Powell. It shouldn't be difficult to track down English editions of Jun'ichirō Tanizaki's, Ryūnosuke Akutagawa's, and Sōseki Natsume's well-known books, particularly *Kokoro*, one of the most loved novels in Japanese literature. You can find stories by many of the other authors Takako discovers in the major anthologies of Japanese short stories, each of which is almost a bookshop unto itself.

This translation owes its existence to many people, especially its eminent editor, Sara Nelson, and Setsuko and Simon

Satoshi Yagisawa

Winchester, without whom I never would have met Sara. I could not have done it without my parents: my father, Yuichi, who answered every question I had, and my mother, Susanne, who first taught me the pleasure of reading. The text was immeasurably improved by my whole family, particularly my brother-in-law, Bruno Navasky, and my sister, Melissa, who each read multiple drafts, and by my friends Hiroko Tabuchi, Junko Suzuki, and Ayaka Kamei, who patiently offered their insights. I would also like to thank my wife, Nicole, whom I met one day by chance in a bookstore and who is always my first reader.

More Days at the Morisaki Bookshop

SATOSHI
YAGISAWA

Translated from the Japanese
by Eric Ozawa

1

It's my day off from work, and I'm walking down the same familiar street. There's a feeling of calm in the air, like everything is at peace on this warm October afternoon. With a thin scarf loosely wrapped around my neck, I feel myself starting to sweat a little bit.

Even on a weekday around noon, the people I pass on the street walk at a leisurely pace and so do I. And from time to time, we come to a stop and disappear silently into one of the many bookshops along the way like we've been swallowed up.

The Jimbocho neighborhood is a little unusual for Tokyo because most of the stores there are bookshops. Each of the used bookshops has its own particular specialty: some carry art books, or play scripts, or philosophy texts; others handle rare items like old maps and traditionally bound Japanese books. Altogether, there are more than a hundred seventy stores. It's impressive to see all those bookshops lined up one after the other down the street.

If you cross the avenue, you'll find yourself in an area of offices, surrounded by tall buildings, but within its borders the neighborhood has done a good job keeping the rest of the city at bay. Only here are there rows of picturesque buildings. It's like the neighborhood exists in a different time, enveloped in its own quiet little world. Which may be why when you're walking around here, going wherever your fancy takes you, you look up and suddenly realize how much time has passed.

The place where I'm headed is on this corner. If you pass the street with the row of secondhand bookshops and turn onto the side street a little ahead, you'll be able to see it.

It's a used bookstore called the Morisaki Bookshop and it specializes in modern Japanese literature.

Once I turn the corner, I hear someone eagerly calling my name. "Hey, Takako, come here!"

I look over and see a small middle-aged man looking my way, waving me over enthusiastically.

I hurry over to him and whisper my objection. "Didn't I tell you on the phone that you didn't need to wait for me? I'm not a little kid."

He's always like this, treating me like a child even though I'm a twenty-eight-year-old woman. It's obviously embarrassing, as you can imagine, to have someone shouting my name like that in the middle of the street.

"Well, it was taking you so long to get here. I got to worrying that you might've gotten lost."

"That's why I told you, you didn't need to wait for me in front of the shop. I've been here dozens of times. How could I possibly get lost?"

"Sure, I guess, but you know you can be a little bit absent-minded sometimes."

"You mean *you* can, don't you? Take a good look in the mirror sometime. You'll find a very absent-minded man staring back at you."

This is Satoru Morisaki, my uncle on my mother's side, and the third-generation proprietor of the Morisaki Bookshop. The original store, started by my great-grandfather back in the Taishō era, no longer exists. The current store was built almost forty years ago.

At first glance, my uncle Satoru might seem a little sketchy. He's always dressed in threadbare clothes, with slip-on sandals on his feet, and his shaggy hair makes you wonder if he's ever had a proper haircut in his life. And on top of all that, he's always saying off-the-wall things, and he ends up blurting out whatever he's thinking like a child. He is, in short, a tough man to figure out.

And yet, in this peculiar neighborhood, his odd personality and unusual appearance strangely seem to work in his favor: he's surprisingly well liked. It would be difficult to find someone around here who doesn't know my uncle.

His Morisaki Bookshop is an old-fashioned store, in a two-floor wooden building untouched by time, every bit the image of a vintage bookshop. The inside is cramped. You could get five people in there, but just barely. There's never enough space on the shelves; the books are piled on top, and along the walls, and even behind the counter where the cash register is. And the intense, musty smell particular to old bookshops penetrates everything. For the most part, the books on the shelves are cheap, running from around a hundred to five hundred yen, but the store also sells rarer things like first editions of famous writers.

The number of people looking for secondhand books like these has dropped since my grandfather's generation. From what I've heard, there were some extremely difficult times. It's only thanks to the customers who love the shop and have kept coming back over the years that it's still in business.

I first came to the shop more than three years ago.

Back then, my uncle let me come live on the second floor, and told me I could stay as long as I liked.

I can still vividly recall the days I lived here. At that time in my life, I was feeling desperate although the cause now seems insignificant when I look back on it. At first, I often lashed out at my uncle and locked myself in my room like some tragic heroine, crying all alone. Yet he patiently endured it all and offered me kind words and caring instead. As time went on, he taught me how thrilling reading can be, and how crucial in life it is to not hide from your emotions but to face them.

Naturally, my uncle was the one who introduced me to Jimbo-cho. At first, I was confused to look down the street and see just one bookstore after another.

"The great writers have always loved this place too," my uncle said, sounding like he was boasting about himself. "It's the best neighborhood of bookshops in the whole world." To be honest, I didn't get what he was talking about then. I couldn't see what there was to boast about.

But as time passed, I came to understand what he meant.

Jimbocho is brimming with charm and excitement. There's no other place like it in the world.

My uncle and I are still bickering back and forth in front of the shop when I hear a loud voice shout from inside, "Hey, what are you two doing?" When I peek in, I see a woman with a short, stylish haircut sitting at the counter, staring at us, with an irritated look on her face. That's Momoko.

"Quit dawdling out there and come in already, will you?"

She waved us in impatiently. She didn't seem to enjoy waiting in the shop for us by herself.

Momoko is Uncle Satoru's wife. You'd think she wouldn't be so different in age and appearance from my uncle, but she has such a straightforward and candid way about her that she seems much younger. My uncle is no match for her. Whenever she's around, he's always on his best behavior, like a little lapdog. It's only when she's there that you ever see that side of him.

Actually, Momoko lived apart from my uncle for almost five years, as a result of some unfortunate circumstances, but about a month ago she returned home safe and sound. Since then, she and my uncle have been running the shop together.

"So, Takako, what's new with you?" Momoko asks with a smile. She has such fine, straight posture that she somehow looks elegant even wearing just a sweater and a long skirt. I don't think I ever want to become someone who fills a room the way she does, but I do wish a little bit that I could have some of her grace.

"Things are good. Peaceful and calm. Work's going well. How are you?"

"I'm doing great," she says, flexing her arms to show off her biceps, like she's doing her Popeye impersonation.

"That's good to hear," I say, feeling a sense of relief. Years ago, Momoko had had a serious illness, and we're still watching her prognosis. My uncle is always very careful about Momoko's health, but it seems like his constant concern ends up irritating her.

"I've got some sweet daifuku mochi with me. Shall we have some?"

"Oh, maybe we should."

My uncle checks that Momoko has gone to the back and then complains to me in a whisper. "It's awfully cramped with Momoko here with me at the shop, but that's how it goes, I guess. It's just so much easier to work alone."

"But weren't you lonely when you were actually left all by yourself?" I'm only trying to tease him, but he gets all worked up and argues with me like a little kid.

"That's nonsense! I mean when she's back behind the counter, where am I supposed to go? These days, I'm just pacing back and forth by the entrance like a guard dog."

"Is that by any chance why you were standing out in front today?"

"Take a guess." He confesses this pitiful fact with a straight face, then leans forward like he's going to whisper in my ear. "But I've got more important things to tell you, Takako," he says.

"Like what?"

"The other day I got some pretty good stuff at auction. I haven't put it on sale yet at the shop, but for you I'll make an exception and let you have a little look."

He might've tried to sound reluctant, but I know there is no way he isn't going to show me those books. Yet I've been so thoroughly converted that I'm excited to see them. I almost wonder if this love of books is hereditary. I sometimes think that might be why I'm still coming so often to the shop on my days off from work.

"Show me!" I shout without meaning to. "I've got to see them!"

"Hey, I just made tea for you two." Momoko looks at us dumbfounded, with the teapot in her hands.

"This is a bookshop," my uncle says bluntly. "How are we not going to look at books? Right, Takako?"

"Right," I agree with a laugh.

My aunt gives us an annoyed look and grumbles, "You two are the worst."

This is my beloved Morisaki Bookshop. It's been an inseparable part of my life since the days I lived here.

In its own modest way, it's a place that holds so many little stories within its walls. Maybe that's the reason I keep coming back.

2

The Morisaki Bookshop bills itself as a store specializing in modern Japanese literature. The shop does stock some contemporary novels, but those are kept on the hundred-yen cart at the entrance. Inside the shop, there are basically only novels that date from the Meiji era to early Showa. (Which is why the interior is permeated by such a damp and musty smell, but that comes with the territory.)

Maybe it's because the shop deals with a special type of book that it tends to attract a lot of customers who are a bit *eccentric*.

Now I'm perfectly accustomed to them, but at first, they threw me off. It's not that they're hard to deal with. In fact, for the most part, they're perfectly harmless. They're just a little unusual, that's all. They come in now and then, hardly saying a word, lost in their single-minded search for a book. These customers, who are overwhelmingly elderly men, are, without fail, solitary figures. There's something about them that makes it impossible to imagine their everyday lives—so much so that if someone told me they were harmless ghosts, or some kind of otherworldly creature, I might actually be persuaded to believe it.

Whenever I visit the shop, I find myself weirdly concerned about whether they're still healthy enough to come in. I've never been close to them, but I can't help but hope they're well. I feel a kind of sympathy for them since we all love the same shop. And given the advanced age of most of these customers, I worry about them.

So, if they happen to come in when I'm helping out at the shop, I feel a secret relief when I see they're doing well.

Back when I was living on the second floor and working at the shop every day, the "paper bag man" was the one I worried about most of all. As his name suggests, he always came in carrying a tattered paper bag in both hands. Sometimes it was a bag from a department store, but occasionally it was a bag from one of the larger bookstores, like Sanseidō. He must have been going from store to store before he came to us, because the bag was often already full when he showed up. It looked quite heavy for his skinny arms. He invariably wore a dress shirt under a mouse-colored sweater.

If that was all, there wouldn't be anything so peculiar about him. The problem was that mouse-colored sweater. It wasn't simply frayed, no, it went far beyond that to the point where this article of clothing was so ragged that it was a miracle he was even able to wear it. Now, there was nothing about the old man that seemed unhygienic. In fact, he seemed neat and clean, aside from the absurd condition of his sweater, which looked like it had been dug up from some archaeological site.

The first time I saw him I was quite shocked. I snuck glimpses of him as he silently selected his books, and several times I felt the urge to shout, "Sir, you should be buying clothes, not books!" But he didn't seem to notice. He bought ten books, stuffed them into his paper bag, and left the shop without saying a word.

Ever since that day, I haven't been able to take my eyes off him when he comes in. Some weeks he comes in multiple times, but he's also gone a month without coming. He wears the same clothes every time. He's always gripping his paper bag of books in both hands. At the Morisaki Bookshop alone, on occasion he's bought books that cost ten thousand yen apiece. And yet his sweater only becomes more and more ragged. I couldn't help wondering who on earth this old man was. I was unable to muster the courage to talk to him, so I always ended up silently staring at his back as he walked out.

I tried asking my uncle about him once. "He's buying so many books—what if he has his own used bookstore in another neighborhood?"

"Nope. He's buying them to read them himself," he replied with certainty.

"Really? I guess you can tell the difference."

"That much I can tell whether I want to or not."

I guess that's how it goes. I could hardly distinguish one type of customer from another. But when a new customer walked into the shop, my uncle seemed to be able to tell at a glance whether they'd come to buy a book or if they had just wandered in on a stroll. He said his intuition was the result of years of experience.

"So," I said, letting my curiosity get the better of me. "What does that old man do for a living? Can you tell that too just by looking at him? It's not like he spends all his money on books and can't afford new clothes, right?"

"Hey." He spoke in the tone of voice you use to reprimand a child. "Your job isn't to start getting so nosy about the customers. The purpose of a bookshop is to sell books to people who need them. It's not right for us to start wondering what kind of job people have or what sort of life they lead. It's not going to make these older customers feel very good if they know the salespeople have been prying into their lives."

When I thought about it, my uncle's view seemed like a perfectly legitimate way of thinking about a business that caters to its customers. Even though he was usually making little jokes and chuckling to himself, after running a used bookshop for so many years, when something needed saying he came right out and said it. In moments like that, he could be kind of cool.

Anyway, that's the reason why the paper bag man's origins remain a mystery to us.

———

These eccentric customers each have their own distinct reasons for searching for books. It's truly fascinating. I'm always impressed by the wide range of circumstances that lead people to seek out second-hand books.

Take, for example, people who set out to collect rare books, without regard to genre, era, or region. They simply accumulate unusual volumes. When a well-known collector came into the shop, he seemed dissatisfied with what we had in stock. On his way out of the store, he said something that left me dumbfounded. "It doesn't matter if it's a masterpiece. If the volume isn't rare, it's worthless to me."

And then there are what we call the brokers. They acquire valuable books at as low a price as possible and then sell them to another bookshop, pocketing the difference in price. Basically, their trade is buying books. For these customers, the quality of the work is secondary. They probably never even read them. There are others too, people who aren't interested in novels, but instead seek out the work of the obscure artists whose illustrations appear alongside a text. Some of those collectors will rely on the barest of leads in their single-minded pursuit of those pictures. And then there are the people who won't put anything that isn't a first edition on their bookshelves. Even if they want a book, they won't buy it until they can find a first edition of it.

The one who takes the cake is the old man who only showed up once during the period when I was living above the shop.

He wandered in at dusk and went straight to the shelf in the back where we keep the most expensive books. As he pulled each volume off the shelf, he looked only at the colophon (that's the last page of the book) and then put it back on the shelf. He repeated the same action again and again. Occasionally, his hand would pause, and he would stare intently at some spot on the colophon, nod a few times, and then chuckle to himself with an evil grin. To be honest, I found it pretty creepy.

After the old man had finally finished inspecting every book on the shelf, he suddenly walked out. I turned to my uncle, who was sitting next to me, grabbed him by the sleeve, and asked him what in the world that man was up to.

"Oh, he's looking for the author's seal," he said without looking up from the account books, as if there were nothing particularly unusual about this.

"He's a seal collector. They rarely come to the shop, but there are some pretty famous ones around here. I'm sure I told you about Nosaki, didn't I?"

"A seal collector?" I was puzzled by this unfamiliar term.

"Yeah, the seals are stamped on the colophon."

My uncle pulled a book with a rather old-looking binding from the shelf and showed me the last page. It was Osamu Dazai's *No Longer Human*. Near the left edge of the colophon, I could see "Dazai" had been stamped in red. My uncle explained that back when bookbinding was still generally done by hand, the author would verify the number of copies and give his approval to the printing by stamping the books with his own seal. He said that in general they were just stamped with the author's name, but there were some that incorporated elaborate, elegantly designed patterns.

All of which is to say that the old man was after the seals. I had never known about the existence of these seals until my uncle explained it all to me. But still, what was the point? Was he going to cut out all of these seals and paste them like stamps into an album so that every night he could stare at them with that big smirk?

"Yeah, something along those lines," my uncle said nonchalantly. "Well, I think some of them would hate to cut them out of the books so they just collect the volumes."

"That's totally insane."

There are people in this world whose hobby is astronomy and who find the vastness of the universe thrilling. And then, on the other hand, there are people whose hobby leads them to go to great lengths to collect these insignificant little seals. It's kind of hard to fathom.

"Uh-oh, Takako. You might be getting a little too worked up about this," my uncle said at the end, giving me a sideways glance. When he saw the perplexed look on my face, he burst out laughing.

"Hey, I'm back." And with this cheery greeting, Sabu appeared. He closed the door behind him with a loud noise and said something I didn't quite understand. "Ah, great weather, isn't it today? It makes me feel like reading Kōsaku Takii." Then he plopped himself down on the chair in front of the counter like it was his. My uncle, who was accustomed to this, said, "I'll put on the kettle," and started to make tea.

Of all the regular customers of the Morisaki Bookshop, Sabu was probably the most regular of them all. Although that didn't necessarily mean he was making all that much of a contribution to our sales figures. Only that he was the one who came in more than anyone else. More of a regular browser. A short and stout man with a friendly face who loved to talk. I didn't know exactly how old he was, but I'd say somewhere in his midfifties. Except for the area around his ears, he's spectacularly bald. He'll sometimes joke about it himself.

"Oh, where's Momoko today?" he asked my uncle, while he looked all over the shop for her. Of course, Momoko was wildly popular with the men who were our regular customers. She was such a good listener and a straight talker that she seemed to have stolen their hearts. The result has been a curious phenomenon: a sharp increase in the number of customers who come to see her. Sabu, of course, is one of the many she has in the palm of her hand.

"If you're looking for her, she's over at the other place," my uncle said, gesturing toward the doorway with his chin. Sabu immediately looked disappointed.

"What? That's a shame."

Momoko recently started helping out in the evenings at the little restaurant less than ten steps from the shop. After the head chef suddenly quit, the owner turned to Momoko, who was both a good cook and good at handling the customers. I don't know if this is true or not, but I heard that the restaurant was doing amazingly well, far better than before. When we said we were concerned that a hectic job like that might be too much for her health, she said, "I can handle this. It's my choice. You and Satoru worry too much."

Sabu wasn't paying any attention to me, so I had no choice but to say hello.

"Oh, Takako, you're here."

Even though I had been right in the middle of his field of view, he seemed just now to be noticing I was there. Ever since Momoko's return, his treatment of me had been openly shoddy. Before that, he had taken such a liking to me that it was actually becoming a bit concerning. He'd even been telling me I had to marry his son.

"I'm helping out today," I said.

"Helping out? What's a young person like you idly frittering away a weekday afternoon? Don't you have a real job?"

"That's rude! It's easy to take a day off at my office."

He giggled when I took offense. That's how Sabu was. He was nice, but he had a sharp tongue.

In this neighborhood, however, he had a reputation for being someone who knew everything that was going on. It's something he took pride in. So whenever he came by the shop, he always asked my uncle first about the other regular customers.

"How's Takigawa doing these days?"

"He hasn't been in recently. Before, he'd always come in once every couple of weeks."

"I hope he's not ill."

"It would be a relief if he dropped by sometime."

"How about Professor Kurusu? That guy's figured out how to deduct his book allowance from his research budget. A clever move."

"The professor was here two days ago."

"How about Yamamoto then? The other day, he was so proud that his book collection had hit fifty thousand books that I got a little annoyed. He was definitely boasting."

And so on . . . Inevitably, the conversation came down to this:

"Everyone's getting older, huh. If this shop doesn't find some new customers, it's doomed."

"You said it."

And then Sabu and my uncle would laugh together as if they'd said something funny. Those two went through the same routine every time. It was weird to me that they never got tired of it.

For a long time, I'd had my doubts about Sabu.

Like, who exactly was Sabu?

He always seemed to have free time. I had never once seen him busy. And even if the books he bought were not big-ticket items, he'd been buying books for an awfully long time. Unless he had an extremely large house, where on earth was he keeping all these books? The fact that he had a beautiful wife, who always looked nice in her kimono, was another mystery.

Which naturally brought up another question. What did Sabu do for work?

The more I thought about it, the more it seemed that Sabu was the most mysterious character around.

At the shop, Sabu was essentially no longer treated like a customer. My uncle probably wouldn't get upset if I tried asking him about it.

So, at some point while the two of them were still sipping their tea and talking about this and that, I interrupted.

"Sabu, may I ask you something?"

"Why so polite all of a sudden?"

"What do you do for work? You talk a lot about people idly frittering away their days, but aren't you the idlest of them all?"

It was as if Sabu had been waiting for me to ask this question.

He slowly turned up the corners of his mouth and smirked at me like a detective in a hard-boiled novel. It was incredibly annoying.

"You want to know?" he said as he leaned forward on the chair in front of me, bringing his face closer to mine.

"I do."

Even though I already regretted bringing up the subject, I nodded just like he wanted me to. Interacting with Sabu often led to these extremely irritating situations.

"Why do you want to know?"

"Actually, I don't really care."

"You won't reel me in like that."

"Ah, come on, enough already. Okay, I've just got to know. I can't take it anymore. If you don't tell me, I won't be able to sleep tonight. There, satisfied?"

"Really?"

"Sure. I really, really want to know. What on earth do you do for a living?"

I was getting tired of asking, when Sabu nodded with a satisfied look, leaned closer, and whispered, "I'm ... not ... telling."

I stood there with my mouth opening and closing over and over like a goldfish. When he saw my reaction, Sabu doubled over laughing, *mhahahahah.* "Wait ..." He was truly an infuriating old man. He was totally mocking me.

"No, it was too perfect. A masterpiece."

"Hey, Uncle Satoru knows, doesn't he?"

"Ah, um, I do, sure ..."

"Hey, Satoru! You can't tell her!" Sabu shook his head fiercely side to side, looking flustered as he tried to command my uncle not to tell me. "It's too soon to tell Takako."

"Whoops, my mistake."

"What are you talking about?"

"A man with more of a mysterious side has more charm, don't you think? That's why I'm not going to tell you. Your curiosity will grow and grow until it becomes an obsession, and you'll end up dreaming about me."

"Absolutely not. It doesn't mean anything to me at all anymore."

"Such a headstrong woman."

"No, I really don't care. I'll never ask you again," I said indignantly.

"Well, I think I should be going now. I've had my fill of teasing you, Takako," Sabu said. Then he downed the rest of his tea and walked out of the shop, cackling to himself as he went.

"Good grief, that guy," I said, dumbfounded.

My uncle seemed to agree. "Well, he's a strange guy."

This shop really does attract one strange guy after another.

3

Near dusk, my uncle suddenly started to get agitated. "Where's Roy?" he shouted, his ridiculously loud voice reverberating in our tiny shop. "I haven't been able to find him since I got back from my delivery!"

My quiet moment reading a book while I worked at the register was now ruined. "How should I know where he is?" I said sullenly.

As far as my uncle was concerned, it didn't matter if someone was trying to read, he had no problem striking up a conversation with them. The idea of leaving them alone never even entered into consideration.

It was always fun spending time at the bookshop, only it was a shame that my uncle had to ruin it by being noisy like this. Back when I lived here, my uncle would go to the hospital to undergo treatment for his lower back, so we didn't actually overlap much at the shop. But now we were almost always here together. Which meant that I had to interact with him constantly. It might seem harsh to think of my uncle as being in the way in his own shop, but he's the kind of person who gets riled up by the tiniest things, so these annoying outbursts happened at least once a day.

"Roy was here the whole day until I went out!" My uncle was walking around the shop making a commotion, then he chased me away from the chair behind the counter where I'd been sitting and started desperately looking around.

"I told you I didn't know. You must've left him somewhere."

"Roy is as precious to me as my own life right now. I would never do such a thing." My uncle was still rattling on, when he suddenly shouted and bolted up to the second floor.

"That Momoko!"

After a moment, my uncle came stamping down the stairs, clutching a brown-colored cushion to his chest. I can't think of any other adult I know who would make such a fuss over a single cushion like that.

Recently my uncle hadn't just been suffering from back pain, he'd also developed a case of hemorrhoids, which, according to him, made the long hours sitting in a chair "absolute torture."

Still, running a used bookshop means you spend the better part of the day sitting in a chair waiting for customers. It was going to be impossible for him to do his job in this condition. What saved him from his predicament was this: a cushion with a hole in the center, otherwise known as a donut pillow. The cushion was so good at easing the pain that my uncle had absolute faith in it. He said he couldn't just call it a cushion. That would be heartless. And because it was for his hemorrhoids, he started calling it Roy. He wasn't doing it to be funny. No, he was totally, absolutely, 100 percent serious.

"Ooh boy." My uncle placed Roy on his chair and then lowered himself onto it with the care you'd expect from a bomb squad in an action movie. Which didn't stop him from grumbling and cursing Momoko's name. Apparently, while my uncle was out making deliveries, Momoko had left Roy drying on the veranda just before she went to the little restaurant to help out. Which was why my uncle was now furious with her.

"Well, it's good you found it, isn't it?" I felt obliged to ask. My uncle was catching his breath after his brush with danger.

"It's tough getting older. All these little ailments pop up."

"Stop talking like an old man."

"I am an old man," my uncle said with a hangdog look on his face.

"Uncle, you're still in your forties," I said, exasperated. I wanted him to stay healthy forever and not let the whole hemorrhoids thing drag him down. "You're still young. You've got time. Old people are older than you."

"These hemorrhoids are hopeless." The only people who can understand the pain of hemorrhoids are the people who have them. My uncle spoke these words like he was reciting a maxim. I'm sure it must've been terrible. Any type of hemorrhoids come with a considerable amount of pain. But it was impossible to take what my uncle was saying as anything other than a joke. "That reminds me. Should I get one ready for you?"

"I'm fine, thanks. I don't have hemorrhoids at the moment," I replied brusquely. I was getting a little tired of him, and I decided not to pay him any more attention. Why would he be getting one ready for me? I had absolutely no idea what he was thinking. Did he plan on naming it Roy Jr.? This wasn't my uncle's only weird fixation or obsession. He had many, many others too. Every single one of them was annoying. For example, after his midforties, he started insisting that whenever they ate curry at home, it could only be the Vermont Curry brand, and only the "mild" flavor. When Momoko inadvertently bought the "medium hot" version, he spent the whole day pouting sullenly. According to Momoko, he became so irritating she wanted to give him a giant kick in the butt. I knew exactly how she felt.

Anyway, we'd found Roy, so I assumed my uncle would quiet down a little. I let out a sigh and tried to go back to the world of my book.

However, just as the thought crossed my mind, I saw an innocent smile appear on my uncle's face, and he sidled right up next to me with his chair. As incorrigible as ever, he couldn't resist poking his nose in again to interrupt me.

"So, Takako."

I said nothing.

"Whatcha reading?"

"What? Come on. Does it matter?" But whether I tried to ignore him or get angry, it had absolutely no effect on him.

"Hey, is that Sakunosuke Oda?"

He'd snuck a look at the copy of *Sweet Beans for Two!* in my hand, nodded, and gave me a knowing look.

"You like the book?"

"I do. It's actually my second time reading it. There. Are you satisfied now? I'm reading, please don't interrupt."

But naturally, my uncle made no attempt to listen.

"Now there's another writer with a tragic fate."

My uncle's eyes narrowed like he was staring off into the distance as he went on in this earnest tone. "Ah, Takako, you like Sakunosuke Oda too . . . But I'm sure you don't know anything about his life yet. That's such a shame."

At this point, it was already too late. I could tell how eager he was to tell me. I knew there was no way he'd let me go until I'd listened to the whole story. My uncle knew an extraordinary amount about Sakunosuke Oda—his whole life, not just his books. When he liked a writer, he loved nothing more than to read their autobiographies, memoirs, biographies, collected letters, etc. It had nothing to do with the business of running a used bookshop. He did it purely to satisfy his own interest. One thing he loved about books was that they could tell him what kind of lives the writers led, how they lived, how they loved, and how they left this world.

To me, there was something wonderful about that. However, my uncle really loved to make people listen to him recount all this as if it were something he'd witnessed firsthand. That's how I ended up hearing about the lives of a lot of writers, people like Osamu Dazai, Takehiko Fukunaga, Haruo Satō. Of course, the lives of writers whose names now belong to history can be fascinating. But the time has to be right. Sometimes I'm not in the mood to listen to all that. But my uncle doesn't care whether or not the time is right; once the switch has been flipped, he gets a glimmer in his eyes back behind his glasses, and he talks and talks until he's had enough.

I gave up and closed the book with a dramatic sigh (which had no impact on him at all). I'd lost my time to read. What can you do? In this case, I could only listen to what he wanted to tell me.

"Sakunosuke had a tragic fate?"

"That's right," he said.

"You get a sense of that somehow from his style."

"A lot of his work is based on his experiences." He nodded deeply, perfectly satisfied now that I was showing interest in what he was saying. Then my uncle began to recount the events of Sakunosuke Oda's life with great enthusiasm.

According to my uncle, Sakunosuke's life had been a series of hardships. He suffered from tuberculosis when he was a student, and his misfortunes piled up until he had to leave college. He fell passionately in love with a woman named Kazue, who worked at a café, and he set his sights on becoming a novelist, but his work failed to find recognition, and for a long time they lived a life of poverty, with all its daily hardships. But their suffering was not in vain; his books *Vulgarity* and *Sweet Beans for Two!* finally won him the recognition he'd long sought. His writing career was on a roll, but a few years later, his beloved wife, Kazue, fell ill and passed away.

He had enough turmoil in his life to be the main character in a TV show.

Having lost Kazue, Sakunosuke would often collapse in tears, regardless of what others might think. Kazue was the first person Sakunosuke had loved deeply, and the one who had loved him in return. Without her love to support him, Sakunosuke's life fell apart. His tuberculosis grew more and more serious. He must have sensed that death was near. Because when Kazue was on her deathbed, he'd cried as he told her he would follow in a few years. In the time he had left, he searched for solace in alcohol and coffee, as well as in the arms of other women. He coughed up blood as he wrote his novels.

My uncle told the story without a pause, as if he'd actually memorized the whole speech.

You could say he had a talent for it. As I listened, I was now completely entranced by the story, hanging on my uncle's every word.

"In his later years, Sakunosuke was so exhausted both physically and spiritually that he started taking methamphetamines to help him go on writing novels. His illness was so advanced that without them, he couldn't even hold a pen. His body had given out."

"And methamphetamines are a kind of stimulant, right?"

"It's hard to imagine now, but at the time it was easy to buy them at the drugstore. He'd inject them and work on his novel for days without sleeping."

"Yikes." That truly is hard to imagine now. Such a heartbreaking story, I thought, no matter how much times have changed.

"And he's not the only one. There were a lot of writers who regularly used methamphetamines. It was fairly well known, for example, that Ango Sakaguchi was a meth head."

"A meth head?" The words somehow sounded kind of cute, but it actually meant—

"Someone addicted to methamphetamines."

I heard myself say "Yikes" again.

"It's a terrible story," he said, shaking his head woefully. "But Kazue always remained in his heart. One of his masterpieces is the story of a man, driven to despair by the death of his wife, who ends up taking money from his company and betting like a madman on whatever horse is in the number one gate at the racetrack. The sole reason he's doing this is because his dead wife's name, Kazue, is written with the character for 'one.' We can't know for certain what Sakunosuke was thinking when he wrote the story, but there's no doubt it's connected to his intense feelings for Kazue, whose name, after all, begins with the same character."

"Yeah . . . it seems undeniable."

I have a weakness for stories like this. Just imagining what happened left me feeling somber.

"Even when he was dependent on drugs, even when he was coughing up blood, he went on writing novels. And when he had a massive lung hemorrhage and was taken to the hospital, he went on a rampage, demanding to be released because he needed to write. But later on, he ended up collapsing at the inn where he was living, and this time he didn't recover. He died in 1947 at the young age of thirty-three."

"Thirty-three? If he'd been healthy, he could've written so many more books," I said, overcome by a sense of loss. "I wonder what he would have written if he'd lived longer."

"But you could also say that he was able to write the novels he did precisely because he lived such a short time, and because death was always on his mind, as he burned through what remained of his life. He had that monstrous tenacity. When you think about it, there are lots of writers who had short lives. I suspect that they were able to write such amazing books because their lives were so short. Sakunosuke Oda didn't write many books, but he left behind some wonderful short stories. Whether that was for better or worse, we can't say. The only way to find out is to ask Sakunosuke in heaven."

My uncle looked deeply moved as he spoke these words, with his butt resting on the donut-shaped cushion.

"Is that right?" I mumbled. I glanced at the spines of the books lined up on the shelf. "If you think about it, most of the authors of the books here are no longer alive. It's a little bit strange, don't you think? Their books are still with us, and we read them to this day, and feel moved by them." It was true. So many of the people whose names lined the shelves here had long ago left our world behind. When I thought about it, I started to feel close to tears again.

"You're right. The way they shaped their feelings made them last. It's amazing, isn't it? And it's not just writers. All artists are incredible. We can learn so much from the work passed down to us from our ancestors."

I nodded enthusiastically in agreement. "It really is true."

At some point, I realized the sun had set. Outside the windows, the world was shrouded in blue shadows. It was nearly time to close the shop. Somehow or other, my uncle had won me over, and I was drawn into his story.

But it wasn't so bad after all, I said to myself, as I thought about the life of Sakunosuke Oda.

I think that my uncle tried to study these authors' lives in such depth because he was trying to learn something from them, and lurking behind that desire was the hope that he might find a clue to help him understand his own life.

From what I've heard, when my uncle was young, he went through a profound existential crisis. He agonized over it.

So, in his twenties, he worked in Japan to save up money to travel, then put on his backpack and went wandering all over the world for months at a time, solo. When the money ran out, he came back to Japan and started over again. I guess you could say he was one of those guys who are searching for themselves. It might sound embarrassing to put it that way, but for someone like me, who can't be bothered to do anything, the way my uncle was able to follow through on this plan without getting intimidated seems pretty cool.

When I visited his house in Kunitachi, he showed me a picture of himself from those days. It looks like it was taken when he had just started traveling. In the photo, he's still a young man in his twenties. Since that was right after I was born, I'd never seen what he looked like at that age.

In the picture, he's standing in a crowd in Nepal or India (my uncle couldn't remember), his face is stubbly, his cheeks are sunken in, and his skin tanned by the sun to a dark brown. He stares into the camera, the pupils of his eyes glinting darkly in the light.

When I saw the picture, I ended up shouting, "Wow. You look like a totally different person." I really wasn't exaggerating. He had such a different air about him, compared to the way my uncle is now.

"I was young then. That's almost thirty years ago."

"It's not just that. I don't know, there's something kind of amazing about you in that picture," I said, still staring intently at the photograph. That young version of my uncle seemed to be staring back at me. To think that that young man today made such a huge fuss because he couldn't find his cushion. Life is strange.

"Well, at the time, I was really troubled. When I wasn't traveling, I spent all my time reading." My uncle scratched the back of his head through his scruffy hair, chuckling to himself, like he was ready to laugh off the concerns of his former self.

"Every time I look at that picture, it makes me laugh," Momoko said with a little cackle when she rejoined us.

Somehow that was the only picture he took during the many years he spent traveling.

"I only took it because it was my first trip, and I got caught up in the moment. From then on, I didn't bring a camera when I was traveling," my uncle said dryly.

"Really? What a shame."

"Nah, what's the use of leaving a bunch of pictures behind?"

"I guess that's one way of looking at it. Is this around when you met Momoko in Paris?"

"I met your uncle later on, I think," Momoko said. "At that point, he didn't look so terrible. There was more gentleness in his eyes. If he'd looked like this, I wouldn't have let him near me."

"I know it's me, but I look terrible."

"This guy looks like he's going to kill someone." After they said this to each other, they both doubled over laughing. Momoko pinched his cheek, and my uncle let her, as they roared with laughter. (Momoko has a baffling tendency to pinch the cheeks of people she's close to.) They're such a weird couple.

"But back in those days, my father and I didn't see eye to eye. We were constantly arguing. I have to admit though, that I gave him nothing but trouble in those days. It's true."

"You and your father have totally different personalities."

"Definitely. Totally different."

My grandfather was a stern man. He hardly said a word and never uttered a joke; his brow was always deeply furrowed. To him, being stern was a virtue. He even thought of it as a point of principle. According to what my mother told me, his wife died soon after his first marriage. He was already nearly fifty when he married my grandmother. Normally, you might think that since he was older, he would spoil his children, but my grandfather was not that kind of man. My mother and my uncle had quite a strict upbringing. My grandfather stuck to his principles when it came to running the bookshop too. He was absolutely uncompromising in his approach to the business. They said he even used to chase away customers who had only come to browse. It was the complete opposite of my uncle's approach.

"But you ended up being the one who took over from Grandpa."

"Strange, isn't it? I hope he's not rolling over in his grave," my uncle joked.

"I'm sure he's out of his mind with rage. He's thinking, that kid doesn't know the first thing about running a used bookshop. He's making so much noise he's driving everyone around him crazy," Momoko said, and the two of them laughed their heads off.

There was no need to worry though. My uncle's personality might be the exact opposite of my grandfather's, but when it came to the important stuff, they were the same. That was for certain.

I gazed again at the photograph of my uncle on the desk. The person in that photo was a complete stranger to me. That glint in his eyes could've been anger, or doubt, or some vague sadness.

I gave a silent message to the younger version of my uncle in the picture:

It's okay. You're going to meet nice people. You won't have to be so sad anymore. Even if you suffer from back pain and hemorrhoids, you'll be beloved as the owner of a bookshop. So you don't have to worry anymore.

4

The Saveur coffee shop is a three-minute walk from the Morisaki Bookshop. Everyone in the neighborhood knows the Saveur, as you might expect of a place that's been around for fifty years. In the old days, many of the great writers who lived in Jimbocho often spent time there.

The stone-walled interior is dimly lit by lamplight alone, and it's filled with the rich aroma of coffee. The effect is quite soothing. Though it's normally bustling with customers, it never feels noisy. In fact, the sound of chatter blends in with the understated piano music playing in the background, and the result is somehow even more pleasant. Since my uncle brought me here that summer three years ago, I've loved the place's atmosphere and the taste of its coffee. I'm still a regular customer.

The owner of the coffee shop is an elegant man in his midforties with a long, slender face. At first glance, he might seem intimidating, but he's actually quite friendly and easy to talk to. When he smiles, he gets sweet-looking wrinkles around his eyes. As soon as I open the door, he calls out "Welcome!" from behind the counter where he's brewing coffee.

Tonight was no different. As soon as I opened the door, he greeted me warmly, just like he always did. "Hey, Takako. Welcome!"

"Good evening. Seems busy again today." I looked around the store as I said hello.

"Thank you. We're heading into the busy season for the coffee shop. It's when we make more money," the owner said as he polished a glass. He flashed a slightly mischievous smile.

"I guess when it gets colder, people crave coffee."

"So it goes."

Actually, it didn't matter if it was spring or summer; this coffee shop always seemed to be bustling. Still, there was a particular pleasure in drinking a good cup of coffee during the colder times of the year. I supposed the other customers must have felt the same way.

"So, are you meeting someone?"

"I am."

"Oh, how nice. Well, enjoy."

I smiled and bowed slightly.

The waitress came over right away, as if she'd been waiting for me, and led me to a seat by the window that had just opened up. As a matter of fact, this coffee shop was also the place where my boyfriend, Wada, and I would arrange to meet. His office was nearby, so it was a perfect spot. Whenever he was working late, I would pass the time by reading a book and having a cup of coffee. As usual, I had tucked a favorite book into my bag tonight. I took it out right away and started to read. The time I spend this way is quiet, but also exciting—waiting for the person I love to arrive. It somehow feels incredibly luxurious to sit in your favorite coffee shop, reading a book, waiting for your boyfriend.

I had read for about a half hour, waiting this way, when I heard the sound of someone tapping on the windowpane. Wada was standing outside the window. Our eyes met, and he waved. When I waved back, he turned and headed to the entrance.

"Sorry to keep you waiting." He sat down across from me, a bit out of breath, as if he'd come in a hurry. There was no dress code at his work, so he was dressed casually today as usual. For the most part, Wada's clothes followed the same set pattern: a jacket with slim-fitting pants or slacks. If you asked him, he'd tell you it was because it was "too much of a hassle to pick what to wear," but that chic style was really what looked best on him. Today, he was wearing a stylish black jacket with gray slacks that fit him perfectly.

"I just got here," I said with a smile as I shut my book.

"Oh, I hope so." Wada looked at me for a long time with a smile on his face. He just stared at me without saying anything. He kept staring at me for so long that I started to feel embarrassed, then I realized his attention was actually directed at the book in my hand.

"Is that a collection by Taruho Inagaki?" Wada asked with a tinge of admiration in his voice.

"Oh, um, well, yeah . . ." I said, struggling a bit to figure out why these were the first words out of his mouth after we hadn't seen each other in a week. Wada, however, didn't seem to notice my reaction at all.

"*One Thousand and One-Second Stories* is pretty good, isn't it?" he said.

"It is." Wada seemed so happy that I quickly regained my composure and agreed with him. "They're perfect to read in a place like this. They're short and kind of cute. And it seems like they'd go well somehow with a cup of coffee."

"You're right. Absolutely," Wada said enthusiastically. "For starters, even the titles are funny. 'How I Lost Myself' or 'How My Friend Turned into the Moon.'"

"They're so funny. I mean that's why I've read this book five times now."

Wada was a proper book lover too. He had a particular weakness for old Japanese novels. He was far more knowledgeable than I was, since I had only just begun to read seriously. And like most people who love to read he seemed interested in what other people were reading too. He was always curious about each and every book I read. Whenever it was something he loved, he would start smiling like this, and when it was a book he hated or hadn't read yet, he would grimace like a child in the cafeteria being served a dish they hated. The look on his face was so earnest that I would end up feeling embarrassed, as if I were guilty of some awful betrayal. To be honest though, I sometimes looked forward a little to seeing that look on his face. On this particular day, my book seemed to be a hit, and I didn't get to see Wada's sad grimace.

"That reminds me, the first day we met here, you were reading Taruho Inagaki."

"Wait, is that right? I remember I was reading a book."

"No doubt about it. I remember that day vividly."

Hearing Wada tell me that so emphatically made me feel embarrassed somehow. I tried to hide it by laughing.

My relationship with Wada started when we ran into each other here at the Saveur one night and ended up having coffee together. I knew him by sight because he was a customer at the bookshop, but this was the first time we had really talked. Looking back, I think that's when I first felt attracted to him. We've been close since then, but we didn't officially decide we were a couple until sometime before the summer. So, at this point we'd been going out for only a matter of months.

I've tried to call him Akira, which is his actual first name, but even now I still find myself calling him by his last name, Wada, the name I've been using from the first time we met.

It's thanks to the owner of the Saveur that things turned out this way. Which is why I still feel indebted to him.

Wada is an exceptionally courteous person. He hates to be in the spotlight any more than is necessary. In crowded places, for example, he tends to withdraw to the background, listening quietly to everyone talk with a smile on his face, throwing out a clever comment from time to time. That's the kind of person he is. But there's also something quirky about him. Suddenly his stubborn side will emerge, and he'll declare, "Today I want to eat calamari. I decided this morning, and my decision is firm. I won't let anything else into my stomach." He could be a difficult guy to read. But I adored the way he was a little bit weird.

We had different days off from work, and Wada's job got busy at the end of each month, when it was common for him to work on his regular days off. So, we could often only meet for a period of time like this in the evenings. Our mismatched work schedule was proving to be a substantial stumbling block in our relationship. We were both the kind of people who take their job seriously. There was no way for either of us to just cut out early and call it a day. So, the time we were able to spend together was, by necessity, limited. While I couldn't help being frustrated by this, I also knew that there was really nothing I could do about it.

At any rate, this was our first time seeing each other in a week. We were having a cup of coffee and talking about going to get something to eat soon when Takano made a rare appearance outside the kitchen.

Takano was the kitchen manager at the Saveur. He was a tall and gangly young man who had such a timid way of speaking that he came off as completely helpless. I'd heard that he wanted to open his own coffee shop one day and was being trained here by the owner.

"Nice to see you, Takano. It's been a while."

"Good to see you too, Takako, and, er . . . um, you as well, Wada."

Takano tended to be pretty shy around strangers, and it seemed that he was only slightly familiar with Wada and still not used to speaking to him.

"Good evening. It's Takano, right?" Wada replied with a warm smile. I could see from the look on Takano's face that this put him at ease too. Wada had a knack for this. He could talk to anyone easily and make them feel comfortable.

Yet even after we finished greeting one another, Takano continued to hang around for some reason, lingering nearby like a hyena eyeing a lion's leftovers. It was getting a little weird, so I asked him what was going on.

"Ah, no, it's okay. We can talk next time."

Just as he was mumbling his response, the owner called, "Hey, Takano!" from the other side, his voice radiating anger.

As soon as Takano heard him, he panicked and rushed back to the kitchen.

"What was that about?" I was left shaking my head as I watched Takano's spindly frame abruptly disappear into the back.

Wada looked equally confused. "He did seem to be acting kind of suspiciously."

"Still, acting suspiciously is hardly a new thing for him."

"In that case, I guess there's nothing to worry about."

After saying these rather rude things about Takano, we managed to convince ourselves, and left the Saveur.

We sauntered into the Sanseidō bookstore at closing time, then after we'd finished our meal at a nearby set-menu restaurant that Wada liked, we went on a little walk around the neighborhood. We both had to work the next day. I had an early meeting in the morning, so we decided we'd both go home afterward. Wada walked me to the station.

Wada's apartment building was located about a fifteen-minute walk from the neighborhood of used bookshops. I'd only been there a few times, but the first time I went it gave me quite a shock. "My apartment's a mess," Wada tried to warn me repeatedly on our way there, and it truly was.

The moment I first set foot inside the door, I saw the leftover bento containers from the convenience store and discarded clothes scattered all over the floor. His substantial number of books were not only stored on the bookshelves, but had been left all over the sofa and the table. The kitchen area was even more disastrous. The sink was overflowing with dirty plates and frying pans. It was an appalling sight. While it would be an exaggeration to say there was nowhere to step inside, at the very least there was nowhere to sit. The closet door had been left half open, and there were huge cardboard boxes piled on top of each other inside. I peeked in the boxes, with his permission, and found lots of secondhand books. It looked like there might be some valuable ones there, but they'd been thrown in so haphazardly that it looked like it would be an ordeal just to get them organized. In any case, given how disorganized they were, it probably would have been better to have the Morisaki Bookshop pack it up and take the whole pile away.

"I'm really sorry. I'd planned to clean up, but this week has been so busy at work, I just didn't have time."

I'd been anxious about coming to his place, but my anxiety vanished once I saw what it looked like. I was laughing about it to myself for a long while. I felt like I'd seen an unexpected side of him, but it was so unexpected I didn't know what to make of it.

"Well, I guess this is just what single guys' apartments look like," I said.

Wada, who had been panicking, now seemed to relax a bit. I'd been surprised because it was Wada's apartment, but this level of disorder is pretty common in general. Of course, it would be nice if he'd cleaned it for the first time his girlfriend came over, but . . .

"What did you do when your last girlfriend came over?" I asked nonchalantly.

"Ah, well, she always cleaned up for me whenever she noticed. She was the kind of person who liked things to be clean," Wada said, smiling grimly.

I suddenly regretted asking the question. You ask too many questions, I said to myself.

Wada had brought that woman several times to the Morisaki Bookshop back then. She had beautiful features and a tall, slender figure. At the time, I only knew them by sight, so I would casually look at them and think, "Oh, what a beautiful couple." Now that the situation had changed, I wanted to take that image and stick it in the cardboard box in the closet along with all the books. Burning with petty jealousy, I decided at that moment that I would clean his apartment. I wouldn't let that woman beat me. So, that afternoon, while Wada stood by unsure what to do with himself, I transformed into one hell of a cleaning machine.

That was how I ended up spending the night at Wada's place.

In Wada's arms, I became aware of something within the core of my being. And it felt like that core was being touched. It was probably the first time in my life that I'd ever felt that way.

At the same time, I worried whether Wada could really be enjoying himself with an ordinary person like me. In Jimbocho, I had met so many truly fascinating people, starting with my uncle, (even Sabu, I had to admit, was fascinating in his own way), but the flip side of that was that it made me realize just how dull and ignorant I was. Which left me worrying that Wada would soon realize it too.

I wanted to spend more time with him, to share all kinds of things together. But I wasn't sure if Wada felt the same way. I'm terrible at romance, forever a late bloomer. That might be to blame for my last relationship, which came to a terrible end. It turned out I was the only person who had thought we were going out to begin with. Now, I was 100 percent certain that Wada wasn't that kind of guy, but I still couldn't tell how much he needed me.

Wada wasn't the type to show his emotions. So I sometimes became extremely worried trying to figure out what he was thinking. What was he looking for in a girlfriend? Did he love me more than he'd loved his previous girlfriend? It's not like I was as beautiful as she was. These thoughts weren't getting me anywhere; they just kept going around and around in my head. But one thing was quite clear. I knew what I felt, and I wanted to express it to him in my own words. And what I definitely didn't want to do was just muddle my way through that feeling or the relationship I'd begun with him.

Reading had started to affect me in ways I hadn't expected. I had been touched by the kinds of love I read about in books, and that had strengthened my belief that I needed to take my own affections more seriously.

"*It gets so* much colder at night."

"Yeah."

We were slowly walking up the slight hill that leads to Ocha-nomizu Station. Jimbocho Station is much closer, but we had purposely gone the long way. Unlike the neighborhood of bookshops where everyone goes to bed early, this side of the street was still lit up with its many restaurants and shops selling musical instruments. There were many walking down the street and a constant stream of cars.

I wanted to stay with him.

But I had to go home.

In my head, the same thoughts kept coming back over and over.

I was watching Wada out of the corner of my eye as he walked beside me. Wada took each step so smoothly, without any wasted movement. His footsteps hardly made a sound. It was just like him. Was he feeling a little sad too? The expression on his face looked the same as always.

As we continued our walk, we had a conversation about the right book to read before going to sleep. Wada surprised me by saying he couldn't sleep if he read in bed. He told me with a straight face that if you had to read something, then the phone book would do. After a long deliberation, I suggested Kōtarō Takamura's book, *The Chieko Poems*.

"Though I think it would be a waste of a great book because you can't actually read that much before you go to bed."

"Somehow neither of us can come up with a proper answer," Wada said with a smile. "But I see that *The Chieko Poems* is a really important book for you."

"I mean I don't know of another book that's so filled with love."

"I agree. Chieko's mental illness only strengthened his love for her, and as if in response, his poems became more beautiful."

An excerpt from *The Chieko Poems* was included in my textbooks in school, so of course I was familiar with it. But once I started to read the book from the beginning, I was surprised by how moving it was. The days Takamura spent with Chieko, all the happiness, worry, sadness, and pain of their love, all the emotions, from their first meeting to their wedding, the outbreak of her illness, and her death, were turned into lines of poetry. There's a light within those poems that shines so brightly it's almost blinding.

I think that probably for a lot of people, a great many actually, *The Chieko Poems* is an important, even irreplaceable book. And I am certainly one of those people. Whenever I read it, I'm overcome with emotion. So much so that I no longer feel the need to put it in words.

That's why I only allow myself to read the book when I'm really compelled to. Because I want to hold on to the part of me that finds reading this book so moving. Whenever I read it, I always end up crying. No matter how many times I reread it, the tears always well up. I get tears in my eyes, just thinking about the book.

I think about how wonderful it must be to be able to put one's thoughts into words like that.

As the thought crossed my mind, I realized the station was already in view. It was time to say goodbye.

We said good night and went our separate ways. This was the most painful moment in the day for me. Try as I might, I can't find another word to describe it.

I stood for a moment in front of the turnstiles and watched Wada gradually recede into the distance. I thought that I might read a little bit of *The Chieko Poems* before bed. It had been a while. I thought about it all the way home.

5

Day by day, we went deeper into autumn. Winter was closing in. The dry wind was cold enough to make us shiver. Along the road, the trees had just begun to change color. Before we knew it, the sun would set earlier with each passing day, and the nights would grow longer and deeper.

This was my favorite time of the whole year, the period before winter had truly arrived, the time to mourn the passing season. It made me want to stand still and stare up at the pale blue sky and its soft light. That's why lately my morning routine had been to walk to work with my gaze turned to the sky.

I was working at a design studio in Iidabashi, the same company that had hired me when I moved out of the bookshop. It was a very small firm whose main business was designing pamphlets and leaflets. If you include the time in the beginning when I was part-time, I'd been working there almost three years.

Since many of our jobs were basically solo projects, we didn't have strictly defined hours or workdays, and as long as we maintained basic office etiquette, we were relatively free to do as we wished. At the company where I worked before, our personal relationships were kept secret, and they definitely even had cliques, all of which I was truly terrible at navigating. In part because my new firm was small, I could keep clear of those sorts of entanglements. My income was significantly lower than at my last job, but I was able to work at my own pace, and I felt like the new place was definitely a better match for me.

Staying late at night at the office slogging away at work isn't my favorite thing to do, so I was usually the first one to arrive in the morning, and I would try to finish up early in the evening. I'd have conversations with my coworkers, but I didn't get involved with them any more than was necessary. I rarely met them outside of work.

Perhaps because of all this, on one of the rare occasions when I was invited out for drinks with my coworkers, one of them said to me, "You kind of keep to yourself, don't you?" The others seemed to have formed the same impression of me. In their view, I didn't talk much, and I always went straight home early in the evening. It caught me a bit by surprise, but when I thought it over, it seemed a major reason for this might be that I had found a place where I felt at home.

Before I mostly would just go back and forth between home and work. I didn't have any real hobbies or any strong attachment to anything. I wasn't especially unhappy, but I did have the slight sense that my life was missing something. Looking back, I think I always felt that way and didn't know what to do about it. But I didn't feel that way anymore. Of course, it would be foolish to say that I felt perfectly fulfilled right now. It was just that when I thought about it, I no longer really felt that anything was missing.

There were places I wanted to go and people I wanted to see. And there was a place that was always ready to welcome me back.

I can't think of anything more wonderful than that.

I was able to do my job working at my own pace. I liked the job itself, and things at the office weren't too bad. I felt confident that things were headed in the right direction.

But more recently, I did run into a little bit of trouble. Deep down it was a trivial matter. If I told anyone about it, they'd probably laugh it off like it was the punchline of a joke. But the truth is it was pretty upsetting to me.

It all started one day at lunch. The company didn't have a cafeteria or a set lunchtime. It was up to each person to spend their lunch break as they saw fit. I generally went to a nearby café. It was empty even at lunch, and I never saw anyone from work there, which made it the place I felt most comfortable eating.

One day, however, I unexpectedly bumped into a senior colleague. He was a guy who had a sarcastic, condescending way of talking to people. I'd already had a feeling that he was someone I'd have a hard time with. So, I casually said hello and tried to find another seat, but he called out to me.

"Hey, come sit here."

I didn't have any other choice but to sit with him. As I might have expected, it was not exactly festive at our table. It was partly my fault for not making an effort to keep the conversation going, but I really didn't know how to respond when he went on talking and talking, boasting and complaining about work. "The problem is our clients are too idiotic to know better. I need a bigger job to put my talents to work. With our current projects, I barely feel like putting in fifty percent of what I'm capable of." We spent the whole lunch break with him going on like this with a revolting look on his face. In the end, I could only muster a simple "uh-huh" in response.

That should have been the end of it. I thought to myself, it's just one of those things—you run into someone you don't like; today's not your lucky day. But afterward, he started looking for ways to talk to me whenever he could. Even at the office, if I was busy working at my computer, he'd go out of his way to come over and start talking to me. If I pretended not to hear him and kept on working, he'd come over and hit me on the back to force me to pay attention to him. Then he started asking me out to lunch as if that were perfectly normal. I had absolutely no idea what could possibly motivate him to want to spend another dull hour in my company. And in my position, I couldn't very well turn him down every day, so I got stuck going back to that same café with him many times after that day. Of course, all that was waiting for us was a total waste of time.

What was the point of it all? What did he find amusing in all this? Was this just some new form of harassment? I was getting more and more irritated.

On the fourth time he forced me to take my lunch break with him, in a pause between complaining and boasting, he suddenly asked me, with a mouthful of sandwich, "So, what do you do on your days off?"

"I . . . um . . . go to secondhand bookshops a lot." I was caught so off guard that I made the mistake of giving him an honest answer.

"Why? What would you want to go to a place like that for? What are you, an old man?" He burst out laughing like I'd just told him the funniest joke he'd ever heard. *You have no right to ask me what I do on my days off!* I said to myself, but then I remembered he was still above me at work. There was no way for me to say that out loud.

"How about we go for a drive on your next day off?"

After another surprise attack, I felt more and more upset. "Um, why would we do that?"

"What do you mean 'why'? If you're not busy, wouldn't it be nice?"

"No . . . I have, um, plans."

"Plans?"

"I just told you about the bookshops."

"Come on. Nobody goes to bookshops that often."

"People who like them do though. There's nothing wrong with that," I replied. I was definitely getting annoyed. He scratched his head in confusion and took a deep breath. He let out a sigh rich with pity, like a teacher coming across a high school dropout in the guidance counselor's office.

"Do you enjoy life?" he asked.

"What?"

"I mean it's like you're always under a dark cloud. You can't keep up a conversation. It's like what's the point in talking to you? Even when I try to help you out and invite you places, you start squirming and say something about used bookshops or whatever. You need to get a more positive attitude, or you'll end up wasting your life."

After this parting shot, he didn't give me a second to reply before sniping, "This is boring." Then he got up and walked out. For a moment, I couldn't move at all. I just sat there stunned, with my mouth hanging open.

"Oh, how annoying!"

That night, I went to see Momoko at the little restaurant where she was working and sipped sake as I went rattling on about the incident at lunch. Recently, I'd started to frequent the restaurant, drawn by Momoko's cooking. Mr. Nakasono, the restaurant's owner, was an affable guy who had a way with words. In that sense, he and Momoko were a pretty good match. But maybe because he couldn't keep track of all the names and faces of his customers, Mr. Nakasono just could not remember my name. Every time I came into the restaurant, he would start calling me "Mikako" or "Yukako" or something like that. No matter how many times I corrected him, the next time he saw me, he always mixed it up again. I finally resigned myself to it.

That night, after being called "Teruko," which is quite a long way from my actual name, I shook with rage before quickly deciding it didn't matter.

On the other side of the counter, Momoko was busy at her work, looking quite at home in her apron. "Hey, don't come into someone's place of business jabbering on when you've had too much to drink," she said, like she was telling off a drunk customer.

I was, on this rare occasion, actually rather drunk.

"But it's so incredibly annoying. Of course it's annoying to have to hear that from him, but the most annoying thing of all is that I couldn't even respond."

"Yeah, I get it, sure. It's annoying. I get it."

The drunker I became, the angrier I felt about what I saw as his high-handed attitude. And what made matters even worse was that his name, by some twist of fate, was Wada. That was another thing I found extremely unpleasant.

"I wouldn't call it a twist of fate. Wada's a common name. It's not as if it was his choice to be named Wada," Momoko said in disbelief.

"But I can't stand it. I mean when you think of him, doesn't Wada end up popping into your head too?"

"So you've been thinking about this guy, have you?" Momoko said, with a malicious grin.

"That's not what I mean. I mean like when we're talking about him now," I said, taking offense.

"Well, I guess it is inconvenient. Shall we call him Wada #2 then?" Momoko said, giving him an impromptu nickname. "So, basically you're saying Wada #2 asked you out and you didn't realize it?"

"No, I knew, but I didn't know why he was suddenly talking to me about all that."

"He asked you out because he thought you wanted him to, and then you got angry at him."

"It doesn't make sense, does it? Like is that how people really see me?"

"Well, that's how Wada #2 did," Momoko said dryly. She shrugged, as if to say, Don't get mad at me. "But you can be a little like that, you know, Takako."

"Like what?"

"You know, careless."

"What do you mean, careless? I wasn't doing anything."

"Sometimes that's the same thing. And sometimes that can invite an even more thoughtless response."

That startled me. I'd been guilty of that in the past. "I guess you're right . . . I did run into some trouble that one time."

"Ah, are you referring, for example, to the case of the girl who locked herself away inside the secondhand bookshop?"

"What, that? Please let's not start giving the events of my life weird case names."

Momoko burst out laughing. "But although you can be a little slow . . . and careless . . . and, well, tactless, I do love how sweet you are." Momoko stared at me with a smile. Her soft, short hair gleamed in the fluorescent light.

"I can't quite tell if you're complimenting me or insulting me."

"Nah, I'm complimenting you, more or less," Momoko said, laughing out loud again. "Coming back to what you were saying before though, even if Wada #2 saw you like that, it doesn't necessarily mean that he truly saw you for who you are as a person. He just saw you from his own preconceived point of view. The point is, if you'd been a little more aware, you could've steered clear of someone like that who was going to put you in a difficult position."

"That's easier said than done. He's above me at work."

"Which is why you've got to do your best to give off an aura that says you're not interested in getting any closer to this guy. You can project that. And even as dumb as he is, he'll get the message."

"Oh, I really am terrible at that sort of thing."

"That's what I meant when I said you were so sweet. And I want you to be yourself. I like you just the way you are," Momoko said as she reached across the counter and patted me on the back.

"What do you mean?"

"You might often end up on the losing side that way, but isn't it better to be true to who you are?"

"I guess." I didn't really understand what she was talking about, but I figured she was saying she wanted me to remain the same.

"But there are people like that, you know, people who are so self-centered. To someone like that, it doesn't matter if it's you or somebody else who's there with them."

It was painful to hear, but I knew she was right. I'd had a bad experience like that in the past. I thought that person had chosen me, but in fact, it wasn't true. He would've been satisfied as long as it was *someone like me*. It was deeply upsetting, because it felt like my very identity was being negated. On the other hand, it's clear that I bore some of the responsibility.

"There are all kinds of people in this world. A person like Wada #2, he's the main character in the story of his life. Of course, personally I'm not that interested in reading a book about that Wada #2." Momoko stuck out her tongue like a naughty little kid.

"Listen, life is short. In the story of your life, you've got to avoid people like that. Choose to be with the people who really choose you, people who see you as irreplaceable. That's the story you want—you know what I'm saying?"

"I do. I know exactly what you mean."

I really did feel like I understood. It seemed to me to be deeply connected to what I'd been thinking lately about my relationship with Wada. Someone who chose me for who I am. Was that how Wada (and, of course, I'm not talking about Wada #2) thought of me? Wada was the only one for me. There was no way someone else could take his place.

"That's good. Take it to heart. It's a little advice from one of your elders."

"Okay."

Our conversation had taken a strange turn, but I knew what Momoko had told me then was true. I nodded obediently, accepting what she'd said.

A few days later, a last-minute request for edits came in from a client, and it brought with it so many new deliverables that it led to a series of hectic days at the office. Thanks to that, I guess, though maybe "thanks" isn't the right word, I didn't have any time to give Wada #2 another thought.

Then, one night, after things had started to look up again at work, I left the office feeling exhausted and found myself walking automatically to the Saveur. It's not because I was planning on meeting Wada there, I just had an overwhelming urge for a cup of coffee. You're a real addict now, I thought. I laughed a little to myself as I made my way to the coffee shop.

Opening the door, I heard the familiar sound of lively conversation, and I realized that Sabu was there. And of course, there he was, sitting at the counter, talking to the owner.

"Hey, good to see you." After a brusque greeting, I sat down beside him and ordered a blend coffee and Japanese-style Napolitan spaghetti with a salad because I was feeling incredibly hungry.

The owner turned to the kitchen and yelled, "Hey, Takano! One Napo on the double!"

"Okay!" Takano replied a bit sheepishly.

"By the way, that idiot has been trailing around after you, Takako.

47

Is he talking nonsense to you again?" the owner asked, maybe thinking about Takano's odd behavior the other day.

"No, not particularly."

"If he bothers you, feel free to give him a smack on the head."

"Sorry, I don't think I could do that," I said, taken aback. It made me wonder what it must be like for Takano to work there, having to put up with such harsh treatment.

Sabu was in fine form as usual, chatting about one thing or another as he sat beside me.

"What's wrong—are you tired?" Sabu asked, more or less admitting he was bored when I failed to keep up my end of the conversation.

"Yeah, things have been a bit busy at work. You look well though, Sabu, as always."

Sabu giggled. "You need to take a vacation. I, on the other hand, am so powerful, so robust, that I don't need time off."

I guess it must've been my imagination then that he seemed to be on a permanent vacation.

"I take days off all right."

"Is that so? And then you're always hanging around Satoru's place. If anyone, it's Satoru who never takes a day off. Momoko came back, but nothing's changed. If he keeps it up, she'll run off again. I'm always taking my wife on trips or taking her out to eat, bringing her to all kinds of places and whatnot to keep her happy."

"After all, when she's unhappy, she throws away your books," the owner muttered, sending Sabu into a rage.

"Shut up, old man!"

"The only old man here is you."

"Ah, that's true. I'm the old guy," Sabu said, slapping his bald head. Then he burst out laughing like an idiot. To my surprise, the owner, who had been polishing glasses with a blank expression, couldn't keep from laughing a little. These two had a weird relationship. It was hard to know if they liked or hated each other.

Nonetheless, what Sabu said touched on something I'd been concerned about for a while. Momoko had come back, but despite the fact that they now had time to spend together, my uncle was just working nonstop. Even on the days the shop was closed, he would go out in his run-down little van, traveling long distances to buy books. He didn't seem to be setting aside any time at all for them to spend together. He was extremely worried about her health, and yet I couldn't see any sign that he was actually trying to take care of her.

As I sipped my coffee, I thought about how hopeless my uncle was and sighed. "My uncle should take some time off. What with his hemorrhoids and all."

"Right, think of his hemorrhoids. He ought to go to the hot springs and really relax. What if he took your aunt with him?"

It sounded like it might be a good idea. I forgot all at once about feeling tired, and was now bounding with energy.

"That's great. That's an amazing idea."

My uncle was too busy at the shop to realize it, but what if I offered them a little trip as a simple gift to thank them for all they've done for me? Momoko was just saying that their wedding anniversary was in November. It might be a little early, but I could say it was my present for them. I could take care of the reservations for the inn and the train tickets for my uncle, because that was too much of a hassle for him. That ought to make both of them happy.

"Ah, wouldn't that be nice?" the owner said. "It would be good for Momoko, of course, but even Satoru should take a break every once in a while. He might seem carefree, but when it comes to the bookshop, he's so devoted to his work that he might be taking it too far."

I felt encouraged by what he'd said. And at that moment another idea popped into my head that made me even happier. I was getting extremely excited.

"Sabu, on occasion you say something smart."

"Hey, what do you mean, 'on occasion'?"

"I ought to thank you though," I said, sincerely expressing my gratitude.

It was rare to see Sabu looking slightly embarrassed by the attention. He turned away and mumbled, "Okay, that's enough," chewing his words. He seemed unaccustomed to being thanked, maybe because he was always needling people.

"Thank you, Sabu." I pushed it a little more and said it again.

"No, really, that's enough." Sabu looked truly embarrassed now as he brought the coffee to his mouth, mumbling.

He looked unbearably funny.

"Look at you laughing all the time. You haven't got a care in the world."

"Though someone told me recently that I was an extremely gloomy person."

"Must be something wrong with his eyes. The only time you've ever been gloomy was back in your sleep monster days. Now you're Miss Carefree."

"Hey, you might be right. Thank you, Sabu."

"I told you to quit that. It makes me all itchy. If you keep going, I won't say another word!" Sabu said, scratching all over his back.

"Takako, I see you too have figured out how to tease Sabu. And here is your Napolitan." The owner placed my spaghetti with plenty of ketchup on the table in front of me.

I ate in a trance.

By the time I was full, my fatigue had vanished, and the anger I'd felt toward Wada #2 had long since disappeared.

6

My uncle and I got into a fight.

It was the first time in all the years we'd known each other that we had ever had a real fight like this. And yet the reason for this fight and the issue we fought over were fundamentally stupid.

It began with the aforementioned trip.

After I hit upon the idea at the Saveur, I immediately went home and selected several promising-looking hot springs resorts online and arranged everything so that once they made their choice, I would make the reservations.

Then on the afternoon of my day off, I headed over to the Morisaki Bookshop, bubbling with excitement.

"Wait, aren't these all weekdays?"

"It's fine. There are a lot more openings than on the weekends. And you could use some time away from the shop."

"But I can't close the bookshop."

I'd been expecting that response. "I knew you'd say that," I told him proudly. "I will look after the shop for you."

The truth is that I had a bit of an ulterior motive for my plan. With Satoru and Momoko away, they'd naturally need someone to look after the shop. I had secretly been wanting to spend a few days there. Of course, if I'd asked my uncle, I could've stayed on the second floor above the shop whenever I wanted, but that would be a completely different thing. Even if it was for a short stay, I wanted to manage the shop from morning till evening, and then spend the night in that room upstairs that made me nostalgic now. That way

I could soak it all in, and there'd be no one to shout, "Where's Roy?" and ruin the mood. My uncle could let his weary body get some rest, and to top it off, I could enjoy myself. It was two birds with one stone—at least it should've been.

"No way. You've got your own job, Takako."

"My days off match up, so it's okay."

"Well, we'll take you up on your generous offer then, Takako," said Momoko, who had been listening nearby. "How thoughtful of you." She had a gleam in her eye and seemed as pleased as I'd expected.

"Hey, don't just decide for both of us," my uncle grumbled.

"What's wrong with the idea? It's good to take a day off every once in a while. Besides, Takako's gone to a lot of trouble. She wants to do this for us." Momoko gave his cheek a good pinch as if to say, *What a hardhead.*

"Nope. It's out of the question," my uncle insisted stubbornly, even as his cheek turned red. "I mean, what'll we do if something goes wrong?"

"So you won't even go on a day the shop's closed?"

"That's right. Next week I promised Yoshimura I'd go to buy stock from his place in Saitama."

"Then a regular weekday should be fine. If it's just a day or two, even I can take care of things. Please have a little faith in me."

"Absolutely not," my uncle flatly refused.

"But why not?"

"It's hopeless," Momoko said, throwing her hands up. "When he gets like this, there's no sense in talking to him."

I'd prepared myself for a little resistance, but not this level of stubbornness. Although I might have had a slight ulterior motive for my offer, I truly wanted to show how grateful I was to them by giving them some time off. I stared at my uncle with resentment, feeling profoundly disappointed.

"You really hate the idea that much?"

"Hate it? What's out of the question is out of the question."

"God, I can't stand you!"

"It's out of the question!"

"Stop acting like little kids, you two," Momoko interjected, looking at us in disbelief. "If that's how you feel," she added, "then Takako and I will go together like last time. Besides, I'll have more fun with her than I will with whatever this is."

"Then what's the point?"

He really was pouting like a spoiled child. But I can be stubborn too. And I was going to make him take time off and go on that trip.

For a very, very long time, my uncle and I went back and forth, repeating these meaningless replies again and again—"Go!" "Out of the question!"—until the original intention faded away, and we were just butting heads, each refusing to give in.

I don't know if there's ever been a more meaningless fight in the world.

In the end, I shouted, "That's enough!" and walked out of the shop, fuming. I got carried away and shut the door behind me as hard as I could, and the sound it made was so much louder than I expected that I was taken aback, but I walked away pretending nothing had happened.

The day after all that, I met up with Wada. It was our first time seeing each other in four days. Naturally, we'd arranged to meet at the Saveur. However, on this particular day, Wada showed up with an oddly stiff expression on his face. Then, as he was about to take his seat, he suddenly asked, "Can we talk for a second?"

I flew into a panic. What on earth could it possibly be? I'd been expecting us to spend some quiet time together tonight, so this caught me completely by surprise. "Huh? What is it?" I asked nervously.

"Could we change tables?" he asked, also looking quite nervous. That made me feel even more uneasy.

"Um, is this a good talk . . . or a bad talk?" I asked, preparing myself for the worst.

"A good talk? No, I don't think so."

What could I do? What had I done? As I started to panic, the thought of my stupid fight with my uncle vanished from my mind.

"W-w-where are we going?"

"Um, I don't know. What should we do? This spot is fine, actually. It's nothing important."

I had no idea anymore what was going on. A minute ago, he seemed so nervous, now he was telling me it was nothing important. When he started, for a second I thought he might even be about to talk about getting married. Lately, my mother had been pestering me on the phone, always asking, "When are you getting married?"

I just realized I'd reached the age where you start to make your parents worry about that sort of thing. But this was apparently going to be a bad talk? It had to be about that. It was too terrible for words. I still wanted to be with Wada. I was still dreaming of being with him forever and ever. Or maybe he was keenly aware of that and felt pressured.

"You won't laugh, right?" Wada asked earnestly, heedless of the fact that my mind had gone blank.

"I can't be sure until I hear what you have to say, but I probably won't laugh," I said, but really, what was there to laugh about? You had to have some nerve to burst out laughing when the person you love has just started talking about breaking up.

"Understood," Wada calmly agreed. There was no change in his expression.

And then he said something I absolutely did not see coming: "I'm thinking about writing a novel."

"A novel?" The word reverberated inside my head, but its meaning would not register. A *nah-vul* . . .

"Yeah. Does that sound weird?"

"Weird? No, but is that what you wanted to talk about? That's it?"

"That was it . . ."

I was ready to fall out of my chair. Wada could really be impossible to read sometimes. I was so exhausted by it all I ended up laughing.

"You laughed," Wada said, looking stricken.

I tried desperately to explain myself. "It's not that kind of laughter."

"Not that kind of laughter? What kind of laughter are we talking about here?" he asked earnestly. It was no use though. We were totally out of sync.

I drained my glass of water and sighed. That somehow managed to calm me down.

"You said this was going to be the bad kind of talk so I was nervous," I mumbled.

Wada looked back at me blankly.

"I didn't say it was bad. I only said it wasn't good."

"Which means it's going to be bad."

"Is that right? I'm sorry. I just meant it wasn't especially good news."

"Wada, you can be a tiny bit strange sometimes," I said sarcastically, trying to get him back for how nervous he'd made me.

"Really?" Wada folded his arms and pondered what I'd said.

We didn't seem to be getting anywhere this way, so I tried to go back to what he'd said a minute ago. "You're going to write a novel?"

"Yes," Wada said, finally coming back to what he was saying. "Actually, I started writing in high school and wrote for almost ten years. But not that long ago, I'd completely stopped writing. Then I got to know you, Takako, and all the people who come to the Morisaki Bookshop, and I felt inspired again. Now I feel this irresistible urge to write a novel that takes place at the bookshop. I'm not aiming to win any awards, of course, or trying to become a professional writer. I thought my drive to write was gone, but then I realized I still had it, and I just feel like it would be a shame to let it all end without really trying." He gave an embarrassed laugh.

Simple as I am, I completely forgot about what had happened a minute ago. What Wada said had moved me. It made me really happy that he'd opened up to me about what he'd been thinking about for some time on his own. Wada is always so earnest. Even if it wasn't a big deal to me, it's clear that he was really worried about revealing this. That alone made it important.

"I think it's a wonderful idea. I want to help."

"Really? I'm so glad to hear that. If it's okay, I'd like to do some research at the bookshop, to gather some ideas."

"Oh."

"Is there a problem?"

"My uncle Satoru and I are in the middle of a big fight at the moment."

"A fight with the owner? I'm kind of surprised that you got angry too."

Apparently, he hadn't noticed that I was a little angry with him a minute ago. But that wasn't the only problem. My uncle hadn't taken kindly to Wada, because he was my boyfriend. Right after we'd started going out, I'd brought him to the shop to introduce him to my aunt and uncle. My uncle completely ignored Wada, even when he greeted him. He stayed stock-still, acting like he was one of those see-no-evil monkey figurines.

"Do you think the owner dislikes me? Did I violate some bookshop protocol without realizing it?" Wada said, cocking his head to one side and furrowing his brow.

"No, not at all. That's just how he always is," I said, desperately trying to bluff my way through.

On our way home, Wada kept muttering to himself about how he'd always thought of my uncle as so bright and friendly.

Later, when I went to the bookshop alone and flew into a rage about my uncle's attitude, my uncle yelled, "He isn't the right kind of customer for the Morisaki Bookshop."

Beside him, Momoko shook her head in exasperation. "Come on, you just don't want him to steal away Takako."

"Don't talk nonsense. All I'm saying is that I can't stand these pseudo-intellectuals. Guys like that are inhuman brutes who think nothing of leaving girls in tears."

"Monsters?" I was beyond outraged now. I was dumbfounded.

"I'm worried he might make you cry. And why does he keep referring to me as the proprietor? It creeps me out. I can't stand it."

"You're unbelievable," Momoko said. "It's about time for you to move on and let Takako go. And Wada seems like a really great guy. He's tall and slender, and he's about a thousand times better looking than you."

"Under no circumstances will I allow him to enter the shop."

"Hmmm . . . You used to be so cool when you said, 'The shop is open to anyone and everyone,' but now it turns out that you want to choose the customers?" I said coldly.

My uncle seemed at a loss for words. Then he repeated the phrase he always said when he was stuck: "People are full of contradictions."

I was determined to help Wada write his novel no matter what. Wada seemed so happy when I offered. And when he was happy, I guess I was happy too.

"Please make up with the owner soon," Wada said as we waved goodbye at the turnstile in the train station. "Not because of my novel, of course. Just because."

———

The next day, on my way home from work, I stopped by the Mori-saki Bookshop around closing time. I had come to make up with my uncle. It was a little annoying, but I didn't have a choice. Besides, Wada had asked me to. If I gave in, that would be the end of it.

When Momoko brought up the idea of my uncle not going on the trip, he really seemed deeply disappointed. He had to go for her sake too. So I decided to try changing my strategy.

"Hey, Uncle?"

"What?"

The storefront was already shuttered, so I stuck my head in the back entrance and called out to him. His voice sounded wary. At night, the damp smell inside the shop was even stronger.

"Come on, can't you let your guard down?" Forcing a smile, I tried to put him in a good mood by asking if he'd gotten any good books in lately. Whenever he gets talking about books, my uncle's bad mood vanishes right away. It's that simple. Soon he'd completely forgotten that we were fighting, and we were on our way.

"Oh, well, something came in yesterday that might be perfect for you."

"Really? What?"

"It's a classic that still hits home with readers today."

My uncle pulled Jun'ichirō Tanizaki's *In Praise of Shadows* from the stack and passed it to me.

"It's an essay, right? What does the title mean?"

"Hmmm . . . if I were to grossly oversimplify it, I'd say that it's about how we shouldn't just pay attention in our everyday lives to where the light is. We should look at the shadows as well. And behind that idea is a whole aesthetic sensibility. And I guess there's something about experiencing a Japanese sense of beauty. It all gets much, much deeper than that though. It might be a little difficult to read, but it's such a good book, you should give it a try."

"Thanks. I'll give myself plenty of time to read it."

"Give it a read now," he urged, briskly leaning in. It seemed like he wanted to sit next to me while I read the book so he could explain it. I recoiled, pulling away from my uncle.

"I'm okay right now. I'll read it carefully soon, someplace quiet and free from interruptions."

"How come? If you want to read it now, I can open up the store again."

"That's why I was saying I want to read it somewhere quiet."

"Where can you find a place quieter than here?"

Apparently, it never would have occurred to him that he was the one guilty of shattering the silence.

"So, about that trip," I said, returning the book to the shelf. My uncle's expression stiffened immediately, as if to say, *Here we go again.*

"It's okay if you just can't go," I said as a preamble, though I didn't believe that in the slightest. I lowered my gaze. "I feel like I always depend on you so much. I just wanted to do something to show my gratitude. So, I'm not asking you to do it if it's not possible, but Momoko wants to go, and it would be great if the two of you could go spend some time together." I said the lines I'd prepared in advance, putting as much emotion into it as I could.

"I want you to be able to keep the store open for a long, long time. And to do that, you have to remember to take time off. Otherwise, you're going to ruin your health. And if you died from working too much, I think my heart might burst."

Telling him all this was starting to make me uncomfortable. First of all, my uncle's the kind of person you couldn't kill if you tried. The idea of him overworking himself to death was too outlandish to believe. But he turned out to be ridiculously vulnerable to this approach. Sure enough, he was soon staring at me with tears in his eyes.

"Takako, you . . ."

"So, you understand what I mean?"

My uncle nodded several times, overcome with emotion. "Is that true? I really mean that much to you?"

"Well, that's why you should go," I said, losing no time.

"Ah, mmm-hmmm," my uncle replied automatically.

"And take good care of Momoko too. How about next week? I'm available then."

"What? Ahhhh." My uncle reluctantly agreed, although looking at the expression on his face, he didn't seem entirely convinced. My strategy had succeeded.

We left the shop and walked together to the station. The whole way, he kept mumbling, "Are you really sure you can run the store by yourself? I don't know."

I stood up straight and said, "Trust me," showing him how confident I was.

Once night fell, it turned thoroughly cold out. I wrapped my scarf tighter around my neck. My uncle was grumbling beside me, his breath making hazy white puffs that hung in the air for a moment and then vanished into the night.

7

The day of the trip, I woke in the morning and headed to the Morisaki Bookshop, bringing a bag with two days of clothes. My aunt and uncle were leaving straight from home, so I would be taking over for my uncle and running the bookshop right from the morning through the evening. Just thinking of it made my heart beat faster.

That may be one reason why I ended up leaving my place almost an hour early, which meant I ran right into the morning rush hour. I normally didn't have to be at work until ten, which meant I missed rush hour by a bit. So this was my first time back in those crowded trains since the days I was working at my old job. I ought to have mastered then how to fight my way onto a packed train, but it had been such a long time that I'd completely forgotten how to do it. As I steamed in the heat of the train, swaying to and fro in the throng of bodies, and got carried off by the current, I must've screamed to myself about thirty times.

Back when I used to spend every morning rocking back and forth in crowded trains, I encountered some strange people. People who muttered to themselves, or screamed in rage, people who threw themselves into you with clear malice. There was always some kind of trouble, and the whole train car would get drawn into it whenever someone was accused of groping or a fight broke out. Seeing something like that so early in the morning would leave me feeling profoundly exhausted. Now that I found myself back in a train car in that menacing environment for the first time in a while, that response didn't seem unreasonable. Being locked in with such misery every morning could definitely take a toll on your mind.

After enduring fifteen minutes in hell, I got off the train in Jimbocho and headed to the bookshop. It was still just a little after nine. The shop didn't open until ten so I was too early.

With nothing else to do, I went around inside cleaning every nook and cranny. I ended up becoming so focused on cleaning that before I knew it, it was time to open.

"All right, let's do this," I said, getting myself fired up as I raised the shutter and started my first day. Open up in the morning, tend the shop all day, and then at night, put the day's proceeds into the safe and lower the shutter. Of course, I wouldn't be able to give prices to any valuable books, so if customers came in wanting to sell them, I would tell them the situation and hold on to the books for them. As long as it was only for two or three days, I figured I ought to be able to do a decent job running the shop by myself.

Looking around the street, I saw that the other shops were preparing to open too. The heady scent of a sweet olive tree came drifting in from somewhere nearby. I made eye contact with Mr. Ijima, the owner of the closest bookshop, diagonally across the street, so I wished him good morning.

"Where's Satoru today?"

"He left on a trip."

"Oh my!" the owner said, his eyes wide with surprise. "That's pretty unusual. It's going to rain today, isn't it?"

"I'm so sorry about that," I said, apologizing for the weather in advance.

As usual, hardly any customers came by in the morning. That's how it always was, and I was used to it. I was content to sit back, relax, and wait for the customers to arrive. To be honest, I was happy just being surrounded by all the books, and I would've been content even if no one had come in.

Still, the fact that my uncle had already called three times that morning was more than I could take. It seemed like it made him terribly worried to be far away from the bookshop. I got tired of dealing with him, so I made an effort to reassure him and quickly hung up.

The time went by very slowly. I spent the period before noon dealing with the customers who trickled in, few and far between, dusting and organizing the books piled up along the wall, and stopping to flip through any that caught my eye.

I also picked up Jun'ichirō Tanizaki's *In Praise of Shadows* to give it a try since my uncle had been so enthusiastic about it. The book is a profound examination of the meaning of shadows, which emerges from Tanizaki's account of his own experiences. It's an argument to be skeptical about the brightness of Japan's cities. His writing was so powerful, I felt like he was right beside me, speaking to me. The book had such an irresistible pull that before I knew it, I was completely sucked in.

When the afternoon finally came, it actually did end up raining. At first it was only drizzling, but it became gradually more intense, and before I knew it, the whole of Sakura Street had turned black with rain.

In this neighborhood of used bookshops, there is no greater enemy than rain. It's a serious problem if the books get wet, plus the number of people coming in instantly drops. As I rushed outside to bring in the carts of books, I saw that in front of all the other bookshops on the street, people were racing to bring their merchandise inside too.

Even Mr. Ijima, who had been cracking jokes about it raining earlier, was now battling the rain.

We laughed bitterly as we both pulled our carts under the roof.

"It's really coming down," he said.

"It really is, isn't it?"

Massive clouds covered the sky, bringing stronger rain showers. Maybe it was a mistake after all to force my uncle to go on a trip. I hoped it wasn't raining over there. "Hmmm," I muttered to myself. "It looks like I won't have anything to do till the end of the day." I went back inside.

Once I pulled the door shut, the fierce sound of rain became a gentle whisper. The faint scent of the road wet with rain drifted into the shop, where it blended with the smell of old books.

The flow of customers came to a halt.

For a long moment, I sat in my usual spot behind the counter with my eyes closed. It was quiet, so very quiet. If I concentrated, I could make out faint sounds—the patter of raindrops hitting the window, the low hum of cars splashing through the rain. I had the peculiar feeling then that I had become one with the bookshop. I could feel my sense of self begin to dissolve and my consciousness expand.

No, no, I can't fall asleep, I thought. I'm the person they trusted to take care of the shop. No matter how much free time I have at the moment.

But being surrounded by books that had been around for so many years seemed to change the way I experienced the passing of time itself. I had a clear sense of myself as existing within it. If there are some professions that require stillness and others that call for action, running a secondhand bookshop falls into the first category. Of course, one can't just divide jobs into simple binaries like that. But it's true that the entire image one has in one's head of these bookshops comes down to a feeling of stillness and calm. I felt like I fit here perfectly, like I had come to rest in a spot that was just my shape and size. And I wanted to remain this way forever.

Had my uncle ever felt like this? The feeling must have been even more intense for him. The shop had been passed on to him from my grandfather and my great-grandfather. One of the reasons my uncle was proud of running the bookshop lay in the respect he held for those who had looked after it before him.

These were the thoughts that drifted through my head as I stared out a window misty from the rain.

After four o'clock, just as the rain lightened up, I suddenly heard the sound of the door clattering open.

"Hey, sorry to barge in."

It had been so long since I'd had a customer that I jumped off my stool. But when I realized it was Sabu, I sat back down, mumbling, "Ooh boy," just like my uncle. Apparently Sabu had come to check in on me just to kill time. His face bore a perfectly mischievous smile.

"How's it going today?" Sabu asked, sounding the way he always did when he asked my uncle that same question.

"It's not," I replied.

Sabu gave his usual giggle. The sound of his laughter reverberated inside the shop. Given how quiet it had been up until a moment ago, it all seemed a little strange to me. The atmosphere of the shop felt completely different when it was filled with the sound of people's voices. Which wasn't necessarily a bad thing.

"You're a curious person, aren't you?" he said. "You come every week to this shop that no one ever comes to."

"You're the curious one. You show up at this shop every day."

"Oh stop, you're embarrassing me."

"You mustn't be so modest."

"I give up. You win."

"Once again. And remember you said you didn't mind."

While we sipped our tea, we went back and forth like this, talking nonsense with a straight face. Sabu left without buying anything, as usual. Eventually the sun went down, and the rain, which had eased off, stopped completely. The clock on the wall marked off the minutes, and when I looked up, it was already seven o'clock—time to close. The day had seemed long, but it was over before I knew it. I slowly rose to my feet and prepared to close the shop.

At exactly that moment, my uncle called again, as if he'd timed it precisely. I told him that I'd closed the shop without any issues, and I asked him to please only call me once the next day.

"Okay, let's split the difference. Three times!" my uncle yelled over the phone. Good grief, what exactly were we splitting the difference of?

The room on the second floor was even more comfortable than before. Momoko, who had stayed here for a time, was now living with my uncle in Kunitachi, so no one was using it. Nevertheless, the room had been kept clean, and books were all neatly in order, probably thanks to Momoko. Pots of geraniums and gerbera daisies adorned the bay window, and there was a note Momoko had written, affixed to the window frame with instructions for watering them. I got the impression that if I forgot to water them somehow, it would be a major disaster. And there, nicely enshrined in the center of the room, was that well-used low dining table.

I opened the sliding door a bit to peek into the small connecting room and saw something frightening. In the dim light, I could see the room was packed tight with books from my uncle's collection. The dark silhouette of all those books, looming silently behind the door, was awfully creepy. I shut the door gently, pretending I hadn't seen anything.

Right at that moment, my cell phone started ringing on the dining table, and it startled me. When I looked at the screen, I saw the call was from Wada. I'd told him that today was going to be my first day tending the shop, so he was probably concerned about me.

"How'd it turn out?"

"Perfect. How about you? Things busy at work?"

"I've got my hands full."

"Take it easy. Sounds like you're too busy to write your novel."

"I'm taking my time, so it's not a problem. Hey, I should get back to work though."

"Okay. Don't work too hard. Thanks for calling. I know you're busy."

Afterward, I finished my simple dinner, took a shower, and then I was basically done with everything I needed to do. I lay on my futon, took a book from the shelves nearby, and flipped through it, but I was too sleepy to concentrate. Still, it seemed a shame to go to sleep like this. A tiny spider was crawling slowly across the ceiling above me. I followed him with my eyes for a while absent-mindedly.

Before long, I got up suddenly and opened the window. The chilly autumn wind rushed in. I could see the silver light of the moon shining in the sky in the distance. The noise and bustle of the neighborhood sounded far away. There was the low rumble of passing cars, the sound of people talking as they went down the street. Then came the sudden clatter of someone closing a shutter. After the sound faded, the silence deepened.

In Praise of Shadows.

I wasn't sure if this was the right situation for it, but I found myself murmuring those words. Then I turned off the lights in the room, sat by the window, and closed my eyes.

I had spent so many long nights this way. Back then, I couldn't conceive of the idea that that time in my life would ever end. But those days have passed. That period of my life has receded into the distance. There's no going back to the past. As I told myself this, I felt a sweet sorrow spread through my chest.

But there was no point in dwelling on that, I thought. I'm much happier now.

My life till this point had been simple, but that didn't mean it was trouble-free. I'd had my share of suffering and setbacks along the way. I sank to the bottom of a deep, dark sea, and for a time, I believed I didn't want to come back up. But on a quiet night like this, I could feel keenly how blessed I'd been, how all the wonderful people I have met along the way had lifted me up. I really had met some wonderful people. I opened my eyes a little and saw moonlight shining in through the window. Sitting in the gentle light, I could feel happiness slowly welling up within me.

Then, for some reason, memories from my childhood came back to me, one after another. It was like a door that had been closed had suddenly been thrown open.

In my own way, I was an unhappy child. Or rather, maybe I should say I was far more troubled in childhood than I was after I became an adult. I think it's partly because I was an only child and an introvert, and I didn't get to spend much time with my parents since they were both busy working. It's also because I wasn't able to properly deal with the anxiety and sadness I felt.

Since I couldn't talk to anyone about this, I couldn't find a way out of my problems, and little by little the sadness inside me grew until it felt like a massive balloon pressing down on me every night when I got into bed. Of course, it was always about childish things. They all seem trivial when I look back on them now. Like when I got depressed thinking about having to take a test in gym class right after summer break to see whether I could spin backward over the playground bars. Or when I heard a rumor that people buried dead bodies under cherry trees, and became afraid of the cherry tree in my backyard. Or when I became despondent after the boys in my class gave me the nickname "Bones" (because I was tall and kind of skinny).

There was nothing I looked forward to more in those days than going back to my grandfather's house every long vacation. My uncle Satoru would be there, waiting to see me. It was a huge help. For me, being with my uncle in his room was like a bulwark against the world. Once I'd made it there, I could relax. There was nothing more to worry about.

In his room, my uncle would listen sweetly as I rambled about all kinds of things. When I finally got tired of talking so much, he would pull out the right record from his collection, and the two of us would sing along at full volume. We were awfully noisy, and sometimes we would even get yelled at by my grandfather, who would come rushing up from the hall where all our relatives had gathered, his face bright red with rage. My uncle and I would put on meek expressions and pretend to be sorry, but as soon it was just the two of us, we would break out giggling. At school, I was always so timid, but with my uncle I felt so brave that it was like I wasn't my normal self.

The anxiety that I had trouble putting into words seemed to diminish a little bit. The rest of the world that up till then had seemed to be wasting away, now, with my uncle, was suddenly thrown open wide.

Looking back, I realized all of my memories of my uncle from that time made me feel like I was in some warm, sun-dappled spot. Was it nostalgia? Did I wish I could go back in time? I wasn't sure, but somehow I was on the verge of tears.

In that room lit only by moonlight, I revisited those sweet memories that had lain dormant behind a door within me, and it was like I was opening up one book after another, turning the pages until I finally fell asleep.

8

The next morning, the fair weather returned. Ragged clouds drifted across the clear autumn sky. The puddles glittered in the bright morning light.

"It's not going to rain today, right?" Mr. Ijima said from the other side of the street, not sounding all that confident.

"I don't think so, but . . ."

"If it does rain today, and I ever hear about Satoru going on a trip again, I'll use every ounce of strength in my body to stop him," Mr. Ijima said as he went back to getting ready to open. I couldn't tell whether or not he was joking.

Fortunately, however, the sky kept my fears at bay. Thanks to which, business was much better than the day before. From the morning, there was a steady drip of customers coming and going. I even sold a Hideo Kobayashi volume with a price tag of five thousand yen.

Then, sometime before noon, I had an unusual visit from a pair of girls who looked like college students. They both vaguely resembled each other, but the one in the flowery dress had an expensive-looking single-reflex camera hanging from her neck. They each carefully examined a single book, then asked me if I could recommend anything. After a great deal of thought, I suggested Tōson Shimazaki's *Before the Dawn*. It seemed to interest them and they bought it.

As they were leaving, the girl with the camera said in a polite tone of voice, "Would you mind if I took a photograph?"

"Oh, not at all," I said. The girl's eyes lit up, and she immediately started taking pictures of the shop.

"Um, can I take one of you as well?"

I reluctantly sat down in the chair behind the counter.

Perhaps because I had too stern a look on my face, she said timidly, "And, um, could I ask you to just look the way you usually do?" But there was no way I could do that in front of the camera. For the most part, when I have time to myself at the shop, I sit there with a dazed look on my face. Getting my picture taken like that would just mean making a fool of myself. In the end, I made up some excuse and stepped back, and basically fled to a corner of the shop.

"To tell the truth, I've liked the feel of this store for a while, and I've been wanting to photograph it," the girl told me as she clicked away at the shutter. The girl who came with her stood smiling beside her. They were cute and they seemed really nice.

"Wow. Is that right?"

"It's got a style to it. And the atmosphere inside is really wonderful."

"I guess you're right," I said nonchalantly. I guess you could say that there's something special about the atmosphere inside an old wooden building. Though my original impression the first time I came here was simply that it was falling apart.

"But, there's always, kind of . . ."

"A weird old guy who's hard to talk to?" I said with a wicked grin.

The girl seemed flustered. "Oh no, not, I mean . . . well, yeah, actually."

"I'm not surprised."

I laughed out loud, ignoring the blank looks on their faces.

"You've been incredibly helpful. Thank you so much. We'll be sure to read the book too."

After the girl had finished shooting, she thanked me politely, and the two of them left the shop.

Things like that kept me pretty busy, and before I knew it, it was nighttime. After I checked the ledger and put the day's take in the safe, I finished a simple cleanup and closed the shop. And in a complete change from yesterday, for some reason my uncle never even called once that day. Had he finally started to trust me? I couldn't help feeling something was missing. In the end, I finished preparing to close, then went out so I could buy ingredients for dinner.

That night, Tomo was coming over. When I'd told her that I'd be staying at the shop again after such a long time, she said she just had to come by after work. Back when I lived at the shop, she came to see me many times and had fallen in love with the place.

Since she was coming over around nine, I used the time until then to prepare a dinner that I'd learned from Momoko when she lived here. Momoko still made lunch for my uncle, which meant that there was already rice and seasonings there.

It was a menu of pure Japanese food, passed on directly from Momoko: stewed chicken and hijiki seaweed, fried tofu, salt-broiled mackerel pike, miso soup with deep-fried tofu and turnip slices, and rice with red shiso. There was only one gas burner, so cooking took more time than expected. I was impressed that Momoko was able to make such delicious food every night with a setup like this.

At exactly nine, I heard a cheerful voice call out "Good evening" from the back door, and I went downstairs to welcome Tomo.

"Ooh, something smells good."

"I've just been cooking. You haven't eaten yet, have you? I thought we could eat together."

"I wouldn't want to impose . . ."

"Not at all. I have to eat anyway."

Tomo and I first got to know each other and became close back when she was working part time as a waitress at the Saveur. The first time I met her I had a sense right away that we could be friends. When I told her that later on, to my delight she said she'd felt the same way at the time. Since then, we've developed one of those rare friendships that are hard to come by. There was something in the way she talked that felt calm and reserved. Her black hair was shiny and her skin was pale white. If you looked up the entry for a traditional Japanese beauty in the dictionary, the picture would look something like Tomo. And moreover, she was talented. She had studied Japanese literature in graduate school. I'd heard she was working now as a librarian at some college. Today, she was wearing a stylish black dress and a silver necklace with a bird motif. It struck me that she seemed to have an innate sense of what clothes suited her best.

With Tomo's help, I spread out all the dishes I'd prepared on the low dining table. It was quite cramped with the two of us eating there, but it was the best we could do.

After Tomo sat down in front of the dining table, she looked around the room. "Ah, it's been a long time since we've been here together," she said emphatically. "It's such a relaxing spot, isn't it?" She was quick to notice the book I'd left on the windowsill, Hyakken Uchida's *Train of Fools*, which I'd started to read the night before after getting into my futon, hoping to feel like I was going on a trip too.

"Oh, I've read this too," she said, her eyes sparkling.

Train of Fools is a travel diary written in the 1950s. In the book, the writer sets out on a trip, with no particular purpose and no particular destination in mind. He just somehow finds himself leaving on a trip. And so the trip becomes an end in itself. There's something funny about this man, who's already past sixty, earnestly committing himself to carrying out a plan that simply popped into his head one day, though strictly speaking, the plan is both meaningless and pointless. There's a richness to the writing; the sentences flow like water. Reading them, you get to savor the feeling of traveling, and as a bonus you get a glimpse of the customs and culture of the era.

"Hyakken Sensei is wonderful, isn't he?" Tomo said with a smile.

I could tell how deeply she loved his writing by the way she'd automatically called him Sensei.

"He's the best. And his companion, Himalayas. They're too adorable together."

"I wanted to be on the trip with them."

"They're so hard to please though. Don't you think if you actually went it would be a disaster?"

"But they're so cute—and they seem like pretty cheerful old guys," Tomo said with a sweet smile. There was something so maternal in that smile that it startled me.

Tomo chewed her food slowly as she ate. For some reason, I always tended to rush impatiently through the meal, so this time I followed her example and ate slowly. She said she hadn't eaten Japanese food in a while. She tended to prefer spicy food. She'd always been a light eater, and since she'd been busy at work she'd gotten in the habit of eating whatever she could throw together. Seeing her across from me breaking out into a smile and telling me how delicious it was, I couldn't stop myself smiling in return.

We talked about a lot of things over dinner—about our jobs, about the books we'd read recently. We were always emailing and calling each other on the phone, but it was a joy to talk face-to-face like this. Even after the meal was over, we stayed at the table talking.

"But being a librarian is perfect for you."

"A college library's nice, but my real dream was to work at the National Library."

"Oh, that's the library that has every book that's been published?"

"Exactly. But I flunked the exam for the job."

"Really? What a shame."

"The place I work now might not be big, but the library does have a collection of old and important texts. I get a thrill out of it. Still, sometimes the youthful exuberance of all those college students can get a bit overwhelming," Tomo said. Her voice had a gentleness and a maturity about it. Even the way she used chopsticks was elegant— all that remained of her mackerel pike was the head and the bones. There was nothing to praise about what I'd left on my plate. She must have been raised well, I said to myself. In fact, I'd heard that Tomo's family ran the biggest construction company in the area. Basically, she was the boss's daughter. "It's not as nice as it sounds," she insisted.

"What do you mean 'youthful exuberance'? There's hardly any age difference between you and them."

"I guess I'm no longer that exuberant."

"Haven't you found any college guys you connect with?"

With a girl like Tomo at the library reception desk, there were probably lots of students who were crazy about her. I let myself imagine some male student who saw Tomo in the distance and fell madly in love. But Tomo quickly dispelled my delusions.

"No, not at all. But what about you? Are things going well with Wada?"

"Um, yeah, I guess," I said, flustered to find myself the focus of the conversation.

Right at that moment, my phone chimed like I'd timed it perfectly. I looked and saw it was a text from Wada. Would I mind if he visited me at the shop for a little bit? He was about to call it a day and leave the office.

"Wada says he wants to come over. Is that okay?"

"Absolutely, sure. I want to meet him."

I'd talked to Tomo a lot about Wada, but the two had never met. So, it seemed like a good opportunity. Let's invite him over. Although the room was too small for three people.

Tomo's here, I said, but come over.

Less than ten minutes later, we heard a voice shout "Hey!" from outside the window.

"Welcome," I said to Wada, who had just made it up the stairs and come into view.

"Good evening. It's a pleasure to meet you," Tomo said, with a huge smile on her face.

"Oh, Miss, um, Ms. Tomo, I've heard so much about you. It's a pleasure to meet you as well." Wada bowed quickly to Tomo.

"You don't need to call her 'Miss,'" I said laughing, but in response to Wada's earnestness, Tomo straightened her posture and bowed in return.

"No, the pleasure is all mine."

"Wada, you already had dinner, right? I'm sorry. We ate everything. If I'd known you were coming, I would've prepared a plate for you."

"No, don't worry about it. I'm heading home in a bit."

Wada seemed restless for some reason. He was sitting there in a formal posture in one corner of the room. When I asked him why, he said he was just excited because it was his first time coming to the second-floor room.

"But it seems wrong to barge in and have a look around without the owner's permission."

It seemed like he was trying desperately to suppress his urge to lick every surface in the room.

"You say that, but then you came over anyway, didn't you?" I said, astounded.

"I let my curiosity get the better of me. But I was wrong to cross that final line. One mustn't give in to passion at the cost of courtesy. Moreover, there's a high likelihood that Mr. Morisaki hates me." There was a look of anguish on Wada's face now, but he hadn't budged from his stiff, formal posture.

"You're just as funny as Takako said you were."

"Right?"

We nodded our heads in agreement as we struggled desperately to keep from laughing.

"What? What's funny about me?" Wada asked earnestly, in another display of how serious he was by nature.

We couldn't take it anymore, and the two of us finally burst out laughing.

It was a lively night, a complete change from the night before.

When it was nearly time for the last train of the night, Tomo had to leave, and Wada decided to leave with her. I wanted to get a little air too, so I went with them part of the way.

After we said goodbye to Tomo at the entrance to the subway, I immediately turned to Wada and asked him what his impression of her was. "Tomo's wonderful, isn't she?"

"Oh, sure she is."

Deep down, I had been nervous about how Wada would respond to meeting Tomo, but mostly he just seemed indifferent. On the one hand, I was relieved, but I was also disappointed that he hadn't quite seen how wonderful she was. I was proud to call her my friend. Why couldn't he see how charming she was? It irritated me.

Wada, however, kept talking and looking rather confused. "It's just that she . . ."

"What?"

77

"I don't know. It's just a feeling, but it's like she's there, but she's not really there."

"Huh?"

"I don't know what to make of it. Maybe she's the kind of person who's used to being alone. Or rather, it's like she's the kind who prefers to remain alone."

"You think so? I don't get that sense from her at all."

What Wada had said was so unexpected, I could hardly grasp it.

I'd always thought that Tomo was the kind of cheerful girl that anyone would love.

"I don't know. Maybe it's her way of protecting herself. I'm not sure how to describe it. It might be because I can be like that myself that I was able to pick up on it. It's like the moment we laid eyes on each other, I had a sense she and I were the same type of person. I don't know. It's probably just that she was nervous meeting me for the first time. Sorry. Forget I said anything."

As I listened to him, I was less concerned about Tomo and more concerned about Wada.

What he was saying at that moment . . . I'd secretly sensed that he hadn't completely opened his heart to me. I realized I was right, and it made me feel lonely.

Wada stopped ahead of the traffic signal on the avenue and said, "This is far enough. I can walk back from here by myself."

"Or you could spend the night at the shop?" I asked, pretending I was joking.

"I couldn't. That's the owner's . . ."

"That's okay. I understand," I said, cutting him off.

His answer was so obvious, I couldn't even be disappointed. But the fact that the answer was obvious made me a little sad.

"Good night."

To hide what I was feeling from Wada, I turned on my heels and ran back to the shop without waiting for his response.

The next day, I was in a dark mood right from the morning.

I sat in my chair, staring blankly, lost in thought. Ever since I'd gotten to know Wada, my brain had been split in two, with the affirmative side of me and the negative side perpetually locked in debate. This morning that debate reached a boiling point.

I'd find myself reacting to every little thing he did or said, trying to gauge the depth of his love, and I'd think, What an annoying, clingy person. And yet the moment I fell in love, wasn't that what I became?

On this point, my affirmative side tried to convince my negative side, *This shows how much you love him*, to which, my negative side promptly answered back, *This is further proof of what an annoying person you can be*. Today, once again, my affirmative side had the weaker position, and my negative side was in top form.

"Um . . ."

I was suddenly startled to realize someone was speaking to me.

I looked up, feeling flustered, and saw that Takano was almost hiding behind one of the bookshelves, looking my way.

"Wait, Takano, how long have you been here?"

"I just came in."

Checking my watch, I saw it was almost noon. He must have come by on his break from the coffee shop. Takano was wearing only a T-shirt with three-quarter-length sleeves and a character printed on it who looked like a disintegrating Mickey Mouse. For some reason, he dressed lightly even in the cold months. Probably because in his heart he was still a boy.

"Say something when you come in. Or just don't come in so quietly."

"I'm sorry. I did say something, but you had this look on your face like you were deep in thought." Takano was scratching his head, like he couldn't figure out why I was mad at him. I was embarrassed because I realized that I was taking my frustrations out on him.

After I cleared my throat and regained my composure, I asked, "Is there anything you need?"

"I heard from my boss that you've been running the store since the day before yesterday."

"That is correct."

"So, um, there was something I wanted to talk to you about."

"That's why I was asking. What is it?"

"Well, it has to do with Tomoko Aihara."

"Tomo?"

Was this déjà vu? We had definitely been in this exact same situation before. I was alone in the shop, Takano came in, mentioned Tomo . . .

That's right. Takano was in love with Tomo. Intensely so. Back then, Takano had asked me to act as a go-between since I was good friends with Tomo. But just as they were becoming close, Tomo quit her part-time job at the coffee shop to find a real job, and after that, there were no more signs of progress in their relationship.

I sat there at the counter with my head resting in my hand. "Really? What is it now?" I said, totally indifferently. To be honest, my brain was already at capacity thinking about my own situation. I didn't have any interest in what Takano had to say.

"Could you please not sound so obviously annoyed?" Takano said, like he was losing his nerve. "You don't know what it's like. Your life is one happy day after another."

"Wait a second. You came to the shop to tell me something. Don't just sit there and sulk."

"I can't help but sulk after what happened," Takano said and laughed a little at himself. What a gloomy guy, I thought. He was sulking in such a terrible way that I found myself recoiling a little. It was probably safer not to tell him that Tomo had come over the night before.

"But can I tell you something?" Takano let out a sad sigh after he asked the question. Then he started to tell me this story.

Even after Tomo quit working at the coffee shop, they kept texting each other (mostly about books). Still, Takano was always the one who texted her first, so to avoid bothering her, he made sure to let enough time go by between texts. But about two months ago, he sent her a text for the first time in a while, and not only did he not get a reply, the text itself never even arrived. After that, he tried texting her dozens of times, but he always got an error message in return, and they never reached her.

"Which means she must've blocked my number? I mean otherwise my texts should get through, right?"

I couldn't believe Tomo would do something like that. Supposing she had, did that mean that Takano had done something truly terrible? As a test, I tried sending her a text right then: Thanks for coming last night. See you soon.

As expected, a "transmission complete" message appeared on the screen of my phone. I held up my phone to Takano, who stared at it like he was about to devour it with his eyes. He was silent for a moment, and then he looked up at the ceiling and yelled, "Why!?!?"

"Takano, do you have any recollection of, say, standing watch outside her home, or maybe sifting through her trash, or, I don't know, bugging her room?"

I'd heard a lot of stories about people who were driven to act like that under the strain of a love they could never share with the object of their affection. But Takano turned all red and denied everything.

"What makes you think I could have anything to do with a crime like that? My boss is always saying that I have trouble reading between the lines, but I would never do something so awful to Tomo, let alone anything like stalking."

"You're right. I'm sorry. It's so odd for her to do something like that, that I had to check. There's no way a timid guy like you would pull a stunt like that."

"Exactly!" Takano said, standing up a little straighter.

It was at that moment that Tomo's quick reply came back. It must have been her lunch break. The text said, I want to thank you for dinner last night. Come over to my place next time.

Delighted, I replied, How about next week?

Takano watched me with a look of despair in his eyes.

"Why? But why? Why only you?" he whined. There was an urgency in his voice. But no matter how many times he asked me, I didn't have any answer for him. Still, as I remembered how pretty Tomo had looked last night, I felt sympathy for Takano. If I were a man, I'd probably fall in love with Tomo too. And if one day she blocked my number, I'd probably spend a week in bed. Yesterday, I could only think about my relationship with Wada, but now, listening to Takano talk, I was fixated again on what Wada had said about her.

"Well, Takano, what are you going to do?"

"I'm going to look for a book."

"Heh?"

It was such a random, off-the-wall response that I practically screamed at him. How could looking for a book have anything to do with what was going on with Tomo? "There's a book that Tomoko wants. It was a really long time ago, but she was talking to the owner at the Saveur, and she told him that there's a book she'd always wanted to get, but she'd never been able to find it. I was, um, listening nearby."

"What book?"

"I think the title is *The Golden Dream*. I've forgotten the name of the author, but it sounded like an old Japanese text, I think, probably a novel."

"So your plan is to find that book and give it to her as a present?"

"The fourteenth of next month is her birthday, right? If possible, I'd like to give it to her then. I don't know that much about books like that, but I was thinking that you might know more."

Despite what Takano had said, I'd never once seen a book with that title in the shop.

"Well, let's suppose you give her the book, what would you want her to do?"

"I don't want anything in exchange. It's only for my own satisfaction. I'm not trying to get her attention or win her over or anything. If she's avoiding me, then we can pretend it's from you."

What Takano said seemed laudable to me. I could tell from the tone of his voice that he truly was thinking of Tomo. He reminded me of that song I learned in grade school, "Donna Donna," about a calf being carted away from its mother. I'm sure the look in Takano's eyes at that moment was the same as the calf "with a mournful eye" in the lyrics.

"Tomoko probably just thinks of me as some guy she used to work with at her old part-time job, but to me, her smile is the reason I never quit the coffee shop. It's what made me able to go on working. So I want to find a way to express my gratitude for those years. I'll be satisfied as long as it makes her happy."

"Okay, I understand." After hearing what he felt, there was no way I could refuse to help him. "In that case, I'll help you look for the book. With the two of us, it shouldn't be any trouble. I want to make Tomo happy too."

"Thank you so much." And with that Takano's expression finally brightened a tiny bit.

———

That night, my aunt and uncle stopped by to check on things a little before I closed the shop. It would've been better for them to have gone straight to their home in Kunitachi, but my uncle couldn't help himself. I proudly informed him that there had been absolutely no problems at the shop. Thanks to the effects of the hot spring, Momoko's skin was even more lustrous than usual. "It was really fun," she said as she handed me a gift box of hot spring steamed buns. My uncle, however, was standing nearby, looking gloomy.

"That reminds me. You stopped calling after the second day," I said.

My uncle just mumbled "Yeah" in response. He looked a little unwell.

I was worried and looked to Momoko, who tried to explain. "It's been so long since we've been on a trip. I think we're a little bit tired. Don't worry about him. He really enjoyed it."

"Hmmm . . . really?" I thought it was a little odd, but I didn't pursue the matter any further. If they both said they'd enjoyed themselves, then that was enough for me.

"Well, I can close up. Leave the rest to me."

I wanted to fulfill my responsibilities right up to the end, so I had them go home first.

I had to work the next day too. My days at the Morisaki Bookshop had come to an end. I wanted to go on living at the shop, but instead I closed the shutter tightly and went back to my home and my normal life.

9

The following week, the cold air retreated and the warm days returned for a time. At midday, it felt hot wearing a jacket.

I tried to find the book that Tomo wanted, *The Golden Dream*, just as I had promised Takano.

I asked my uncle about it first, since that seemed the surest way to find any book.

But my uncle said he'd never seen or even heard of the book. I'd taken it for granted that he, of all people, would know it if it was an old Japanese book, but my assumption was totally wrong. And to make things worse, he barely showed any interest, which was so unlike him. Normally, my uncle would've gotten all worked up, searched until he found it. Lately, my uncle had seemed odd (he was odd before, of course, but not in this way). It was like he was profoundly tired. When I got worried and asked him if he was all right, he turned it around and asked me what I was talking about, so I figured there wasn't much to worry about.

With no other options, I made the rounds of the secondhand bookshops on the way home from work, keeping up my search for the book. Takano had assumed it was some kind of novel, but if my uncle didn't know it there was a decent chance that was wrong too, so I even popped into some shops that specialized in illustrated books.

In a mountain of thousands of old books, I was searching for a single volume, with only the slightest clue to go on. I found it surprisingly fun—like a treasure hunt. I wanted to find it for Takano, but I had also become deeply curious about the book itself. What kind of a book would Tomo want so badly? Was it funny? Maybe it was the kind of book that could change your whole perspective on life? I'd been feeling uneasy about things with Wada since last week, which only made me want a book like that even more. But the search proved to be more arduous than expected. As I made the rounds, not only could I not find the book, I couldn't even find a person who knew of its existence. And when I asked, Wada said he didn't know it either. It seemed the book that Tomo wanted to find was only for the true diehards.

But the harder it was to find the book, the more my interest in it grew.

My next step was to ask my uncle to get me into the auction being held at the Rare Book Hall in Jimbocho.

When you run a secondhand bookshop, the auction is your best opportunity to acquire books in large quantities. You could even say that it's nearly impossible to keep a bookshop going if you don't attend the auctions regularly. So, of course, all the bookshop owners of Jimbocho would be at the auction in the Rare Book Hall. It was easy to gather information there, and you could find a rare book without having to walk to all the shops.

To be honest though, the auctions were not exactly my cup of tea. While it was a relatively friendly scene because I knew so many people, there was a solemnity in the air that I found stressful.

I knew I would be out of place once the auction began in earnest. So, during the initial open period, meant to allow people to check out the items on auction, I stayed at my uncle's side and looked around for the book. This was the only occasion when my uncle seemed to concentrate, taking notes as he looked over the items. It didn't seem right to get in his way, so I kept my mouth shut and studied all the titles of the books in front of me. In the end, I didn't find what I was looking for. When I asked the bookshop owners I knew, they all said they'd never heard of the book.

I snuck out of the venue and stood in the hallway, grumbling to myself. If I couldn't find the book in this neighborhood after this much searching, where on earth would I ever find it? Of course, it was conceivable I'd missed it, but Takano had been checking the shops diligently too, and had been searching for more information online. But for all that, he hadn't turned up anything worthwhile.

Talking it over with Takano at the Saveur, we came to the conclusion that our best bet was to try the Book Festival.

Held from the end of October to the beginning of November, the Book Festival was Jimbocho's biggest event of the year.

For this week alone, this neighborhood, where time always seemed to go by so peacefully, was completely transformed. Carts of used books and rows of bookshelves lined the streets, and they even set out stands selling yakisoba and candy-covered fruit. Lots of people came, all looking for books. Once this time of year came around, I couldn't help but feel excited. It made me happy to see that so many people loved books. It often seemed as if only a limited number of people thought of Jimbocho as a crucial part of their lives, but in fact, there were all these people who loved it. I admit I found it all deeply moving.

Naturally, the Morisaki Bookshop was part of the festival every year. As a small shop, we did things differently from the bigger stores on the avenue. My uncle would run a sale on the books on the carts that fit snugly in front of the shop, and he set up a bargain corner inside. This year, Momoko had taken care of all the preparations, so there didn't seem to be much I could do to help. My uncle, who loved a good festival, was in such a frenzy this time of year that he could barely think about business, but this time he said, "Trust me, I've got it all under control."

Because of work I was only able to go to the festival for a single day. On that day alone, I was able to do my part, helping out at the shop from the morning on. Inside, we could hear the lively music coming from the main avenue, where the event booths were set up. From the other direction, the smell of sweet sauces and the aroma of grilled meat drifted to us on the breeze from Sakura Street, where the food stands were lined up.

At lunch, the three of us stood out front eating okonomiyaki and sausages my uncle had bought at the food stands. "This is so good," my uncle said, in ecstasy.

"This kind of food is more about the feeling," Momoko remarked coolly. "The taste is really nothing special."

Later on, after the sun had gone down, I joined Takano, who was now finished with work, and we wandered around searching for *The Golden Dream*. We hurried through the throngs of people, checking literally all the shops from one end of the street to the other. As Takano walked beside me, he turned and mumbled sadly, "When we did this three years ago, Tomoko was with us."

It was true: Tomo had been with us then. And now she had blocked his number. I guess you could say that for Takano that day was *The Golden Dream* itself.

Given the limited time and the large number of shops, it didn't seem possible to go to all of them, so we decided midway to divide them between us and meet up again in front of the Morisaki Bookshop in an hour. In the end, my search was fruitless. Takano's too. As soon as I saw the look on his face, I knew there was no point in even asking.

That evening, after the festival had come to an end, Takano and I went out for curry with my aunt and uncle.

"So, you couldn't find it. I guess that's how it goes," Momoko said as she devoured her beef curry, ignoring the fact that Takano didn't seem to have an appetite.

"It's not a book I know. I apologize I couldn't be more helpful," my uncle said, feeling sorry for Takano. My uncle, of course, had ordered his curry mild.

"There's no need to apologize," Takano said. He was shaking his head briskly, yet it was obvious from the way he let his shoulders droop that he was heartbroken.

I was exhausted, and I was beginning to wonder if there was any point in continuing our search. Wouldn't it be better to ask Tomo instead, rather than taking such a roundabout way? We had no definite proof that Tomo didn't already have the book to begin with. But Takano had done his best, even if it was in vain. And that was one of his finer qualities, so I decided not to push him any further.

"It's a shame we didn't find it, but the fact that you looked for it will make Tomo happy."

"That's right. It's what you did that matters."

"You think so?"

"Besides, you can't expect to seduce a girl with a single book," Momoko said.

Takano leaned across the table and protested frantically. "That wasn't my intention at all. Seduce her? The thought never even crossed my mind."

"Oh, is that right?"

"It is," I said, coming to Takano's defense. "Besides, Takano's texts are getting blocked. Let's not get ahead of ourselves."

"You mean she dislikes you that much? That's tragic," Momoko said, turning her face to the heavens dramatically. What she said sounded like a death sentence to Takano.

"Hey, that's enough out of you," my uncle scolded.

"Takako . . ." For some reason, Takano was looking at me bitterly.

"Oh, sorry, that was thoughtless of me," I said and immediately covered my mouth with both hands. But it was too late. The part about his number being blocked was supposed to be a secret.

"You've got to be careful about this one. She has a pretty big mouth," Momoko said.

"Nah," my uncle said. "Takako's tight-lipped about secrets, just like she's tight about money."

Takano turned to me and bowed his head, ignoring the nonsense coming from my aunt and uncle. "Anyway, I apologize for bringing you into this, Takako."

"I told you there's nothing to apologize for. I enjoyed it. It was fun looking around."

"I'm happy to hear that, but I still owe you an apology."

"I just told you that you really don't. But if Tomo is okay with it, I'll see if I can invite you to her birthday party," I said.

Despite how dejected he felt, Takano was sweet to be so considerate. That's the kind of person he was. And I believe that's why the people around him all loved him. In my heart, I thought, wouldn't it be nice if we brought Tomo and him together for a bit . . .

That Sunday, I paid a visit to Tomo's home in Nezu. It was my first time there. She didn't work on the weekend, so I stopped by on my way home from the office. Her apartment was less than five minutes from the train station, a corner unit on the second floor of a two-story building only for women. I pressed the intercom button, holding the cake I'd bought as a gift at a shop near the station. Tomo came out right away with a smile on her face and welcomed me in.

Tomo's apartment was not all that different from what I had imagined: simple, clean, and stylish. The warm-toned curtains, furniture, and bedspread were all color-coordinated. It was the apartment of a young woman of refined taste. Except for one thing: the bookshelves were enormous. They went all the way up to the ceiling. I had the urge to ask if she had ordered them from a trade supplier. Of course, they were tightly packed with books with no space left to spare. It looked like she was ready to open her own little bookshop. When you visit a friend's place, it's normal to take an interest in the contents of their bookshelves. While Tomo made us tea, I took the liberty of thoroughly examining the contents of those enormous bookshelves. It was mostly old Japanese novels, but there were also books by foreign writers like Baudelaire and Rodenbach, and fantasy series like The Lord of the Rings and The Earthsea Cycle. (As far I could tell, the book Takano and I had been looking for wasn't there.)

"It seems like it must've been hard to move in," I said, looking over the bookshelves.

Tomo understood what I meant. "Oh, absolutely!" she said. "These books alone filled ten cardboard boxes. I'm trying not to get any more books now. But what do you do, Takako, to organize your books or pack them up when you move?"

"I don't have that many books yet. I don't worry much about holding on to them, so I tend to gather them up and sell them."

"I see." Tomo fell quiet. "I'd better start selling more, or I'll be in trouble. But once I like a book, I just can't let go of it."

After tea, while we ate the elaborate Southeast Asian dinner that Tomo had prepared, I said that since her twenty-sixth birthday was coming up so soon, we should go out to dinner again to celebrate. Surprisingly she had almost nothing planned for her birthday, so it came together quite quickly.

"I wonder if we should invite Takano," I asked, trying to take advantage of this moment in the conversation.

At the sound of his name, Tomo, who was reaching with her chopsticks to pick up a fresh spring roll, suddenly froze. She turned and looked at me with a pained expression on her face. "Did you say Takano?"

"Yeah, is that a bad idea?"

"It's not a bad idea, it's just . . ." Tomo said hesitantly. I could tell by the tone of her voice how troubled she was, and I hesitated to go any further. The situation might be more serious than I'd thought. But for Takano's sake, I wanted to find out what he'd done wrong. Speaking quickly, I told her what I'd heard from Takano and politely asked if something had happened.

"But look," Tomo said, hesitating even more. "I'd quit my job at the coffee shop, and I didn't expect we'd be in touch after that."

It was hard to believe Tomo would block his number for such a trivial reason. She and Takano had gotten along so well that I thought it might develop into a romantic relationship. Unless Takano had committed some unpardonable mistake, there was no way to explain it.

"Did he, by any chance, do something that upset you?"

"Absolutely not," Tomo said, looking up in surprise. That was the one thing she flatly denied. And I was relieved to hear it. At some point, I had started feeling like Takano's mother.

"Nothing like that happened. Takano is really purehearted. I admire that. There's nothing wrong with him. There's something wrong with me," Tomo said. She cast her gaze downward, pursing her lips so tightly they formed a straight line. I saw tears welling up in her eyes, and I felt myself trembling all over.

"That's not true, Tomo. There's nothing wrong with you. It's not your fault if you don't feel the same as Takano."

I realized I'd let slip something I shouldn't have. Takano had never said a word to her about how he loved her.

"I'm sorry, I, um . . ."

"It's okay. I was well aware of the fact that he cared for me. I sensed it somehow that day the three of us went to the Book Festival such a long time ago. But even though I knew, I always pretended not to notice. I took advantage of the fact that Takano never said anything, and I feigned ignorance, so we stayed friends."

"That's why I don't think you did anything wrong."

"That's not true. There's something wrong with me. The moment I receive that kind of attention from a member of the opposite sex, I suddenly become frightened, and I try to close myself off. I'm frightened that if I reciprocate I won't be able to handle it. I know it's crazy, but I can't help it."

Tomo no longer paid any attention to the food on the table. She fell silent and just kept looking down. The tears that had been welling up in her eyes now seemed about to fall. I felt as if I had accidentally driven her to this point. My chest hurt just looking at her. The room became so silent we could hear the faint buzz of the fluorescent light on the ceiling.

I was unsure whether I could ask anything more. Perhaps sensing this, Tomo said, "Can we talk just a little bit more? I'm not sure I can put it into words well, but I want to tell you."

"Shall I make us some tea?" I said cheerfully, in an effort to keep her from getting more depressed. "You'll feel a little better with something warm to drink."

"Oh, I . . ."

Tomo started to get up, but I stopped her and went into the kitchen, where I quickly cleaned the teapot and cups we'd just used, and made us a fresh pot of black tea.

"Thank you," Tomo said, accepting her cup, and she slowly brought it to her lips. "There's nothing wrong with Takano. There's something wrong with me." She repeated the same words she'd said a moment ago, sounding a little calmer. "I told you before about how I started reading."

"Um, yeah, you said it was your sister's influence."

"That's right. I had a sister who was five years older. From when I was little, all I did was imitate her, not just with books, with everything. Unlike me, my sister was smart and beautiful. She was the kind of person who could do anything. She had a little bit of a wild temper, but she was always kind to me." Tomo closed her eyes for a moment, as if she were recalling her memories of that time in her life. Then she started to speak again. "My sister had a boyfriend she went out with from when they were in high school. He was a very quiet person, the opposite of my sister. To tell the truth, it was because of his influence that my sister started to read books. And then I let myself be influenced so much that I started to love him the way she did. He was my first love. Still, I was in grade school, and I didn't recognize it. I just played with them a lot. I was in middle school when I became aware of it. But anyone could see how well suited they were for each other, and for a long time I never even considered uttering a word about what I felt. I was happy enough that they were there, and that sometimes they would let me into their little world."

Tomo took a sip of tea and glanced at me, as if to check my reaction. I nodded silently, as if to say, *I'm listening*, and she smiled sadly in response.

"Right after I turned seventeen, my sister died in an accident. The driver of the bus she always took to the university fell asleep and collided head-on with an oncoming car."

Tomo pursed her lips and closed her eyes, like she was mourning the death of her sister. I started to say something, but she shook her head and cut me off. "When my sister died, I was so sad that I thought I would die too. It really felt like my chest would burst. But after a while, I noticed that somewhere in my heart I was feeling another emotion. It was hope, hope that after what happened, he might turn his attention to me. It was such an ugly, ugly, sinister feeling."

"But Tomo . . ."

Tomo was still looking down, her gaze fixed to a point on the floor. Like she was staring into a vast, black ocean beneath her. No matter how many times I turned it over in my mind, I couldn't find the right words to say, something that might weaken the hold this had over her.

"I couldn't forgive myself for feeling that way. Nothing anyone tried to tell me could change that. That in the midst of all the sadness I felt after losing the sister I loved so much, I could still . . ." At that point, Tomo abruptly stopped talking and looked up. "I'm sorry. It's such a depressing story," she said apologetically.

I kept shaking my head. "And your sister's boyfriend, how did he . . ."

"I haven't seen him at all since her funeral. He's a friend of the family, and I hear he still visits my parents sometimes. Even after he got a new girlfriend, he still comes. After all this time. And they say he wants to see me. But I'll never see him again as long as I live. I don't ever want to remember what I felt then. And that goes for whoever else I might feel that way about."

"So when you see that someone like Takano has feelings for you . . ."

"I get frightened and I run away. I want to scream at him to stop it. I'm not the kind of person who can be loved. I try to live my life guarding against the possibility of anyone falling in love with me. But Takano is always so kind and pure. I'm afraid I let myself take advantage of that a little. And because of that, I ended up hurting his feelings. I'm the worst. I need to apologize to him when I see him."

"I don't know, Tomo. Doesn't it make you sad to live like that?"

"When I'm sad, I read. I can go on reading for hours. Reading quiets the turmoil I feel inside and brings me peace. Because when I'm immersed in the world of a book, no one can get hurt," Tomo said and smiled. But her smile made her look sadder than I'd ever seen her before. Or maybe after I'd made up my mind early on that she was this cheerful, good-natured girl, I never once thought to look at what lay beneath the surface.

But now that I knew, was there something I could say that could thaw her frozen heart?

In reality, after she smiled for me and said, "Thank you for listening. I feel a little better," I couldn't say anything in response. It was too painful to realize that this was the reason she read so much. All I could do was remember the pain that seemed to squeeze itself deep inside my chest.

It was a drizzly evening, two days after I went to Tomo's place. I was on my way home after dropping by the Morisaki Bookshop. Wada and I didn't have any plans to meet, so I stopped at my second-favorite coffee shop, Kissaku. What Tomo had told me was still swirling around inside me, and I was in a dark mood. I didn't feel like going straight home.

After idling away almost an hour there, I decided it was time to go, so I opened my umbrella and started walking on the avenue heading to Jimbocho Station when the figure of a man walking a little ahead of me caught my eye. Seeing him from behind in that familiar jacket . . . it was Wada, without a doubt. He must be on his way home after work.

I jogged after him, and I was about to call his name, when Wada stopped right in front of a drugstore at the traffic light. And then a young woman came rushing over and stood in front of him. It looked as if they'd planned to meet each other there.

I only caught a glimpse of her face in profile underneath her red umbrella, but I knew right away who it was. Without a doubt, it was the woman Wada went out with before me. The way she was dressed, the way she looked—she hadn't changed at all from the last time I saw her at the Morisaki Bookshop.

The two of them seemed to be discussing something. Wada looked at her and nodded. I promptly hid behind the sign of a restaurant. I had no idea why I felt the need to hide, but that's what I found myself doing. And while I was hiding, the two of them walked away, side by side.

What was I doing? I asked myself that question as I walked behind them, leaving a little distance between us. Am I just going to follow them? I thought it over. It was true though. If I wasn't tailing them, then what could I call what I was doing? In the light rain, Yasukuni Street was so full of men and women holding umbrellas on their way home from work that there was no reason to believe Wada and his ex would notice me. The two of them kept walking along the road, paused for a moment, and then walked into a Doutor coffee shop like it was a perfectly appropriate thing to do.

I walked back and forth in front of the entrance for a while, thinking they might come out soon. As I wandered aimlessly in front of the coffee shop, salarymen passed by on their way home from work, casting sidelong glances at me like I was in their way.

I might have stayed for ten minutes. In my head, I felt calm, but I was also terribly confused. Looking around, I saw the rain had mostly stopped. The people walking down the street had closed their umbrellas.

I could hear myself muttering as I put away my umbrella. Then I trudged wearily back to the station.

10

What happened that evening hit me harder than expected. I felt restless during the day, and at night I couldn't sleep. I didn't feel much like reading.

It got so bad that at work I made a ridiculous mistake, and they discovered a major problem with the data I sent to a client. That caused me to get yelled at mercilessly by Wada #2. But it was all 100 percent my fault.

I was utterly useless. I couldn't concentrate on anything.

At night in my apartment, when I was all alone on my futon, I couldn't stop going over these foolish things in my head.

What did it mean to be in a relationship? I wondered as I stared vacantly at the ceiling. We went to the movies, we went out to eat, we slept at each other's places. But if I never got inside his heart, would we ever really be together? What exactly did I mean to Wada? For example, did I have the right to interrogate him about what happened that night? Even thinking of it as a right made me feel like there was something wrong with me.

Because of all this, I was afraid even to talk to Wada. I used to look forward to his calls, but now I wanted to run and hide when I saw his name show up on my phone.

Wada's voice still sounded exactly the same on the phone after that night. Calm and kind as always. Before, whenever I heard his voice, I felt at ease. Like I was looking out over the calm surface of a lake. But now, his voice felt awfully far away.

"What's wrong?" Wada asked me, sounding worried. But I was never good at expressing myself. "Are you not feeling well?" I could hear in his voice that he was confused.

"No. It's nothing. Well, good night."

Right before I hung up, I told him I had to cancel our date next week because I was going to be working late.

Soon, I'd reached my limit for being stuck in my head and depressed. I found myself heading toward the little restaurant where Momoko worked.

"Oh dear, you mean Wada would do something so shameless?"

I'd told her that all this had happened to a friend of mine, but Momoko saw through me easily. There was no way I was going to pull one over on her. While she watched over me in her white apron, I drank sake, and then the words came easily, as if the tangled thread inside me had come loose at last. I came clean about the whole story, including how I still couldn't get over it.

"Good grief, this place is turning into a relationship counseling service."

"I'm sorry."

"Well, as long as it's for my adorable niece," Momoko said with a grin, though I had my doubts whether she truly meant it. "You're afraid to confirm this with Wada?" she asked.

I nodded silently.

"But Wada's not that kind of person, is he?"

"It's because I believe he isn't that kind of person that it's so scary. Because the thought that he could cheat on me is really terrifying."

"Hey, Takako." Momoko came around from behind the counter and sat down next to me. "Listen, I'm no great scholar. I'm not very well-read. It's all I can do to read one book in the time Satoru reads ten. But I think I'm a pretty good judge of people. As far as I can tell, Wada would never deliberately hurt you. You can see that in his eyes. But I think maybe the bigger problem here is the wall you've built around yourself."

"The wall?" I repeated.

Sitting beside me, Momoko stared at me, trying to look me right in the eye.

"You know what I mean, don't you?"

"I think I might."

After what happened with my previous boyfriend, I had unconsciously been avoiding trusting anyone completely. And I was scared, scared because I'd been careless in trusting someone before, scared of being hurt again, of cursing myself for my own foolishness and wanting to throw it all away again.

That's why I was always overreacting to everything Wada said or did, and not just on this occasion.

"*If you won't* open your heart, it's selfish to expect the other person alone to open theirs to you, don't you think?" Momoko said. "Unless you take that first step, I don't think anything's going to get better. Wada's a human being, after all. He might get tired of living with your chronic indecisiveness, and if that happens, you'll be the one to regret it."

What Momoko said cut me to the quick. I'd asked so much of Wada, but I hadn't offered anything in return. And like she said, I had gone to great pains to read into every little thing Wada did or said, searching for what the look in his eyes could have told me.

As I mulled this over, I heard a high-pitched shriek coming from the kitchen. Mr. Nakasono, the owner, was yelling, "Momoko, help me!"

"Yes, right away," Momoko shouted back, and got up from her chair.

"Well, I've got to run, but do me a favor and try not to worry your aunt Momoko too much. Hurry up and put my mind at ease." She pinched my cheek, and without giving me a moment to respond, she ran at full speed to the kitchen, where Mr. Nakasono was still yelling, "Help! Help!"

It was Thursday night, a few days later, that we held Tomo's birthday party. We called it a party, but it was a cozy night with just the three of us. At Tomo's request, we'd decided to have dinner on the second floor of the Morisaki Bookshop, and had brought the long table normally used as a counter upstairs to set up our hot pot.

We tried to invite my uncle and Momoko, but they declined, claiming the party "was no place for old folks like them." Takano refused to come at first, saying that Tomo probably wouldn't want him there, but I persuaded him that it wasn't true, and half forced him to join us. He showed up with a nervous look on his face, dressed lightly, of course, in only an orange hooded sweatshirt. I couldn't help thinking that he ought to have dressed a little more stylishly for a night with the girl he loved.

Although Tomo knew that Takano was coming, the two of them only said hello at the door to the bookshop and seemed awkwardly nervous after that. I couldn't say things were great with Wada, but things were looking really bad here, so I forced myself to be cheerful. My cheerfulness was purely superficial though, and it only seemed to end up dampening the mood further.

In this gloomy atmosphere, we picked at the hot pot, barely saying a word. Takano and I drank beer while Tomo, who didn't drink alcohol, had orange juice. Tomo ate only vegetables; Takano ate only tofu.

But we've done all this for Tomo's birthday, I thought to myself. As I watched the two of them sitting there silently with only their chopsticks moving, I got more and more irritated. And naturally, the one to bear the brunt of my irritation was Takano.

"Takano, can you quit eating only the tofu? Eat some vegetables and chicken."

Takano had just taken two big, round pieces of tofu and was eating them by himself.

"What? Oh, I'm sorry. I just thought there was too much tofu left. I assumed you two didn't really like it." Takano was flustered, but I kept pushing him.

"Don't make that decision on your own. I'm trying to eat a nice balanced meal. Tomo, you want some tofu too, don't you?"

Tomo was startled as she was suddenly drawn into the conversation. She looked up at us. "No, I'm fine," she said. "Takano, you can eat it."

"You can't be too polite, Tomo. It's your birthday," I said.

Takano nodded frantically in agreement. "That's right. I promise not to touch another piece of tofu. Please eat as much as you like."

He was about to put the tofu slices back, so I rushed to stop him.

After that, we left our leading lady alone and went back and forth bickering over tofu. Tomo watched us, looking like she had no idea what to do. In the end, just after I complained that Takano was a guy who couldn't even dress for the season, Tomo couldn't take it anymore and intervened.

"Um, the tofu is really not a problem. What's more important is I need to apologize to Takano," she said, turning to face him. "I was awful to you. It's entirely my fault. I'm sorry," she said, bowing deeply.

Takano panicked, as one might have expected, and at the moment he tried to stand up he banged his kneecap on the corner of the table.

"No, please, I'm the one who needs to apologize," he said, in agony from his throbbing knee. Tomo apologized again. As I cleaned up the mess Takano had made of the table, I said to both of them, "Let's leave it at that, shall we?"

Takano had tears in his eyes, from his feelings for Tomo or from the pain in his knee, and he seemed to want to say something else, but he reluctantly sat down and stopped talking.

In any case, after that the heaviness in the air seemed to dissipate. I seized the chance to give Tomo her birthday presents. Mine was a brooch in the shape of a lily that I thought she might like; Takano's was a stained-glass lamp. The lamp was intricately crafted in the shape of a lighthouse. It was kind of a wonderful item, the kind of thing a guy who wore seasonally appropriate clothes might choose. Tomo smiled at last, and said both presents were wonderful.

"Actually, Takano originally wanted to give you a different present," I said, ignoring Takano's attempts to stop me. There was no need to keep it a secret now. "But we couldn't find the book, Tomo. *The Golden Dream*. You've been looking for it all this time, right?"

Tomo's mouth hung open. She looked flabbergasted. She turned to me and asked wildly, "What? You were looking for that book?"

"Well, yeah, but . . ."

"I apologize. I'd always remembered what you said about it back at the Saveur. I guess I went too far," Takano said. "I'm sorry."

Tomo looked flabbergasted again as she listened to Takano. "No, it's not that, Takano. That book doesn't actually exist."

Now it was our turn to be shocked.

"What? Really? But . . ."

"I'm sorry. I described it in a way that invited this misunderstanding."

"But when Takano looked it up online, he found a post from other people who were searching for it too." Takano nodded along with me.

"That must've been other people who believed it existed too. In part, it's become almost a rumor. You could think of it as a phantom book," Tomo said apologetically.

In that case there was no way we could have found it even searching in the greatest neighborhood for books in the world. It was no wonder my uncle didn't know it either. Leave it to Takano to jump to conclusions like that. I gave Takano a look full of loathing as he sat there astonished. Then again, I never had the slightest suspicion that the book might not exist so I couldn't lay the blame entirely on Takano.

In any case, Tomo gave us a detailed account of the book that did not exist.

In the early years of the Showa era, an unknown writer named Mitsuko Fuyuno published a book called *A Moment of Twilight*. It's the story of an isolated and blind old man, who is facing death, and the middle-aged woman he hires to read to him. Perhaps the story was too romantic, because neither the literary world nor the general public paid any attention at the time of its publication. *The Golden Dream* is the novel the woman reads to the old man when he's on his deathbed. That text is the key to the whole book. At the time, there were a number of people who became obsessed with finding it, and among them it was a bit of a craze. But after several years, they established that the book was actually the author's creation.

"In *A Moment of Twilight*, *The Golden Dream* is described as a breathtaking masterpiece. After the book is read to him, the novel ends with the old man, who up till then had never known love, realizing that the woman at his side, who had served as his eyes for many years, is the person he's in love with.

"It was my sister who first told me about the novel *The Golden Dream*. She said it was a wonderful book, and I absolutely had to read it. This was about half a year before the accident. I always believed everything my sister told me. So I was fixated on finding that book. But then I discovered that no such book actually existed . . ."

Tomo turned to me and laughed like it was all a joke.

"It seems likely that my sister knew from the start that the book didn't exist. I mean she said she'd borrowed the book from her boyfriend and read it.

"Why would my sister lie to me? My sister wasn't the kind of person to lie about insignificant things. So then why? Was it only to make fun of me? Or maybe she had noticed my forbidden love I felt for her boyfriend, and she wanted to pay me back? Either way, now that my sister's dead, there's no way I'll ever know.

"And even though there is no book, I still find myself looking for it whenever I go into a used bookshop. Whenever someone asks me if there's a book I want, it's always the first thing I mention. Some part of me hopes that if I ever find that book, something inside me will change, like the old blind man in the book. I know it's an extremely infantile thing to believe, but still . . ."

"I had absolutely no idea you were looking for that book. I'm really sorry." At the end, Tomo apologized to us again.

"There's no need to apologize. After all, we took it upon ourselves to look for it."

To think that we spent two weeks searching for the book without the slightest idea of the real story behind it. It all seemed perfectly meaningless now. Tomo wasn't just looking for that book. Deep down, she was searching for an answer she'd never find. And it was all connected to events around her sister's death. Or rather, she was trying to connect it to them.

When Tomo talked about her sister she always gave that lonesome smile. She seemed so sad.

"Happy birthday!" Takano suddenly stood up and yelled. "Your smile always gave me courage. I never quit my job and tried to do my best at the coffee shop because I wanted to see your smile." What was this guy talking about all of a sudden? I tugged hard on his sleeve still in shock, but he was so excited, I couldn't stop him.

"I mean, what I'm trying to say is that, even if you didn't realize it, you helped someone, and that person is here right now with you. Someone who's sincerely happy to be with you on the day that you were born is standing right here with you now. I want you to remember that if you can. That's all I wanted to say." After saying all that without pausing to breathe, he ended by uttering another feeble "Happy birthday." Then his face turned bright red like he was angry, and he sat down with a thud. All at once the room fell silent. He wanted to cheer up Tomo so badly it hurt, but I think, no matter how you look at it, this might have been too much at once.

In front of us, the hot pot had reached a rolling boil, so I turned off the flame on the burner. Tomo hadn't opened her mouth. She was still looking down, staring into her lap.

Then she slowly got to her feet. She opened the sliding door to the room buried under the book collection, went in, and suddenly slid the door shut from the inside.

"Did I say something wrong?"

There was no sound coming from the room next door. We waited for a moment, but she didn't seem to be coming out. I was worried, so I knocked on the door and peeked inside. I had no idea why, but there in the dim light, Tomo was sitting upright, reading with intense concentration. Even though I had opened the door, she made no attempt to look my way.

"Um, Tomo?" I said with her back toward me.

"Yes?"

"What are you doing?"

"What do you mean? I'm reading," she replied, sounding perfectly composed.

"Yeah, but why now?"

"I felt a sudden urge to read," she said without looking up from the book. Was this her way of avoiding reality? The reality that Takano's speech could be seen as a declaration of love?

As Takano drew near to her from behind, Tomo brought her face closer to her book, as if she were trying to immerse herself in reading even more. Takano and I turned toward each other, but we had absolutely no idea what to do.

Then before I knew it, Takano abruptly sat down beside Tomo, grabbed a nearby paperback, and began to read in silence.

For an instant, Tomo looked up and saw Takano, then she returned to her book without saying a word.

"What? . . . You're scaring me . . ." I muttered aloud without meaning to. Neither of them showed the slightest reaction. I started to worry a little about what I'd do if I was stuck waiting for them like this until morning.

Takano abruptly opened his mouth to speak. "Um . . . Tomoko, I'm not good at explaining myself. I might not know how to say this, but I can stay with you like this without talking. You call when you need me. I'll come right away."

Tomo didn't look up from her book, but there was a slight stirring in the shadows. It even seemed like she nodded slightly. When Takano saw this, he smiled a little and then went back to reading silently.

Surprising as it may seem, perhaps it was Takano who understood Tomo, or maybe even human beings in general, far better than I did. While I was worrying about how I could bring them together, he was thinking about how to make her feel better. Rather than trying to force open the door that she had wanted closed behind her, it made more sense to start by getting her to open it from her side. Maybe he's right, I thought. As I watched the two of them sitting silently side by side, it seemed that someday soon Tomo might open the door herself.

I picked up a nearby book and leaned against the wall. As I flipped through the pages, I reached a decision. I would call Wada. I would tell him that I wanted to see him soon. I had to be the one to tear down the wall I'd built.

As it grew late on the night of Tomo's birthday party, the only sound was the turning of pages.

11

Because of a typhoon that swept across Western Japan, we had days of strong rain and wind. The trees on the streets lost most of their leaves. They looked a little embarrassed with their bare branches sticking up into the sky.

Wada was very busy at work for a while, and it wasn't until four days after Tomo's birthday party that we were able to see each other. Normally, it would have been his day off, but Wada had to rush to work and stayed into the afternoon. It was close to evening by the time we met.

Apparently Wada thought that I'd been acting strangely recently. As soon as we were together, he asked me apprehensively if something was wrong. I decided I would ask first about what happened that night.

After I'd finished telling him what I saw, Wada murmured, "So, is that the reason you've seemed so down?" He seemed to understand at last. "It's no wonder," he said. He let out a long sigh, as if he realized he'd made a terrible mistake. Then he sat there with his eyes shut, not moving at all.

The Saveur was packed again that day. Sitting next to us, a man in a suit sipped his coffee as he leisurely spread out his newspaper on the table. Across from us, a young couple huddled together talking. The rain had cleared up early that morning, and the sun was peeking through the clouds at last. Through the window, the soft dusk light quietly streamed into the dimly lit interior.

Wada hadn't touched his coffee. He sat there with a grim expression on his face. His shoulder, closer to the window, glowed gold in the sunlight. He hadn't moved in so long that I began to worry. "Are you okay?" I asked.

Wada opened his eyes, and sounding even more serious than usual, he said, "I'm okay . . . I was wrong not to tell you about it. It was thoughtless. I don't know. I just imagined it from your point of view, and I thought it would make you feel bad. But it looks like, by not telling you, I ended up worrying you instead. I'm really sorry." Wada said all this incredibly fast. He tried to recount the sequence of events that led to him seeing her . . . That evening when he was at work, she'd contacted him out of the blue, saying she wanted to return a book of his. It was the first time he'd heard from her in a year. He said she could keep it, but she said she was already nearby, and she insisted on returning it. When he met up with her, she urged him to come back to her . . .

But before Wada could say more, I interrupted him. "That's enough."

"Enough?" he said, his eyes wide with surprise.

"I mean it's okay. I see clearly that it was nothing," I said, smiling. The smile came naturally; there was no need to force it. To tell the truth, I'd been pretty anxious about seeing Wada again. But with him right in front of me, I felt so much better somehow, and it really seemed things were okay.

"What? But . . ." Wada furrowed his brow. The look on his face showed he didn't understand how I'd been convinced so quickly. He always made that face whenever he was baffled by something. The man sitting next to us looked up from his newspaper, reacting perhaps to the sound of Wada's voice, and gave us a glance. But he quickly lost interest and went back to his own little world.

"It wasn't because I wanted you to tell me about that that I asked to see you today. The truth is, I just wanted to see you."

"But you were worrying about it."

I shook my head. "It really doesn't matter. It was a shock, for sure, but the biggest shock for me was that it made me realize I didn't trust you. I wasn't sure how to face you today . . . So, you see, I was the problem, not you."

"The problem?" Wada frowned again. It was starting to seem like he'd been making that face all day.

"That's right. Because I was a coward. I've been holding back from opening my heart to you. Without realizing it, I was afraid of getting hurt. I finally understood when Momoko pointed it out to me. That's why I've decided to put an end to all that."

Once I put it into words, it felt like all the pointless anxiety that had been building up in my body was suddenly released. I felt at ease. It was okay. Really. I could see that when I took a good look at Wada. I hadn't tried that before. Not once in the whole time we'd been going out.

Wada stared at me for a long time, blinking again and again, before he finally mumbled, "Is that right?" He sounded deeply moved.

"Hmmm?" I asked.

"I was just thinking that you spent this week thinking all this for me," he said, and finally brought the coffee to his lips.

"Hmmm," I said, leaning my head to one side as I thought it over. "Maybe it was for you, or maybe it was really for me. If I hadn't done that, I think at some point I would've started to hate myself. If that happened, I wouldn't be able to be with you. And I couldn't have that."

Wada listened to me, scratching his head. He gave an embarrassed laugh. "I feel like I've been on a roller coaster today."

"I'm sorry. I think it all must sound weird," I said, and finished the last of my coffee, signaling that we'd reached the end of that part of the conversation.

Before we left the coffee shop, Wada, conscientious to a fault, added one last thing, fidgeting a little as he spoke: "It's really my fault. Anyway, there's nothing going on with her. I won't see her again. Believe me." I couldn't help letting out a little laugh.

After that, Wada and I took a long stroll through the neighborhood at twilight. We were headed to his place. We both had to be at work in the morning, but tonight we wanted to be together.

Wada was walking along as he always did, with his back straight and his head held high, when he suddenly said, "Can I confess something? I'm really jealous of you, Takako."

"Me? Why?" I asked. What he'd said was so unexpected it astonished me.

"You have so many people you can rely on, so many people you can trust."

"You mean people like my uncle Satoru?"

"Yes," he nodded with a smile. "It's obvious. You mean so much to everyone."

"You think so?" It's not that I hadn't felt it before, though I'd felt there were a lot of people who liked to make fun of me. Especially Momoko and Sabu.

"It's because you draw all of these people to you. You have that magnetism. And because you value them too."

"I'm not so sure about magnetism," I said, embarrassed. "But it's true that after I came up to Tokyo, there weren't many people in my life whom I'd known for very long. It was the same when I was at home too. I didn't really have anyone I could speak to freely the way

I can with my uncle and Momoko or people like Tomo. I'm kind of amazed by it myself."

When I first went to my uncle's bookshop, I never dreamed I'd meet all these people. That includes Wada too. If not for my pathetic broken heart, I never would've come to the Morisaki Bookshop, and I would still be estranged from my uncle, and I probably would never have met Wada. Thinking about it made me feel strange. It was all interconnected, and now we were walking side by side through the streets of Jimbocho at twilight.

But the idea that Wada felt jealous of me was still hard to imagine. And Wada was someone who could endear himself to a multitude of people no matter where we went. He was the kind of person who could get along well with everyone.

Wada strongly disagreed when I told him what I thought. "That's not true at all. From the time I was little, people always told me I was so serious. It's true that I might be able to get along well with people anywhere I go, but on the other hand, I'm constantly positioning myself as an outsider, and I can't do more than interact with people. My mind is always calm. I don't really have many memories of joy, even as a child. I don't know why that is. I think it might be the effect of growing up in an emotionally distant home. I distanced myself from my parents at times, but I don't think that was the only reason for it. I was probably just born like that. It's just the kind of person I am." Wada went on talking, his eyes fixed on the palm of his right hand, like he was trying to see what he was made of. "Everyone gets tired of being with a person like that, even if there's a novelty to it at first. It doesn't matter who it is. That's why everyone ends up going away. The first time you saw my place, it was in a terrible condition, wasn't it? I don't know. I think it shows what kind of person I am. For all the ways I've learned to keep up appearances, on the inside I'm a mess. And there's nothing I can do about it.

"But when I look at you and the Morisakis, deep down I know I want to be a part of that world. It's what I long for. The idea I told you about—to write a novel set at the bookshop—I think that was my own modest way of trying to be a part of it." As Wada said those words, he looked at me. He seemed a little bit embarrassed. I found myself looking back at him, staring at his face. Until this moment, I hadn't the slightest idea that he felt this way. I felt like I finally understood why he'd looked so anxious when he confessed that he was writing a novel.

"I want all of you to accept me. I want to share the joy and sadness with all of you. This is really the first time in my life I've felt that way."

I gently squeezed Wada's warm hand in mine.

"Of course, we will. I mean, you're a wonderful person."

"You think so?" Wada muttered without any conviction.

I turned to look at him and said definitively, "You are. I promise."

Wada looked at me, a bit surprised, and smiled fondly. "Thank you," he said. But I felt like I was the one who ought to thank him. I was happy that Wada had told me how he felt. I was happy he cared about me and the people who are important to me. I kind of felt like I was being rewarded. For finding the courage to confide in him what I was feeling.

Sharing your thoughts with someone seems so simple, but at times it can be surprisingly difficult. Even more so when it's someone you care so much for. That's what I thought about as I walked next to him. But if you can find the courage to do it, it'll bring you closer together.

We turned the corner, and Wada's apartment building came into view. We walked straight for it, hand in hand.

In the space of a few days, it felt like winter had arrived, and my favorite season was over. But that wasn't so bad.

Because from here on, whether it was winter or spring or whatever season might come, I believed these gentle days would continue. And all the people I love would spend them laughing together.

As we walked down the street at twilight, this was what I told myself, though I had no grounds to believe it.

12

I have something to tell you.

It was past the middle of December when Uncle Satoru suddenly made this announcement. I had come into the Morisaki Bookshop in the morning on my day off. With one thing or another, I hadn't been there in two weeks. The hours before closing went by peacefully, but just as I was getting ready to leave, my uncle called me over. "Do you have a minute?" my uncle said, looking ill at ease.

"Sure, that's fine, but . . ." Recently, my uncle had become a little bit more taciturn, compared to earlier. I was concerned without really knowing why. To be honest, with everything going on with Wada and Tomo and the normal everyday busyness, I hadn't been paying much attention to it. Still, my uncle had definitely seemed odd recently. More than anything, just for him to say that he had something to tell me was weird. If he wanted to tell me something, he was the kind of person who would just come out and say it.

We decided that first the two of us would work together and quickly close the shop, and then we'd go out.

The moment we were outside, we could feel the cold night air on our cheeks. A pure, unadulterated winter night. The kind of night where everything around seems quieter, and the air makes you shiver all over. Stars were shining in the black sky.

"Shall we walk a little?" I suggested. I thought it might make us feel better to breathe the air outside and move around a little.

"But aren't you cold?"

"That's why I want to walk a bit."

"Well, then let's do it together."

We left Sakura Street, turned after coming out onto the avenue, and then followed the road. For someone with short legs, my uncle walks pretty quickly, and there was no way he was going to attempt to match his pace to that of a less fleet-footed person. As a result, when we walked together, the gap between us would widen step by step. But I knew that after we'd gone a certain distance, he would always stop and wait for me, so I never needed to rush. I went at my own relaxed pace, following behind my uncle, with his back to me. It was just like the old days. Whenever we went for a walk when I was a child, I would end up following him with my eyes as his skinny little back went on ahead of me.

When we came to the moat of the Imperial Palace, we decided to take a rest before heading back.

In the moat, the streetlights shone dimly on the surface of the water, where a black, silhouetted bird swam by gracefully. Back behind the hedges, the Imperial Palace looked dark and deserted. My uncle bought us two bottles of Hot Lemon and passed one of them to me. "This is so you won't catch a cold," he said.

That was another thing that hadn't changed since the old days: he still liked Hot Lemon.

"Ooh boy," my uncle said wearily as he sat down on one of the benches lined up along the moat.

I smirked and said, "Is your butt okay?"

"Ah, this is nothing." He gave me a thumbs-up.

From there, we had a good view of the night sky. We could see the slender crescent moon, and a little past that, the twinkling stars of Orion. There were still many lights on in the newspaper building across from the Imperial Palace. Along the avenue parallel to the moat, runners ran, gasping for breath. My uncle and I sipped our Hot Lemons, now and then letting our gaze follow a passing runner.

"Thanks, by the way, for the trip. All in all, I'm glad we went. Momoko was happy. When I think about it, maybe it hadn't been ten years since we'd gone on a trip like that."

The trip was over a month ago, but my uncle was just telling me this now.

"You're welcome. Thank you for always looking out for me."

"Nah, I don't do all that much."

I looked up at the night sky and said, "You've been looking after me since I was a kid." I got a little embarrassed thinking about how well he knew me as a child.

"Is that right? I guess we've known each other for more than twenty years altogether." My uncle and I were both staring up at the sky now, squinting as we looked back with nostalgia. "Time goes by quickly, doesn't it?"

"Well, we didn't see each other for a long time. To tell you the truth, once I got to puberty, I really couldn't stand you. I couldn't figure out what you were thinking. You were old enough to know better, but you were always just dithering around."

"That's harsh. I'm in shock." My uncle gave the same flat laugh he always did, his breath forming round white cottony shapes in the air.

"Sorry. But when I was a kid, I adored you. When I think back to those times, I have only happy memories. I can see now just how kind you were to me."

He laughed. "But then you hated me and I didn't realize it. And I guess that's why you didn't come see me for quite a long time."

"I didn't hate you. I just had trouble dealing with you. But I don't feel that way at all now."

"That's a good thing, I guess, but . . ."

As we talked, for some reason I remembered that uncomfortable feeling again. Beside me, my uncle was laughing the way he always laughed, and talking the way he always talked. His kind voice was the same as always. But something was definitely different. He was perplexed about something. Spending a quiet evening together like this, I could feel it distinctly, and it left me deeply worried. And then, deep inside my chest, the feeling grew a little stronger.

"Um, Uncle, what was it you wanted to tell me?" I hesitated to ask the question, but my uncle didn't seem like he was going to get to the point on his own.

"Ah, yes."

"I'm guessing maybe it's not very good news?"

I realized that I was tightly squeezing the plastic bottle in my hand. Although my body was cold, my hands were sweating. My uncle glanced at me from the corner of his eye, and then nodded slightly.

"Well, I guess not."

"So, what is it?"

My uncle nodded again. "Actually," he said with a serious look on his face. "My hemorrhoids are really hurting me something fierce again. No, really, it's gotten to be a serious problem."

I was a fool to be so worried. Without saying a word, I gave him a big shove with both hands. As he was about to fall from the bench, he gave a weird shriek. "Ta . . . Takako, what are you doing? I'm begging you, please don't give my butt any more excitement."

"Jerk."

I let out a big sigh, like I was releasing all the stress that had been building inside me. I felt both incredibly angry and incredibly relieved. Is that right? All this is about your hemorrhoids? I thought to myself. They hurt. I'm sure it's terrible, but if that's all it is, we're lucky. Really lucky.

"Tomorrow," I said, "you've absolutely got to go to the hospital."

"Okay, I'll do it."

"Absolutely."

I sprang to my feet and said, "Well, should we get going?" If we didn't get home soon, we really were going to catch a cold. But my uncle made no attempt to get up from the bench. Did his hemorrhoids hurt that badly? I guess that's how it goes. I reached out my right hand to try to pull him up.

However, my uncle just sat there staring at my hand; he made no attempt to take hold of it. When I got impatient and called out, "Hey," he muttered, "It's about Momoko."

"Huh?" I replied, taken aback.

"Actually, she told me when we were on that trip." He pursed his lips then, as if to pause for a moment. Then he slowly opened his mouth again and went on. "She said the cancer came back before all that. She'd found out much earlier from her doctor. But she couldn't say anything about it for a long time. And, she, um, said it's pretty advanced."

My uncle's breath turned white, floated up into the sky, and then vanished.

"I'm still the only person who knows, but sooner or later everyone's going to find out. Before that happens, I thought I'd just tell you . . ."

I was struck then by the strange sensation that the ground had suddenly been yanked out from under my feet. I was having trouble standing. My hands and feet suddenly felt cold. The hand I was still holding out to my uncle, now, without my willing it, went limp and drooped down.

"That isn't true, is it? It can't be. I mean, she looks so healthy . . ."

I wanted it to not be true. I was pleading with him. But it was true. The misery in his eyes said it all.

13

A flock of migrating birds flew across the featureless winter sky. They formed a single column, propelling themselves with big flaps of their black wings. When it seemed they'd risen high in the sky, they circled and receded into the distance, carried by the wind until finally they were only tiny black specks that vanished into the clouds.

Where were they going?

I contemplated the question as I gazed at the birds from the hospital window.

The winds were strong today. They'd built a relatively large courtyard in the hospital, where the patients could take walks. On warm days, you'd often see people there, but no one was out today. The fierce wind blew through the line of pine trees, bending their branches till they creaked wildly. Cold outside air poured in through the window I'd left slightly ajar.

"See something interesting?"

When I looked, I saw Momoko, sitting up in bed, peacefully knitting as she watched me standing at the window. I closed the window gently.

"No, I was just noticing how windy it is today. Is it okay that I shut the window?"

"It's fine. Thanks."

Momoko's knitting needles moved lightly back and forth in a nice rhythm. Lately, she seemed to be lost in her knitting, her gaze focused always on her hands.

"What are you knitting?"

"Gloves."

"Even though it's the end of February?"

"It's okay. I'm only doing it for my own enjoyment. It's perfect for killing time."

"Hmmm . . ." I sat down on the folding chair beside her, and the two of us watched her hands as she knit.

"Takako? Could I give you these? I don't need gloves."

"Sure. I could use them. But how long will they take to finish?"

"I might be done in March? But you could wear them again next year too, right?"

Next year.

I repeated the word to myself. It was impossible to imagine that Momoko might not be with us next year. Or rather, I didn't want to imagine it. Trying to negate that unpleasant thought, I said cheerfully, "Yes, please."

"Got it."

She lifted her head for a moment and gave me a smile. A perfectly innocent smile, overflowing with affection. She was staying in a four-person room at a general hospital in the city. She'd had surgery before in the same hospital. The room she stayed in then was different, but apparently it was on the same floor. At that time, she was still separated from my uncle, so she would've had no one at her side. It must've been so lonely.

The room itself smelled of medications and that antiseptic particular to hospitals, and also slightly of sweat. Behind the cream-colored curtain, the walls were bright white. A little bit cold and indifferent. "That's what hospitals are like," Momoko said. She had an exasperated look on her face, as if to say, "That's just how things are."

"Well, you should go home. I can't bear you sitting there forever."

Momoko gestured with her chin toward the door. Her hands never stopped moving. When I came to visit her at the hospital, she always sent me home within the hour like this. I couldn't tell if she was doing it for my sake or if I was really annoying her.

"You don't need to look after me like that. As you can see, I'm fine," she always said at the end of my visits, giving a little snort. I'd end up leaving the hospital like I'd been shooed away.

But Momoko's complexion was good, and her skin was firm—she looked like the picture of health. She ate up all the food they brought her, and even in bed her posture was as good as always. It's strange to say this, but there was so little change in her appearance it almost seemed anticlimactic.

On the night I went for that long walk with my uncle, he kept grumbling all the way back, "She's such a troublemaker," sighing a little each time. We walked along the road to the station, shoulder to shoulder, moving slowly as if it were against the law to walk any faster. I have absolutely no memory of the route we followed from the Imperial Palace. But afterward, I could still hear the sound of him quietly sighing as if he couldn't keep his emotions from overflowing from inside him.

Then I came to know a few things I'd never imagined could be true.

Momoko's cancer was already fairly advanced; they had detected that it was already spreading through her lymph nodes, which meant surgery would be difficult. That's what the doctors had informed her. Momoko had accepted this and didn't want to undergo another surgery. At first, my uncle had protested vehemently, but after repeatedly meeting with the attending physician, he started to think that might be for the best. For him, the most important thing was to respect Momoko's wishes.

Walking beside him, I could only respond listlessly with a "Yes" or "Is that right?" Caught off guard by this sudden news, I couldn't gather my thoughts. I didn't know what to think. As I listened to my uncle talk, the only thing I understood was that the situation was far more serious than I'd thought.

The sound of my uncle sighing blurred together with the sound of passing cars. For a while, I just stared at the asphalt without saying a word.

"You said she told you on the trip, right?" I asked, suddenly preoccupied by this possibility.

"Yeah, she dropped it on me with no warning. I was shocked. I mean you know how she jokes around a lot, but she would never joke about something like that. I realized pretty soon that she was serious."

"So, you've known for a long time." All I'd wanted was for that trip to be a chance for the two of them to rest. To think that this was what they were talking about. Looking back, I realized that it was after that trip that my uncle became noticeably quiet. He held that secret in his heart for a long time without saying a word. I could sense how difficult it was for him to tell me. To say it aloud would mean fully accepting the truth. That had to be scary.

"It must've been hard for you to be the only one who knew," I said.

"Nah, not really." He laughed dryly.

"Like I told you, it's not something that's going to happen right away. In a little while, she'll probably have to go to the hospital. And then they'll have to see how things go from there.

"Oh, I see . . ." So when he said they weren't going to operate, it wasn't that she was going to make a full recovery—it meant she didn't have much time left.

That came as the biggest shock for me. The thought that the disease lurking inside her would soon grab hold of her and carry her away from us to the other side. That before long, Momoko would be gone from this world. It was impossible to believe such a thing. I'd already let myself imagine the kind of sweet old lady she would be one day. And I imagined that she would run the Morisaki Bookshop forever together with my uncle, who would've aged like her and turned into an old man.

I realized I was sighing softly now just like my uncle. As if on cue, my uncle muttered, "I give up. Just when I thought she'd come home after five years, it turns out she's sick. And even worse, we're nearly at the terminal stage. She's acting like nothing's happening, so it hasn't sunk in yet at all. It would help if she could let herself act a little more like a patient."

My uncle shook his head miserably and let out another little sigh.

"Yeah," I said.

"I can't win with her."

He said it again and again until we made it to the station.

But for a long time after that, the days went by as if nothing had happened, just as my uncle had said. At the bookshop, Momoko looked after the customers, just as she always did, and a few days each week, she went over to help at the little restaurant nearby. Sabu and the other regulars were always stopping by the bookshop, looking for Momoko's polite smile. On the surface, not a thing had changed.

Even when I went to see her at the bookshop after I knew about her illness, her response was matter-of-fact.

"Well, that's how it goes," she said, sounding unconcerned.

"But, um . . ."

I wanted to say something, but before I could open my mouth, she said, "There's just nothing we can do about it. I'm prepared. And I'm halfway ready for it. So please don't look at me with that grim expression on your face. You'll end up getting me down too," she said, smiling, and slapped me on the back. It felt like she was the one cheering me up.

Since she herself was acting that way, it didn't seem right for me to be depressed.

The day was coming, but until it arrived, I felt strongly that I wanted to spend as much time as possible being Momoko's niece, and her friend, however far apart we were in age. And I needed to be of help to my aunt and uncle in whatever way I could.

And then, a little while later, they decided it was time for Momoko to be hospitalized. It happened after the start of the new year.

At first, it was supposed to be temporary, but they said it could become long-term depending on her condition. She explained the situation to Mr. Nakasono, and she took the rest of January off from working at the restaurant. Mr. Nakasono was the one who suggested they think of it as time off, rather than an end to the job, but although they said it would be for a month, it was the last time he would see Momoko in her apron.

My uncle tried to think of all the little things that might make Momoko happy. He even tried to get her to go on a trip before she began her stay at the hospital. But what Momoko wanted was to relax at home.

My uncle suspected she was worried about him, since she knew how reluctant he was to take time off from the bookshop. "One trip is enough," she told him firmly. "Take care of the shop. I could watch you look after the shop all day long." After he'd heard that, my uncle didn't bring it up anymore.

It was around that time that everyone they knew in Jimbocho learned of Momoko's condition. Like me, when they first heard the news, they couldn't really believe it. "Not our Momoko?" People like Sabu pressed for more information—he even called me on the phone and demanded almost angrily that I give more details. And yet, in accordance with Momoko's wishes that we keep things the same, no one acted as if they were particularly worried for her, not on the surface at least, and no one showed her how heavy-hearted they were.

Until she was hospitalized, Momoko had more free time because she was off from her job at the restaurant, so she often dropped by the Saveur. At times, she would get into conversations with Sabu, the owner, and even Takano. Momoko was cheerful there too, and she was even relaxed enough to tease Sabu and the others about being so dispirited. And she adored the milkshakes the owner made for her, and always seemed happy whenever she had one.

Once the two of us had tea with Wada. That was when Momoko deliberately came out and said, "How's Wada #2 these days?" She seemed delighted with the result, and sat back and watched as Wada very earnestly asked, "Wada #2? Who is that? Am I Wada #1 then?"

Then as if she were remembering something, Momoko turned to Wada and said suddenly, "Look after Takako, will you? She can be indecisive, but she's a good kid." It didn't sound like Momoko at all.

I was taken aback, and I sat there wide-eyed with surprise as Wada, sitting next to me, answered, "Of course."

Around this time, my uncle always seemed depressed. He some-how seemed to be feeling much worse than Momoko. Even still, he ran the bookshop as usual, and now and then I went by to see how he was doing.

"Uncle, are you okay?" I would ask, feeling worried.

He would always answer, "Oh, I'm fine."

But he didn't look the least bit fine.

If I said anything more, he would get annoyed and take offense, so instead, I brought up a topic that I thought might make him feel better.

"You don't have any books to recommend, do you?"

"Hmmm? Oh, that's right. I can't think of anything now, but I'll find something for you next time."

Even when it came to a subject he normally would've jumped at the chance to talk about, he could only muster this listless response. And then of course he started sighing again.

"Um, is there anything at all I can do?" It was a sincere offer. Seeing the sullen look on my uncle's face was more than I could bear.

If there was a way I could be of help, I wanted to do it no matter what it was. But my uncle looked back at me astonished, as if to say, *What are you talking about?* "You've already done so much for us. You even accompanied her when she went to the hospital. I can't ask you to do any more than you've already done. It's too much," he said. Then he gave a weak laugh and that was all.

In that moment the Morisaki Bookshop, which used to resound with the sound of my uncle's cheerful voice, now seemed a terribly desolate place.

In the beginning of February, a week after Momoko had been admitted to the hospital, the doctor declared she had six months left to live. But even after my uncle told me this, it still didn't feel real to me at all. They were just meaningless words. I found it impossible to imagine that within that time frame Momoko would be gone. More than anything, I couldn't detect the slightest indication of it from Momoko, who was breathing and smiling at this very moment.

Death itself seemed far off in the distant future. This was Momoko—couldn't she just laugh it off and make it go away altogether? It seemed just about possible when you looked at her.

When I went to see Momoko at the hospital it was mostly to confirm this. When I saw that she looked exactly the same, secretly it would ease my mind. I really said to myself, "Oh, doesn't she look fine, she must be healthy. In October, or even September—once it's cool outside, we should go to Mount Mitake again together."

One day later that month, when Momoko was lost in her knitting as usual, I asked her to go with me. The two of us could climb the mountain on the funicular like we did last time and stay at that same mountain inn that was basically a hostel. Haru and the innkeeper must still be there now. Let's go see them again. Then we could look out from the viewing platform at the mountains stretching across that gorgeous landscape, and at night we could put our futons together and sleep side by side.

"It's a good idea, isn't it? You said yourself that you had a good time," I said, now at the edge of my chair.

"Yeah . . ." Momoko hunched her shoulders as if the whole idea seemed like too much of a hassle. "But Takako, you just complained the whole time that you were tired and your feet hurt."

"I'm not complaining now."

"You *were* complaining."

"I might have complained a little bit, but what if I say I won't complain this time?"

"Doubtful. You'll start whining right away."

"I'll make a vow not to, okay?"

"That reminds me, Takako. Remember when you fell down on the mountain right smack on your butt? That was brilliant," Momoko said with a mischievous grin.

Ultimately, the conversation came to an end without her offering a definitive answer about where she would or wouldn't go.

I could see in the courtyard on the other side of the hospital window that early cherry blossoms had already started to fall. Their petals spun in little whirls, dancing at the edge of the path.

14

Even after spring turned to summer, Momoko seemed as healthy as ever. I worried her condition might deteriorate in the intense summer heat, but her appetite was unchanged; even her complexion was good. She was in and out of the hospital for a while, but she even dropped by the Morisaki Bookshop, though she had to pause now and then to rest. One night when Tomo came to visit, the three of us went out to eat at Mr. Nakasono's place.

Yet, at the beginning of fall, when we would finally get a cool breeze in the afternoons, her condition took a turn for the worse. Momoko collapsed while she was recuperating at home. Her week of convalescence at home was canceled, and they quickly decided she needed to return to the hospital that day.

"It's time to prepare for the end. That's what the doctors told us yesterday," my uncle told me in a stiff voice over the phone. "Takako, when you have time, could you go see her again?"

This brief phone call from my uncle was all it took to obliterate the fleeting hope I'd held on to for half a year. And it was also in that instant when things finally became clear, the parts I'd been trying not to shine a light on, the reality I'd been trying desperately to turn away from.

The next day, I used one of my vacation days at work and rushed over to Momoko's room at the hospital. The anxiety and worry were tearing me apart as I opened the door to her room.

"Oh, Takako." I was struck by the sound of her voice. "You're back again?" It was the same speech she always gave. But there was no comparison between her voice then and how feeble she sounded now. There was no strength in her voice. Until then, I had rarely seen her lying down in bed, but today, perhaps because she was in pain, she didn't get up even when I came into the room. And only a week ago she'd seemed so healthy.

When her eyes met mine, she let out a laugh, almost like a shy little girl.

"Momoko . . ." Without meaning to, I said her name like I was about to cry. But I immediately regained my composure and did my best to smile. "My uncle called. It gave me a scare."

"I look pretty awful, don't I?"

Her new room was a single. Momoko was alone, lying in the middle of a white bed. The room was relatively large, but its size made it feel strangely oppressive. A great number of people had spent time in this room, in this very bed, and now they were gone. Somehow you could feel that keenly just by being in the room.

"Uncle Satoru?"

"He went back to the house a bit ago to change. It was so sudden we didn't have anything prepared."

"Oh . . ."

I waited there until my uncle returned. Unlike before, Momoko didn't try to hurry me and tell me to go home early. She lay there quietly.

When I was leaving, she muttered, "Takako, thank you for always coming to see me. Will you come back?"

"That doesn't sound like you, Momoko."

"I mean, it's embarrassing, don't you think? I only talk this way when I'm feeling weak."

"Sincerity is more becoming."

"Hey, you're talking to an old lady, you know."

"I'll come back soon. So, get some rest. Okay?"

Momoko turned just her head toward me, smiled, and said "Yes" meekly. I felt a warm lump inside. It was somewhere in my chest, throbbing. I could feel it rising inside me, like it was trying to find a way out. I left the room and leaned against the wall in the hallway. I looked up and stared into the fluorescent lights on the ceiling until the feeling passed.

From that point on, because my uncle often went to be with my aunt at the hospital, the Morisaki Bookshop was closed more frequently. Momoko objected, but no matter what she said to him, my uncle stubbornly refused to stop coming to the hospital.

I could see my uncle was getting skinnier. He was skinny to begin with, but he was far beyond that now; his body was shrinking so much that it was painful to look at him. Dark circles formed under his eyes, and his cheeks sank in; he seemed to age five years over the course of a few months.

He was always absent-minded—even to the point that at times a customer would be holding out a book in front of him, and he wouldn't notice.

"Uncle, you've got a customer," I'd say, gently nudging his shoulder.

"Oh, forgive me. I'm sorry," he'd say as he hastily accepted the book and rang it up. Once he was finished, however, he'd go back to staring off into space again.

There was no change in the shop's appearance. The books were put on the shelves where they belonged following my uncle's system of classification, and the place was scrupulously clean. Yet I couldn't help feeling that the shop now felt suffocating to be in.

I tried to tell my uncle gently that he might try to take a little break. But he wouldn't listen. "If I'm working," he told me, "I don't have to think about everything."

"But if you keep this up, you'll collapse."

"I'm fine. I'm not that fragile."

Even though he was normally so fragile that he was always whining, right now he was pretending to be tough.

"You know Momoko was trying to apologize for everything she put me through. Hearing her actually say it aloud threw me off. I didn't know how to respond. That's why I have to prove to her that I'm doing just fine."

"Uncle . . ." I couldn't find the words to say.

"I'm useless," my uncle mumbled to himself. He was sitting astride Roy, still staring off into space, lost in grief. "The past six months, I wanted to resign myself to letting her go, but it's no use. As the moment gets closer, I just want to be with her for as long as I can. I keep selfishly wishing for her not to die yet. She's already resigned herself to it. In the end, I'm the one who can't accept it. I'm just being greedy."

"You're not greedy," I said firmly.

My uncle shook his head.

"No, I am. Lately I find myself thinking that I'd sacrifice anything if it meant she would live even a little bit longer." My uncle smiled grimly. "I'm hopelessly selfish," he added in conclusion, and then he suddenly seemed to come back to himself, and he looked at me.

"I'm sorry. I'm just complaining."

"It's okay. The only thing I can do to help is to listen."

It really was about the only thing I could do. It broke my heart to be so powerless.

My uncle, ignoring how despondent I was, suddenly shouted "Oh" and stood up. "It smells like sweet olive blossoms," he said, and inhaled deeply and closed his eyes.

I took a breath too, caught up in the excitement.

"I guess it's already that time of year," I said.

My uncle gave his first proper smile of the day.

"Momoko's always liked this scent. I hope she can smell it at the hospital too." My uncle closed his eyes for a long time, like he was making a wish.

The days went by, and time kept on passing. No one can stop that.

The last time I saw Momoko was a quiet afternoon in the beginning of October. The autumn air blowing in through the open window felt pleasant, and the scent of sweet olive blossoms was carried into the room. The curtains swayed slightly in the breeze. Surrounded by this quiet, you could hear the soft sound of rustling fabric. That's the kind of afternoon it was.

When he saw me come in, my uncle mumbled something about having an errand to run and quickly left the room. Looking back, I think it was probably his thoughtful way of giving us some time alone, since he knew it might be the last time Momoko and I saw each other.

"Hey, can I talk to you about something?" Momoko said, once she opened her eyes after nodding off for a while. "I feel much better today. And I'm in the mood for a story."

"What kind of story?"

"Any kind. How about a memory from when you were a kid?"

Caught short by the sudden request, I thought through what kind of memory might fit the situation. A funny story would be good. Something to make her laugh. Something to let her forget about the pain she was in, even if only for a moment.

"Now that you mention it, there was this one time that my uncle took me to a summer festival. It was before you two got married."

"Really? Satoru did this?"

"It was the last night of our usual summer trip to my grandfather's house. In the distance, we could hear the music from the festival in their neighborhood. I was whining because I wanted to go so badly. My mother said we had a flight the next morning so we should go to bed early, but I loved being with my uncle, and the thought that we wouldn't be there the next day made me miss him so much. And so he brought me to the festival. My uncle was in high spirits too, of course. Ultimately, the festival ended right after we arrived, but I was content that I got to go. It was this incredible feeling, like I'd won something. We couldn't buy anything at the stalls, so my uncle bought us ice cream at a convenience store nearby, and the two of us walked back together, eating our ice cream and feeling sad."

As I talked, I could vaguely recall the light of the paper lanterns, the sound of the crowds of people talking, and even the way the afternoon heat lingered in the evening air. I'd forgotten about that, but now it felt like a really precious memory.

"That's all. I'm sorry. I wish I'd thought of a more interesting story."

Momoko was gazing up at the ceiling as I apologized. She slowly shook her head. "I can imagine it somehow. That scene . . . It's wonderful. I wish I'd been there. I wish I'd gone to a festival with Satoru and you when you were a child."

"No way, Momoko. I told you we barely even made it there."

"But isn't that just so like the two of you?" Momoko said and giggled, and I ended up laughing too. At least I meant to laugh, but then I felt something cold drip on the back of my hand. Before I had time to react, it was like raindrops were falling from my face onto my hands. No, I can't, I thought, but it was already too late.

I had decided I wasn't going to cry in front of Momoko. I thought it would be shameful, since she was the one suffering the most. Although I'd decided I wouldn't cry, on that afternoon alone it was no use. Once I let go, there was no stopping it. That lump that had been growing inside my chest had found a way out.

"I'm sorry," I apologized as I tried to find a way to stop my tears. But once those emotions had found an outlet, there was no reasoning with it, the tears kept coming and coming.

"I'm sorry. I'm so sorry." I hung my head, repeating the same words over and over, and Momoko reached out her hand and touched my hair, and stroked my head like she was taking it in her arms.

"It's okay," she said, almost whispering in my ear. "Don't apologize."

Hearing Momoko whisper gently to me like that made me cry even more.

"But . . . I am sorry."

"Takako, don't apologize, okay?"

I managed to nod through my tears. Momoko weakly pinched my cheek. Her fingertips were very cold. On impulse, I took her pale, cold hand in mine and held it tight. Such a small hand. Momoko had always had small hands, like a little girl. But now they felt so much smaller. As soon as I held her hand, it seemed to shrink, and it seemed like it might go on shrinking until it vanished like a dusting of snow.

"Thank you for crying over me," Momoko said. "When you're sad, don't try to hold it in. It's okay to cry a lot. The tears are there because you've got to go on living. You're going on living, which means there'll be more things to cry about. They'll come at you from all sides. So don't ever try to hide from the sadness. When it comes, cry it out. It's better to keep moving forward with that sadness; that's what it means to live."

Yes, I nodded, holding her hand tightly in mine. The scent of the sweet olive blossoms lingered faintly in the room. Even as I went on sobbing, I could smell it.

"Hey, Takako, I don't regret anything. I think I was really lucky that I got to see Satoru again, and I got to spend the time I had left with him at my side, and I was given the time to say goodbye.

What's more, I even got to become close with you. I couldn't wish
for any more than that."

So that was it. Momoko had come back to my uncle because she
wanted to say goodbye. Maybe the reason why she didn't seem any
different after she found out about her relapse was that her wish
had already come true. And even after she was hospitalized, and she
lived under the watchful eye of the people around her, she always
seemed dignified. Because she truly had no regrets.

After she told me this, she went on talking. "But, um . . . there's
just one thing I still worry about after I die," she said abruptly. "I feel
bad asking you this because I've already imposed on you so much,
but I do have one final request. Can I ask you one more thing?"

"A request?" I looked at her, with my nose running and my face
wet with tears. She stared back at me intently, her eyes full of deter-
mination.

"You know Satoru hasn't once let me see him grieving since he
learned my cancer had relapsed. He smiles, and I can see in his face
that he's always carrying the whole burden himself. But I'm painfully aware how sad it makes him to see me like this. He denies it, of
course. But my worry is that after I'm gone, he won't let himself cry,
and he won't let himself be dependent on anyone, and that he'll live
trying to bear the burden of this grief himself. Because he's a very
kind and a very foolish man."

"I see."

In the back of my mind, I pictured my uncle's pained smile, and
it made my heart break.

"That's why if it seems like Satoru isn't able to cry after I die, I
want you to be with him. We never had any children, so you're the
only person I can think of to ask. If Satoru closes himself off from
the world, yell at him and make him cry. What I hope more than
anything is that if he cries, he'll be able to move forward."

Momoko squeezed my hand hard. Her face contorted like she was in pain.

"I'm sorry. It's selfish of me to ask this of you."

I looked Momoko in the eye and said, "I'll do it. I promise." I wanted her to know that I'd understood.

"Thank you. That's a huge relief," she said, and the look on her face finally softened into a smile. It was a tender smile that showed how deeply relieved she felt now. Then she gently wiped the tears from my face with her handkerchief. Like a child with its mother, I closed my eyes and didn't move a muscle as she wiped all my tears away. We stayed that way for a long time.

It was a truly peaceful afternoon. The cream-colored curtains swayed quietly in the breeze.

Momoko died in the early morning, three days later.

15

The funeral was held at my uncle's house. It was a bright and sunny October day, worthy of Momoko. Momoko's parents had passed away when she was young, and the few relatives in attendance were people like my parents, but instead, there were many people she knew from Jimbocho: Sabu and the other bookshop regulars, then the owner of the Saveur and Takano, Mr. Nakasono and the familiar faces from the restaurant, plus the innkeeper and the people she'd worked with at the mountain inn . . . and of course, Wada and Tomo. Tomo and the innkeeper rushed over right away to assist with the preparations for the wake, and they were a tremendous help when my mother and I found ourselves shorthanded.

From that alone, I could see how much everyone loved Momoko, how precious she was, and it made me profoundly happy. And everyone was in agreement that it should be a cheerful sendoff. Right up to the end, Momoko had kept smiling her reassuring smile, as radiant as a flower in bloom. Clearly, it would've been wrong to say goodbye to a person like that with a grim funeral.

As we gathered around her coffin at the wake, we laughed together like we always did. Sabu, who was quite drunk, launched into an endless monologue that lasted more than thirty minutes about how he wasn't able to fulfill his promise to Momoko to share one of his talents with her: performing some traditional *naniwabushi* ballads for her. In the end, his wife actually told him not to embarrass himself. A woman, who was Momoko's distant relative, scowled at us as if to say there was something inappropriate in us carrying on like this, but she completely misread the situation. There was sadness in it too. We just wanted to express our grief in a way that would make Momoko happy.

It was a good funeral, I think, one that will remain with us. I'm still convinced that it made Momoko happy. Momoko seemed at peace in her coffin, even cheerful. We talked about it. "Momoko looks good," we said; "she kind of looks like she's enjoying this along with us"; "definitely."

Yet there was one thing that worried me.

It was Uncle Satoru. He hardly opened his mouth during the funeral. He didn't touch any of the food or drink. All he did was go around bowing politely to everyone who'd come, expressing his gratitude again and again. Even when Momoko was cremated, he just gazed up at the sky while Sabu and the owner of the Saveur wiped away their tears. He had such a distant look in his eye, it was like he was trying to see to the outer limits of Earth's atmosphere. If he had broken down and cried at that moment, we were prepared to warmly welcome him into the fold. To be honest, I hoped he would. I hoped he would let himself depend on us. To mourn with us, and, if possible, to allow us to offer some words of comfort. But my uncle wouldn't show any weakness in front of others.

My uncle was the one who was with Momoko at her deathbed. I don't know what it was like. I don't know what he thought or what he said at that moment. Yet, based on how he was at the funeral, I got the impression that he was avoiding showing what he was feeling, just as Momoko had feared.

"I think I'm going to close the store for a little while."

It wasn't long after the funeral that my uncle made his announcement. I had stopped by the Morisaki Bookshop on my way home from work because I was worried about him. But the shutters were closed, even though it was still business hours. I got worried, and called my uncle at home right away; I had to wait awhile before he finally answered. When I asked him about it, he said, "I've decided to close for a while," sounding terribly exhausted.

I felt confused, and at the same time, a part of me thought, "Yes, of course." I'd had a slight hunch that he might say something like that soon.

"Are you in physical pain?" I asked.

"No, it's not that," he said, sounding listless on the other end of the line.

"Are you eating properly? Could I come over and make something for you?"

"I'm fine. I'm just a little tired. So . . ."

And with that the line went dead.

But my uncle had wasted away so much in the space of a month that I agreed that he should rest for a while. Get some proper rest, I thought, and when you're feeling better, come back to the shop. My uncle had already decided it was better that way.

I thought it would last a few days, certainly no longer than a week. Yet no matter how long I waited, the shutters of the Morisaki Bookshop remained closed. At some point, a handwritten sign on a piece of white paper had been stuck to the shutter, announcing, "We're closed for a while." The paper now dangled, after being battered by the wind and rain.

"How long is Satoru planning to wait till he opens the shop?" Sabu, who once seemed to come by every day, now seemed sad to have lost his place to go.

"I understand the feeling, but I still want Satoru to open the shop. We might not be much, but as regular customers, we can support him. But if he isn't around, then there's no way we can cheer him up."

On the phone, Sabu asked me to pass on the message when I saw my uncle.

He was right. There were other people who were waiting for the shop to open. But I would think my uncle already knew that . . .

The shop was still shuttered, and my uncle had let it remain closed for roughly a month. What was he doing all this time? He had basically shut himself up inside the house. Until Momoko passed away, he had insisted on running the shop, no matter what happened. Maybe he had put himself under too much strain, and now all at once it had come undone.

I went to the house in Kunitachi to see how he was doing. On the phone, he always told me he was eating right, but his voice sounded so listless that I decided to buy some groceries at the supermarket on the way so I could get him to eat something.

I stopped at a big supermarket near the train station that I'd been to many times with Momoko. She had a deep love for the place, because when they had sales the prices were much cheaper than the other stores nearby. It used to make me laugh when we went there together to see the way she would put the whole weight of her small, nimble frame on the shopping cart and then go gliding swiftly down the aisle. It was trivial little memories like this that kept coming back to me after she died. In those moments, it felt like I had a gaping hole in my heart. That's what it was like losing someone precious to you. I felt it now in so many different places and in so many different ways.

After I finished shopping, I headed for my uncle's house, walking down the alley of their residential street with supermarket shopping bags in both hands. Some dragonflies were flying across the sky, which was now bright red at sunset. One of them came down to me and acted as if it might land on my shoulder, then it flew off into the sky. As I walked, I felt like I was going to cry. I walked faster until I was moving at a brisk pace, rushing to get to my uncle's house.

Although I had told him I was coming that evening, he didn't answer the door when I rang the bell. It wasn't locked. When I let myself in and called to him upstairs, the only response I got was a "Yes" coming from my uncle's room.

Before I went up, I placed my hands together in prayer in front of the Buddhist altar to Momoko in the living room. The photograph on the altar had been taken six months earlier by a regular customer who was an amateur photographer. She was smiling, with the Morisaki Bookshop in the background. It was a wonderful picture. Seeing it brought back so many emotions.

Then I climbed up the stairs, knocked on my uncle's door, and opened it. Although the sun had already begun to set, my uncle was still in a sweatshirt and sweatpants, lying down on his futon. His hair was a mess, and he was so unshaven he looked like a cartoon burglar. He was in such a pitiful state that I blurted out, "Uncle!"

He looked at me drowsily and dumbly greeted me with a "Hey."

Was this how he'd been spending the whole day? There were bags of potato chips and bento containers from the convenience store scattered around the room.

"What are you doing?"

"Sleeping."

From an opening in the covers, my uncle thrust out both of his hands, flashing a peace sign.

"This is hardly peace!" I yanked off the covers, and my uncle curled up in a ball like a roly-poly bug. Undaunted, I threw open the curtains he'd drawn closed.

"Stop! If I'm exposed to light, I'll turn to ash."

"You idiot." I realized my voice sounded like I was about to cry. Why did I feel such relief? My uncle was still perfectly alive, he was still here. It's not that I actually believed that he'd end up following Momoko to the grave. But the way he'd been carrying the burden on his own lately made it seem like that wasn't out of the realm of possibility. Which is why it made me happy to see him there—even if he was acting like a roly-poly.

"Sorry, Takako."

"It's fine. What matters now is I'm making you dinner. Want to eat together? I'm sure you haven't had a proper meal in a while."

"Hey, thanks." He nodded obediently.

I took over the kitchen and made his favorite curry. Naturally, it was the Vermont Curry brand—mild. The kitchen didn't seem to have been used in a while. It was exceedingly clean.

I brought some egg drop soup and a plate piled with curry and salad into the living room and then I called out to my uncle. When I suggested he go wash his face and shave before eating, he obediently headed to the bathroom. I told him he ought to change his sweatsuit too because it was looking a little dingy, and he went up to the second floor and changed into another sweatsuit that was exactly the same color and style.

However, when I came into the living room and saw my uncle, I screamed. The area around his mouth was so covered in blood it was bright red.

"Huh, what?" My uncle's mouth hung open. He tried to approach me, and I shrieked.

"Blood! Blood!"

"Ah, I hadn't shaved in so long, I might've hacked myself up a bit," he said in a daze. He wiped his mouth with a tissue, but when he saw how stained with blood it was, he cried out, "Whoa, that's not looking good."

"Don't stand there 'whoa'ing. Try looking at yourself in the mirror."

"Why would I want to see how terrible I look?"

He was more or less aware, it seemed, of how terrible he looked. But even in moments like this he acted in a way that was hard to gauge, so I stayed vigilant.

Eventually, the two of us sat down at the table. His eyes still looked drowsy, and his expression was still the same as he shoveled the curry into his mouth robotically. It didn't feel like we were really having a meal together. Still, it was better than him not eating at all.

"Sabu and the others, they're worried about you. They want to see you back running the shop again." I passed on the message from Sabu, as I ate the curry that wasn't spicy enough for me.

"Oh, really? I feel bad about that."

"Everyone's waiting for you."

"Oh."

"How about we go together next time? I'll help you."

"I'll think about it."

There was no emotion behind what he was saying. He was just stringing words together. Then he said, "Sorry, I'm full," and put down his spoon. He hadn't even eaten half of it. He was still fairly weak. There was no way I could leave him like this. I had made a promise to Momoko, a promise that I would help him move forward and go on living. But I had absolutely no idea how to go about doing that. All I was able to do was make him meals, do some laundry, and be there for him to talk to. If he would at least open the shop, then I could be of more help to him.

I worried about this, and then I cautiously brought up the subject. "Uncle?"

"Yeah?"

"You aren't thinking about just leaving the shop closed like this, right? It's important to take some time off, of course. You're just taking some time off though, right?"

My uncle looked up as if what I'd said surprised him. But the gloomy look in his eyes returned and he looked down again.

"I don't know . . ."

"Uncle . . ."

"I genuinely don't know. It's not that I don't want to keep the shop. I am perfectly aware that our customers are waiting for me. It's just really hard. Momoko and I started at the bookshop together. Even when Momoko was gone, I ran the shop because I knew she was alive, even if she was living in a faraway place. Because I wanted to hold on to somewhere she could come back to, if she got tired or hurt, no matter what happened."

As he talked, my uncle's expression stiffened again. At times, his face contorted in pain.

"But it's really hard to be there right now. There are too many memories. And all those memories are vivid reminders that she's dead. I don't want the time to pass. Because if time passes, Momoko will drift further away from me."

My uncle stared at the clock on the wall across from me like he was giving it a glare.

The clock had been in use since my grandfather's era, and it was ticking away, still keeping time today. My uncle seemed to think he could stop the hands of that clock.

"I understand how you feel. At least, I think I do a little. I mean, I loved Momoko too. But you're making a mistake. You know it's a mistake, right? We're alive. There's no stopping time. So we have to keep on moving forward, one step at a time, no matter how heavy our legs feel." I felt a lump in my throat, but I kept on talking. "Even if it means leaving behind the person who died."

"Takako . . ."

I tried to look him in the eye as I talked, but he quickly looked away. I went on talking nevertheless. "You don't understand, Uncle. You taught me so many things. All the things you said. That's why even though it might not be clear in my head, I'm trying to find the words to get through to you. It's what you taught me, isn't it? How important it is to talk face-to-face and say what you have to say."

His eyes remained downcast the whole time, so it was hard to tell if he was listening. But in the end, he muttered a few words. He sounded like he'd given up. "You're right. I don't understand. But that's okay."

The Morisaki Bookshop remained closed after that too. The only thing I could think to do was keep the shop clean. If you leave old books shut in a room without air circulation, they'll mildew and become unsellable. I wanted to prepare the shop for when my uncle felt ready to reopen. I knew that was what Momoko would've wanted.

On the way home from work, I used the key I still had from when I lived in the building, and went in through the back door of the bookshop. Because it had been left for a whole month, the air was heavy and stagnant. It was filled with the scent of damp mildew. In the darkness, I felt around with my hands and ferreted out the switch. When I flipped it on, the fluorescent lights flickered to life, and it was suddenly bright inside. When I sneezed from the dust, the sound filled the room.

First, I opened all the windows and aired out the room. Then I took time to sweep the floors with a broom, then diligently wiped down the bookshelves and the floors with a dust cloth. Under the overly bright white lights, the shop looked terribly empty, like some storeroom deep underground. Just being in that room, I felt sadness growing inside me till it was unbearable. Even Roy, the do-nut pillow, neglected by his owner for such a long time, somehow seemed lonely.

My heart ached to see that this place that my uncle loved so much, that mattered to so many people, had now been discarded as if it were no longer needed.

I went upstairs to the second floor and watered Momoko's potted plants on the windowsill with her watering can. Having gone so many days without water, all of them had shriveled and now looked down as if they were cowering. "Sorry guys," I murmured as I watered each one thoroughly.

It was after nine o'clock when I left the shop. The night air was dry, and the wind was so cold it seemed to pierce my skin. I winced. In the darkness, the air I exhaled looked so white it shocked me.

The world was trying to usher in winter.

One season would give way to the next. The loss of a single person couldn't change that. It should've been obvious, but it now felt like an outrage.

I turned to look back at the bookshop and whispered, "Don't worry. I'll be back." Then I walked away.

"Takako, you're doing the right thing." Wada was comforting me on the phone.

Lately, I'd been feeling down all the time. Though I knew it was wrong, I'd find myself depending on Wada.

"But what I said didn't get through to him. I'm at a loss . . ."

What could I really do to get my uncle to move forward with his life again the way Momoko had asked?

"There's only so much you can do. Your uncle lost the person who mattered most to him. Maybe I shouldn't say this, but if it were me, and I knew I would never see Momoko again, then I might give it all up too."

I found myself imagining the reverse scenario. I only imagined it for an instant, but it made everything go black in my mind. He was right; I was truly sad that Momoko was dead, but there was no way it could come close to the sadness my uncle felt. I regretted how I'd righteously told my uncle at his house that I understood how he felt a little bit. For my uncle, Momoko was what Kazue was for Sakunosuke Oda.

"For my uncle, I guess, the Morisaki Bookshop is also a symbol of all the time he spent with Momoko."

There are too many memories in the bookshop. I remembered what my uncle looked like as he said that to me. Memories that stretched across twenty years, of happiness and sorrow, had accumulated in that site, layer upon layer.

"He must find those memories unbearable right now," Wada said. "But the time will come when the place will be precious to him precisely because it holds all those memories. Until that day comes, maybe you just have to put your faith in him, and wait for him to be ready."

"That's all I can do now."

After that, every few days I made time to head over to the shop. All I did was air it out, clean, and check that there were no signs of mildew in the collection. But it was enough to make sure that he could open the shop anytime he was ready.

On one of those nights, Tomo accompanied me. To tell the truth, it was sometimes hard for me to be in the bookshop alone at night; I would find myself remembering all kinds of things. So, I was grateful that she was with me.

Working together, we finished cleaning in less than a half hour. Tomo was so full of enthusiasm she suggested we try to straighten up the collection of books on the second floor, but I dismissed the idea, telling her we'd do it some other time, because if we started now, we'd never make the last train.

I felt indebted to Tomo for coming, and for her help at Momoko's funeral. I was truly grateful. This seemed like a good moment to tell her again how thankful I was.

As usual, she was too modest. "No, no, please. It was nothing," she said.

"But you really have gone to so much trouble on my behalf," I said, insisting on telling her how grateful I was.

"When I go back at the end of the year, I think I'm going to see my sister's former boyfriend again," she said suddenly.

"What? Really?"

"I am. I'm going to apologize to him properly. He's been worried about me all this time, it seems, yet I've been avoiding him. It might sound like an exaggeration, but I feel I need to set things right. I think once I do, I'll be able to see a way forward."

"Oh, I think that's absolutely wonderful."

I was delighted to hear Tomo had come so far. I supported it wholeheartedly.

"It's thanks to you and Takano that I was able to get to this point."

"No, no," I said, flustered. "I really didn't do anything."

She giggled.

"Now you're the one saying that. We're just alike. I'm not here today because I want you to thank me. And the same goes for you. That's just how we are."

Then something happened at the beginning of December, around the time I noticed the neighborhood was lit up in glittering lights for Christmas.

On that night, I went again to the shop to air it out and clean up, following my usual routine. I had more or less finished my work, and had told myself it was time to go home, but I made no attempt to leave. For some reason, I found it hard to go. I thought, Let me stick around a little longer. For no particular reason, I sat down at the counter in my usual seat, staring off into the distance. Although I'd turned on the heat, I'd had the windows open until a few minutes earlier, so it was as cold inside the shop as it was outside. I rubbed my hands together and wondered how long it would take to warm up.

When I looked at the clock on the wall, it said it was nearly ten. I should leave soon, I thought, but my body wouldn't budge. Outside the window, a lively group went down the street, probably on their way home from an end-of-the-year party.

By chance, my gaze landed upon the account book tucked away in the utility cabinet below the counter. Though we called it an account book, there was nothing major written in it. It was the sort of thing where we wrote down the books we sold and the price. The leather-bound book my uncle normally used was thicker and threadbare from years of use. This one was thinner, and still relatively new. What's going on here? I thought, and pulled out the account book that had been pushed all the way in the back like someone was trying to hide it.

When I opened it up, I blurted out, "Oh . . ." On each page, there was something written in densely packed characters.

They were things that Momoko had written. It was not quite a diary, it was more like simple notes, but she recorded the date and the weather, along with things that went on in the bookshop. The dates began not long after Momoko suddenly returned home and started living on the second floor of the bookshop.

"Satoru, sold books again today, in a good mood."

"Setting aside the Ōgai Mori book Mr. Kurada wants."

"Don't forget to organize the book carts!"

"Sold nothing before noon because of the rain. Heartache."

"Takako isn't doing so well today? Worried."

After I read the first few pages, I closed the book suddenly. Some of Momoko's thoughts were still here in these pages. The days she spent with my uncle and me were inscribed in this book. It might not be a masterpiece to be read for generations, or a text left by a great writer, but for my uncle and me it was precious.

I needed my uncle to read it right away. With that thought in mind, I got up from my chair, but in that instant the back door was thrown open with a bang, and I jumped back in surprise. When I looked over, I saw that my uncle was somehow standing in the entrance, breathing heavily. And with a look of shock on his face. But his expression quickly changed to disappointment when he saw me.

"Oh, it's you, Takako," he muttered with a weak smile. "I found myself back in the neighborhood walking past the bookshops. Then I saw the lights were on in the shop . . ."

I didn't have to ask what happened next. I could tell just by looking at the expression on his face. My uncle tricked himself into believing Momoko was inside, despite the fact that there was no logical reason why that should be. I, on the other hand, was so stunned by my uncle's sudden appearance that I couldn't speak.

"Takako . . . ?" My uncle was staring at me with a baffled look on his face.

I couldn't shake the feeling that something strange was happening here, something I couldn't put into words. There must be some other power at work here. The timing was too much. First I find Momoko's writing in the account book, and then at the very moment when I wish I could show it to my uncle, he comes bursting into the room . . .

"So, um," I said, still feeling overwhelmed. I stood in front of my uncle and held out the account book. "This is the account book Momoko wrote in."

"Momoko?" For a moment, my uncle just stared blankly at the book in my hands, then he slowly reached out his hands to take it.

"Maybe I should sit down?"

My uncle sat on Roy, and gently turned the pages of the account book. As he carefully read through each handwritten line, he suddenly cracked a smile. "When did she start doing this?"

"I know, right?"

Finally the heater was kicking in, and the room began to warm up. My uncle turned the pages, as if transfixed. I could hear the rustling of paper. I thought I might make tea, but right when I went up to the second floor to get the teapot and teacups, I heard my uncle suddenly shout, "Ah!"

"What is it?" I peeked suspiciously over his shoulder, then I called out too. There on the last page of the book was a long passage that began "To Satoru . . ." She had noted the date too: it was two days before she collapsed and had to be taken to the hospital in an ambulance.

"It's . . ." I said, and my uncle nodded silently without looking away from the book. His hand was trembling slightly.

"Uh, maybe I should step outside for a bit?"

"No, it's okay. Stay here."

"Got it," I said, and then I stayed quiet.

After my uncle had taken some time to read through what she'd written, he gazed up at the ceiling for a long while. Then he stood up straight and read through it slowly once more. During that time, I walked up and down the aisles, looking around the shop restlessly. I was caught off guard when my uncle suddenly tried to hand me the account book without saying a word.

"That's okay. I don't need to read it," I said.

"It's fine. I want you to." He was looking right at me, holding out the book as if urging me to hurry up and take it.

I hesitated for a moment, but eventually I took the book.

To Satoru,

How long will it take for you to find this? If you've already gotten back on your feet again, then there's really no need to read this. In that case, feel free to blow your nose in it and toss it in the trash.

I thought about leaving a will, but then I'm sure you would've read it right away. That seemed pointless, so I decided instead to leave this for you. So, please read it as an alternative to a will.

Unfortunately, I didn't end up outliving you. I guess this is my fate somehow. I apologize that I had to be the one to leave first.

It breaks my heart to leave you behind because you're such a crybaby. Even when you proposed to me, you cried. "You might be fine without me," you said, "but I'd be useless without you." At the time, I laughed and said, "This guy's a mess," but I was really happy. There's no one else on earth who could have told me something so pathetic and wonderful. After all, I would be useless without you too.

Afterward, through the joy and sorrow, we had many happy times together. But I know I caused you a lot of trouble. Still, you took me in after I chose to leave. And you asked me to come back. You're so infuriatingly kind. So kind that you wouldn't let me go in the end. You never gave up on me.

I've decided that from now until the day I die, I'm going to say "thank you" to you every day without fail. It still won't be enough to express my gratitude for all that you've done for me, but I'd be happy if I can show at least a small portion of how much I owe you.

Um . . . my writing is getting more and more discombobulated. Is that how you write discombobulated? If I'm wrong, please don't snap at me, okay?

Anyhow, here's my request: just as I have wonderful memories of being with you, I don't want you to let your memories of me be sad, I want you to remember the fun and happiness. If you find yourself spending every day in the same anguish you felt when I was in the hospital, you've got to know that's not what I hoped for. I want you to smile. I love the way you smile.

There are a lot of people around you who will support you. Remember that, and lean on them. There's one particular person I trust and love above all, and I'm going to ask her to do a little something for me.

One more thing.

Please give my regards to the Morisaki Bookshop. The proof that we were together lies there. I know how much you love the shop, and the truth is I love it too. If I'd been able, I would've wanted to see you working there just a little bit longer. After all, it's when you're in the shop that you shine the brightest. Of course, it was just a selfish wish on my part. But if that's the case, I hope that after this you and the Morisaki Bookshop can move forward together.

Please look after the shop. It's full of our memories together, and the memories of so many other people too.

Momoko Morisaki

She never played fair, did she? If she had this up her sleeve, she could have at least told me. Did she anticipate that my uncle would close the shop? Or had she left it as some kind of insurance? I didn't know, but what I did know was that this note was full of love for my uncle and the Morisaki Bookshop. And this shop was teeming with the thoughts and hopes and feelings she experienced in her life.

And she referred to me as the person she "trusted and loved above all."

"She really was such a troublemaker." When I handed back the account book, my uncle gave me a bitter smile. "Takako, what did she ask you to do? Was it too much trouble?"

"That doesn't matter now, Uncle," I said and my uncle looked back at me, his eyes wide with surprise.

"What?" he said, and smiled at me.

"Momoko told me, 'I want him to fully grieve, and then look ahead and go on living.'"

"No, Takako, I . . ."

But I went on, ignoring my uncle's attempt to respond. "I can't really do anything for you. I can't do anything but cry with you. So, you don't have to grieve alone anymore."

My uncle stared intently at the account book in his hand as if trying to resist it. He looked hard at it for a long time. And then just as I realized his lips were trembling slightly, he suddenly let out a scream that sounded like the call of some wild beast. He raised his voice as if straining to force out all the air inside him and channel it into a wordless scream. I went to his side and rubbed his back that now seemed so skinny. When I looked at my uncle, my eyes suddenly filled with tears.

"When I went to see her in the hospital, she always said 'Thank you.' I told her to stop because it was disconcerting, but she kept on . . . even at the end . . ."

Now both of us were openly sobbing. We wailed out loud and cried uncontrollably. My uncle crouched and covered his face like he was going to collapse right then and there. I stayed beside him and rubbed his back, ignoring the tears dripping from my face onto the floor.

Our sobs echoed in the bookshop late into the night. Our voices, reverberating inside the room, made the air tremble. It was as if the shop itself joined in to mourn Momoko's death with us. As if it too were grieving.

We went on crying for as long as we needed to.

No matter how much we cried, our tears would not run dry.

That sound will echo in the shop forever.

The night gently enveloped us, my uncle and me, and the whole Morisaki Bookshop.

Surprisingly, it was Wada who told me the following evening that the Morisaki Bookshop had reopened for business.

"I've got good news," he said on the phone, sounding unusually excited. "I finished work early today, so I went by the bookshops in Jimbocho. And then I saw, believe it or not, that the lights were on in the Morisaki Bookshop," he said, almost without stopping to breathe.

"Is that right?"

I was still at work, but as I stood in the hallway of my office, I let out a sigh of relief.

"Huh? You don't seem that happy? Did you already hear it from your uncle or Sabu?"

"No, I just knew it was going to be okay. Thank you, my prince, for your efforts."

After last night, my uncle completely changed, and by the next day he was already opening the shop—that was just like him. I, on the other hand, embarrassed myself by going to work with my face still puffy from weeping my eyes out.

"Oh really? Anyway, it's good news. I was so happy it was like it was happening to me. I got very excited. And even better, when I went in, your uncle brought out tea and said something like, 'Thanks for coming to the funeral.'"

"What? Really?"

"And then I told him I was writing a novel set at the bookshop, and he told me to let him read it when I was finished. He said, 'If it's bad, I'll tear it apart for you.'"

"Hold on there. That's going too far," I said in shock.

"No, I was happy. I was really happy. Whatever the case, it's really good news, Takako."

"It is."

What happened that night seemed like a dream. How I'd suddenly noticed the account book, and how my uncle had appeared right then . . .

Maybe it was all Momoko's doing. She was worried about my uncle being lost in grief . . . The idea briefly crossed my mind, then I decided not to think about it anymore. No matter how much I thought it over, I'd never know. What mattered was that the two of us were looking ahead and going on living. That's all.

"My prince, do you think I should go over after work?"

"Sure, though your uncle will be gone by then."

"Yeah, but still."

"Well, how about the Saveur?"

"Sure."

"Got it."

Outside the window, the sky was already pitch black. The nearly full moon, missing only the slightest sliver, gave off a dazzling light.

16

It's my day off from work, and I'm walking the same familiar street. It may be sunny, but it's still a cold February afternoon. The sky is a soft blue with pale clouds drifting by that look like they were painted with watercolors. I feel warm in the gloves Momoko gave me.

Today, there's a feeling of calm in the air again as I walk through the neighborhood of bookshops in Jimbocho. The people I pass on the street walk at a leisurely pace. I go down a street lined with low buildings and turn onto a side street. And then, just as I expected, I hear someone loudly calling my name.

"Takako!"

I quicken my pace out of embarrassment, and as soon as I get close to the source of the voice, I start to protest. "I told you already—please don't shout my name in the middle of the street!"

"Why though?"

"Haven't I told you it's embarrassing?"

But no matter how often I say it, my uncle will always cause trouble like this. Still, hearing his voice, a part of me feels a sense of security too. This is a place where I belong. A place where I'm welcomed. That's how it feels.

"How are you?" my uncle asks with a big smile on his face.

"I'm good."

"All right, then. Got cold, didn't it? Come on, I'll make us some hot tea."

"Okay."

Satoshi Yagisawa

The Morisaki Bookshop has remained open, keeping its usual hours, ever since the day my uncle reappeared at the shop. It's open for business every day, from morning till night, just like before.

When my uncle initially reopened the shop, he looked at me, on the verge of tears, and whined, "What am I going to do? I've had zero income because I've been closed for more than a month." But despite his griping, there was a bit of excitement around the shop for a while after it reopened. Having heard the rumors, the regulars—Sabu chief among them—started coming by one after another every day. Thanks to which, my uncle's first essential duty after reopening was bowing to each of them to apologize for closing the shop. They were obviously happy, and there wasn't an angry customer among them. My uncle seemed happy to be warmly welcomed back by his many regular customers. The look on his face told me there was no need to worry about him anymore. Of course, he is never going to get over Momoko's death. He'll never fully recover. Yet my uncle has decided to look ahead. He's decided to take in the sadness with everything else and keep moving forward.

There's been a little change too on my end of things. Wada and I are getting married soon. We've already introduced each other to our parents, and now we're looking for a new home. Actually, part of the reason I came to the shop today was to deliver that news. However, my uncle still seems hostile to Wada, and when I casually bring up his name, he suddenly launches into a solemn speech. "What's going to happen to the secondhand book business with the rise of electronic dictionaries and the downturn in the publishing industry?"

Good grief. This guy can bore you to death with this stuff. If Momoko were here, I'm 100 percent sure that's what she'd say. It feels like Momoko's sitting right here, drinking tea with us.

"Well, my uncle's just that kind of guy, isn't he?" As I turn to where Momoko should be and give her a wry smile, my uncle looks at me with his mouth wide open, and says, "Huh? What?"

"Nothing," I lie and smile. "Hey, do you remember when we went to the summer festival together?"

"The summer festival?"

"Yeah, when I was a kid. Didn't we go to one together?"

"Oh, yeah, I guess that's right. We could hear the music, and you just had to go see it."

"That's right. And we ate ice cream from a convenience store and went home."

"You're right. That's it. It was a sad night." He laughs a little, recalling what happened. "But what makes you suddenly think about it now?"

"When Momoko and I were talking at the hospital and she asked me to do something for her, we talked about that night."

"Oh really?"

"She said she wished she'd been there with us."

"Oh."

"I think about that day a lot."

"You do?"

"I do. That's all I wanted to say."

The two of us sip our tea at the same time. I think of the expression on Momoko's face in that moment. My uncle, for his part, seems to be remembering something too. A slight smile forms at the edges of his mouth.

The two of us share this quiet moment thinking of her, and then the door opens with a soft sound. When I turn to look, I say "Hmmm?" aloud in spite of myself. The face that appears in the opening of the sliding door belongs to our mysterious regular: the old man with the paper bag. It's been a long time since he's come in.

The old man carries a paper bag full of books; the look on his face as he comes inside is the same as ever, but I stare at him like I'm ready to devour him with my eyes. That's because the sweater he's wearing is not his usual ancient artifact. It might be the same ashen color, but the one he has on now is a fairly gaudy substitute with a great big deer head stitched into it. On top of that it's new and there's not a single frayed hole in it.

What's even more surprising is that when the old man has rummaged through the shelves and brought several books to the register, he turns to my uncle and starts talking to him. "What's this? You've got things in order again, huh?"

This guy has not once opened his mouth to speak in all this time, no matter what.

Even my uncle looks a little bit surprised.

"Thank you very much. We were closed for a brief period," he says apologetically, as he scratches the back of his head.

"I thought you went out of business," the old man says in a low voice as he fidgets. Without waiting for my uncle to respond, he takes his books, stuffs them into his bulging paper bag, and abruptly leaves the shop.

My uncle and I leave the shop too, as if lured outside by the old man, and stand side by side watching him walk away with unsteady steps.

Overjoyed by our unexpected customer, I say to my uncle, "He looked healthy, didn't he?"

The old man gets farther and farther away until he's finally out of sight. It's cold outside with a chilly breeze, but the little street is lit up in the afternoon light.

"Ah, that was nice."

"He must've come by when you were closed."

"Yeah, I feel bad about that."

"New sweater though, right?"

"It was new."

"It was gaudy though, right?"

"It was gaudy."

"You think he couldn't wear the old one anymore so he got himself a brand-new one?"

"Takako?"

"Sorry, I know. Don't pry, right?"

"Right." My uncle nodded forcefully. He went on talking as if he were admonishing himself. "This is a bookshop. We sell books." The look on his face was cheerful, a little proud.

A writer I like left behind a passage like this in one of his books: "People forget all kinds of things. They live by forgetting. Yet our thoughts endure, the way waves leave traces in the sand." Deep down, I hope that's true. It gives me great hope.

A plane crosses the sky in the distance, leaving behind it a freshly born cloud.

"Hey, Uncle, see that cloud behind the plane?" I pointed to the sky, and my uncle looked up and squinted at it.

The cloud kept growing longer, drawing a bright white line all the way across the pale blue sky.

Here in Tokyo's neighborhood of secondhand bookstores is our little bookshop. It's full of little stories. And it holds within its walls the thoughts and hopes and feelings of a great many people.

Translator's Note

In Satoshi Yagisawa's previous novel, *Days at the Morisaki Bookshop*, Takako finds the book that changes her life by simply closing her eyes and reaching out her hand to pick one at random from the stack of texts beside her futon. One of the joys of the sequel is that it's a novel about the pleasures of searching for books. The truth is, we do not always know why we find ourselves looking for a particular volume. Sometimes, like Sabu, we're returning to an author we remember fondly. Other times we see a title mentioned in another book, like this one, and we're drawn to it as a subtle recommendation. We scan the shelves of some secondhand bookshop for the poetry collection Takako suggests would be ideal to read before bed: Kōtarō Takamura's *The Chieko Poems* (which exists in multiple translations, but I'd recommend the Green Integer edition, translated by John G. Peters, and Kodansha's 1978 edition by Soichi Furuta, which includes reproductions of artwork by Chieko herself). Sometimes looking for one book, we end up finding another. Hyakken Uchida's *Train of Fools* has not yet been translated, but readers can find some of his darker, dreamlike short fiction in Rachel DiNitto's translation, *Realm of the Dead*, or his lighter essays in *The Columbia Anthology of Japanese Essays*, edited and translated by Steven D. Carter. Or they can come to him, like many, through the affectionate tribute Akira Kurosawa paid to his life in his final film, *Madadayo*.

Satoshi Yagisawa

No matter if we are browsing a bookstand in an airport or searching for a rare first edition, our motivation often remains mysterious. The books lie ahead of us; they seem to know things we do not. An old friend once told me how coming across Jun'ichirō Tanizaki's *In Praise of Shadows* in college changed the course of his life. Satoru puts the book in Takako's hands, and tries to get her to read it on the spot. For Takako, reading becomes a way to open herself up to the world, but for her friend Tomoko, literature is a consolation, and, at times, a retreat from the world. Perhaps that's one reason why many of the authors mentioned in this novel are associated with the literature of decadence and the Burai-ha (from Baudelaire to Dazai, Sakaguchi, and Oda). Near the books of fantasy and science fiction on Tomoko's shelves, Takako finds books by the Belgian writer Georges Rodenbach, whose novel *Bruges-la-Morte* has been translated by both Mike Mitchell and Will Stone with its images of the city restored. It has the death-haunted atmosphere of a nineteenth-century *Nadja* or even *Vertigo* (both Sebald's and Hitchcock's).

Later in the novel, Takako and Takano set out in search of a book that, strictly speaking, does not exist. *The Golden Dream* is a book within a book that itself seems to have been invented for this novel, but that doesn't mean we shouldn't go looking for it. Who knows what else we'll find?

We tend to think of reading as a solitary act, but the book you are reading has only found its way into your hands thanks to the ingenuity and diligence of many. I am grateful to Satoshi Yagisawa and to my editor, Sara Nelson, for entrusting me with these delightful novels, and to Setsuko and Simon Winchester, who introduced me to Sara. I'm indebted to my sister, Melissa Ozawa, and Bruno Navasky for their patient and invaluable feedback, and to my father, Yuichi Ozawa, and my friend Hiroko Tabuchi, who helped me along the way. The book was also aided at key moments by my agent, Andrea Blatt, of WME, and at every stage, by my wife, Nicole, who read every word and who always knows where to find the books I'm missing. This translation is dedicated to my sons, Emile and Ilias, who are just discovering the pleasures of reading.

Lying on the floor and scrolling on social media;
wrapped up in bed taking your second nap of the day;
lounging on the sofa and watching TV.
You are not lazy, you are on energy saving mode.

Dancing Snail
Translated by Clare Richards

I'M
NOT
LAZY,
I'M ON
ENERGY
SAVING
MODE

The Korean Non-Fiction Bestseller

After years of battling with depression and
lethargy, author and illustrator Dancing Snail realised the
importance of rest and taking care of our minds when
we feel low. On days you don't feel motivated, are going
through a slump, or simply feel like doing nothing, *I'm Not
Lazy, I'm on Energy Saving Mode*, written in short-form
chapters with charming illustrations, provides you with the
antidote we all need and gives you radical permission to
take the break you don't feel you deserve.

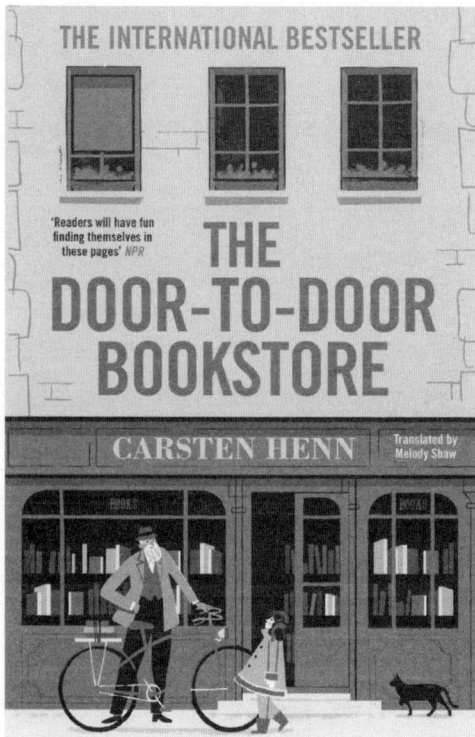

THE INTERNATIONAL BESTSELLER

'Readers will have fun finding themselves in these pages' *NPR*

THE DOOR-TO-DOOR BOOKSTORE

CARSTEN HENN

Translated by Melody Shaw

There's a book written for every one of us...

Carl may be 72 years old, but he's young at heart.
Every night he goes door-to-door delivering books by hand to his loyal customers. He knows their every desire and preference, carefully selecting the perfect story for each person.

One evening as he makes his rounds, nine-year-old Schascha appears. Loud and precocious, she insists on accompanying him - and even tries to teach him a thing or two about books.

When Carl's job at the bookstore is threatened, will the old man and the girl in the yellow raincoat be able to restore Carl's way of life, and return the joy of reading to his little European town.

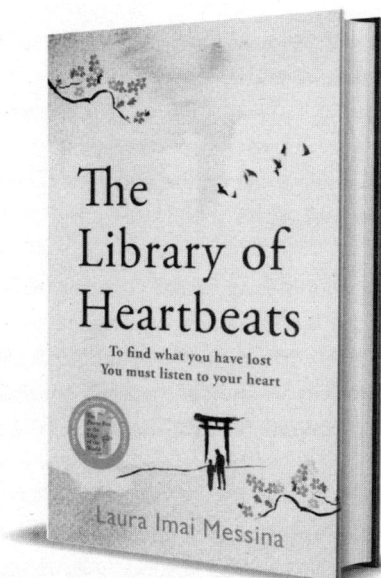

Discover the unmissable new Japanese sensation for lovers of *Days at the Morisaki Bookshop*

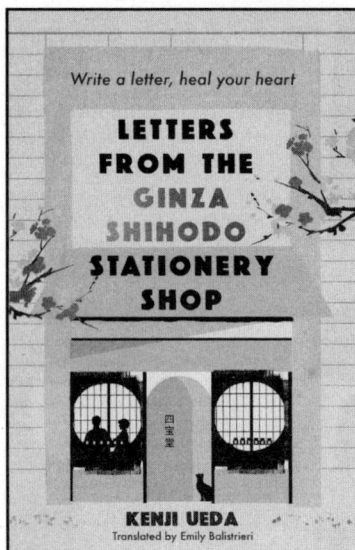

Write a letter, heal your heart

LETTERS FROM THE GINZA SHIHODO STATIONERY SHOP

KENJI UEDA
Translated by Emily Balistrieri

Hidden away in the Ginza neighbourhood is a venerable stationery shop. Inside is everything your heart desires, from the most delicate paper to fountain pens that fit exactly to the shape of your hand. Ken Takarada, the owner, intuits your every need, inviting you to take a seat at a small wooden table on the top floor to write. Here you'll find your words will flow, helping to unlock memories, secret longings and your own mysteries.

Into this shop comes a young man searching for a connection to his past; the hostess of an elegant club, desperate for advice; the lovelorn vice-captain of a high-school archery team; an ageing businessman regretting his choices, and a formerly homeless sushi chef. With his warmth and impeccable manners, Ken helps each of them with more than just their stationery needs.

Ken takes care of his customers with genuine fondness. But while his shop has many visitors, who will look after him?